# Praise for these authors

## Sherryl Woods

On *Waking Up in Charleston*
"Powerful conflict, an interesting subplot and depth
of characterization are this story's main attractions."
—*Romantic Times BOOKclub*

On *Flirting with Disaster*
"A satisfying tale that will leave you smiling."
—*Romance Reviews Today*

## Darlene Gardner

On *Cole for Christmas*
"Fine holiday fare that is mistletoe fun."
—*The Best Reviews*

On *Anything You Can Do...!*
"An enjoyable lighthearted romance...
laugh out loud scenes..."
—*Allreaders.com*

## Holly Jacobs

On *The 100-Year Itch*
"A wonderfully funny story."
—*Writers Unlimited*

On *A Day Late and a Bride Short*
"A beautiful and sweet love story...it will stay
with you long after you close the back cover."
—*Romantic Times BOOKclub*

# SHERRYL WOODS

## Darlene Gardner

## Holly Jacobs

# Dashing through the Mall

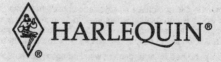
HARLEQUIN®

TORONTO • NEW YORK • LONDON
AMSTERDAM • PARIS • SYDNEY • HAMBURG
STOCKHOLM • ATHENS • TOKYO • MILAN • MADRID
PRAGUE • WARSAW • BUDAPEST • AUCKLAND

ISBN-13: 978-0-373-83733-5
ISBN-10: 0-373-83733-X

DASHING THROUGH THE MALL

Copyright © 2006 by Harlequin Books S.A.

The publisher acknowledges the copyright holders of the individual works as follows:

SANTA, BABY
Copyright © 2006 by Sherryl Woods

ASSIGNMENT HUMBUG
Copyright © 2006 by Darlene Hrobak Gardner

DECK THE HALLS
Copyright © 2006 by Holly J. Fuhrmann

This edition published by arrangement with Harlequin Books S.A.

® and TM are trademarks of the publisher. Trademarks indicated with ® are registered in the United States Patent and Trademark Office, the Canadian Trade Marks Office and in other countries.

www.eHarlequin.com

**Printed in U.S.A.**

# CONTENTS

Dear Friends,

The holidays have always been an incredibly special time for my family. From childhood I remember the preholiday baking, the hiding of gifts—with me trying to hunt them down—midnight Christmas Eve church services, the excitement of opening presents on Christmas morning, the visits to grandparents. There were a few bah-humbug types in the family, but for the most part all of us rejoiced in the season.

So as the holidays approach this year, I wish all of you the joy of the season, the warmth of shared times with family and friends, and a few dozen holiday cookies with not a calorie in them.

All best,

Sherryl

# SANTA, BABY

Sherryl Woods

# CHAPTER ONE

AMY RILEY HAD A FEVER of 102, globs of oatmeal all over her face, hair that desperately needed washing, a screaming baby and a five-year-old who was regarding her with such reproach that she wanted to sit down and cry herself. It was not a promising start to the holidays.

"But, Mom, you said we could go to the mall today and see Santa," Josh whined. "You promised."

Amy clung to her patience by a thread. "I know, sweetie, but I'm sick. I'm sorry."

"But it's Christmas Eve," he persisted, clearly not hearing or at least not caring about the state of her health. "We *have* to go today. If we don't, how will Santa know what to bring us? He doesn't even know where we live now. What if he takes our presents to Michigan and we're not there?"

"He won't," Amy assured him.

"But how do you *know?*"

"Because I sent him a letter," she claimed in desperation.

"What if he didn't get it? Mail gets lost all the time."

"He got it," she reassured him, thinking of the small stash of gifts in her closet. Tomorrow morning, they would provide proof for her doubting son, but today he'd just have to take her word for it.

Thanks to the expense of relocating, she hadn't been able to afford much this year, but she was determined Josh would have at least a few packages from Santa to open on Christmas morning, along with a handful from her folks and the one from his dad that she'd picked out just in case Ned didn't bother sending anything. Unless a miracle occurred and something turned up in an overnight delivery on Christmas morning, she'd pegged her ex's lack of consideration exactly right.

With Josh in her face this morning, she had to keep reminding herself that it wasn't his fault that she and his father had gone through a nasty divorce and that she'd packed up with him and his baby sister and moved to a suburb outside of Charlotte, NC, far from family and friends back in Michigan. Everyone had tried to talk her into waiting until after the holidays, but the thought of spending one more minute in the same town as her ex had been too much. Maybe by next year the wounds would have healed and she and the kids could spend the holidays with her folks, but this year staying there a few weeks longer or making a quick trip back had been out of the question. Amy hadn't had the stomach or the money for it.

She'd convinced herself that things would be better after the first of the year when she started her new job at the headquarters of the same bank she'd worked for back home. At the time she'd been offered the transfer, it had seemed like a godsend, a way to get a fresh start with the promise of some financial security in the very near future.

This morning, though, she was regretting the hasty decision. Money was tight and emotions were raw. She was far from home with no new support system in place. And if it was tough for her, it was a thousand times worse for Josh, who felt cheated not to be with family for Christmas.

But, she reassured herself, Josh was an outgoing kid. He would make new friends in kindergarten. In a few more weeks tantrums like the one he was pitching now would be a thing of the past. They just had to survive till then.

"I hate this place," Josh declared, pressing home a point with which she was already far too familiar. Not a day had gone by in the last week when he hadn't expressed a similar sentiment.

Fighting for patience, Amy lowered the now-quiet baby into her portable playpen, then sat her son in her lap and gave him a squeeze. "It's going to get better," she promised him.

He nestled under her chin in an increasingly infrequent display of affection. "When?" he asked plaintively.

"Soon," she vowed. No matter what it took, she would make this work.

"There's not even any snow in this dumb place. At home, we always had snow for Christmas and Dad would take me out on my sled." He sighed dramatically. "I miss Dad."

"I know you do, sweetie. And I'm sure he misses you, too," she said, though she was sure of no such thing.

Ned had been all too eager to see them gone so he

could get on with his new life with another woman and the baby that was already on the way by the time his divorce from Amy was final. He rarely spared more than a couple of minutes for his calls to his son and even those brief bits of contact had become less routine. Ned was an out of sight, out of mind kind of guy, which was pretty much how he'd gotten involved with a woman he'd met on his business travels. Amy—and his marriage—had definitely been out of sight and out of mind during those trips.

Amy resolved not to dwell on her many issues with her ex today. Even though she felt awful, she was going to do whatever she could to make this first Christmas in their new home memorable for Josh. Emma was still too young to notice much more than the bright lights on their skinny little tree, but Josh needed more. He needed to believe that life in North Carolina would eventually be much like his old life in Michigan. Perhaps even better.

She tousled his dark brown hair, which badly needed a trim. "We can bake cookies later," she told him. "We'll play all the Christmas CDs and tonight I'll make hot chocolate with lots and lots of marshmallows and we can watch Christmas movies on TV. How about that?"

"Sure," he said wearily. "But it won't be Christmas if I don't get to see Santa. We *always* go on Christmas Eve."

Amy bit back her own sigh. That's what came of creating a tradition for your children. They clung to it tenaciously, even when circumstances changed. And seeing Santa was such a little thing for him to ask for.

He hadn't requested a million presents. He didn't make a lot of demands. He even helped with Emma as much as he could. He'd rock her to sleep in her carrier or even show her his picture books accompanied by dramatic reenactments of the stories. He was a great big brother and, most of the time anyway, a big help to Amy.

How many more years would he want to climb up on Santa's lap, anyway, she asked herself. How much longer before he stopped believing?

Maybe if she took a couple more aspirin and a hot shower, she could manage the trip to the mall, she thought without much enthusiasm. Her head throbbed just thinking about the crowds. Still, one look into her son's disappointed eyes and she knew she had to try.

"Will you stay right here and watch your sister?" she asked Josh. "Keep her entertained, okay?"

"How come?"

"So I can take a shower," she told him without elaborating or making another promise she might not be able to keep.

Josh's eyes lit up in sudden understanding, anyway. "And then we'll go see Santa?" he asked excitedly.

"*Maybe* we'll go see Santa," she cautioned. "If I feel better."

He threw his arms around her neck and squeezed. "You will, Mom. I know you will."

He scrambled down, knelt beside the playpen and peered through the mesh at Emma. "We're going to see Santa, Em. You're gonna love him. He's this jolly old guy, who goes ho-ho-ho real loud." He demonstrated, holding his tummy, as he bellowed ho-ho-ho. "He's all dressed in red, and you tell him what you most want for Christmas and then, if you've been good all year, he brings it to you. Santa's the best." He grinned up at Amy. "Next to Mom, of course."

Amy couldn't help grinning back at her budding young diplomat. How could she resist giving him anything he asked for, especially this Christmas? She just hoped she didn't throw up all over jolly old St. Nick.

NICK DICAPRIO WAS NOT having a good week. Hell, he wasn't having a good life. The police department psychologist had informed his superiors on Monday that he was burned out, that he had anger management issues, that letting him go back on active duty in the immediate future would be irresponsible.

Well, duh! After being forced to stand by helplessly while a deranged man had terrorized his own kid to get even with his ex-wife, who wouldn't have anger issues? Nick had wanted to pound heads together that awful day, especially those of the SWAT team who wouldn't allow him to intervene. He couldn't imagine that talking that whole disastrous scenario to death with some shrink was going to improve his mood.

As if all that psychobabble weren't annoying enough, it was Christmas Eve. The whole world was all caught up in the commercialized holiday frenzy. If he heard one more Christmas song, he was going to turn on the gas and stick his head in the oven. Or just get blind, stinking drunk. Yeah, he thought, that was better. Saner. The stupid shrink would be delighted to know he wasn't completely self-destructive.

When his phone rang, he ignored it. There wasn't a

single person in the universe he wanted to talk to this morning. Not one. There were even more he wanted to avoid completely, namely his family, almost all of whom seemed to be possessed by unrelenting holiday cheer. The answering machine clicked on.

"Nick, answer the phone!" his baby sister commanded, sounding frantic. "Dammit, I know you're there. Pick up. I'm desperate."

Nick sighed. When Trish hit a panic button, the whole world was going to suffer right along with her. She'd be over here banging on his door, if he didn't answer the phone. Or, worse, using the key he'd given her for emergencies to barge in and turn his world as topsy-turvy as her own apparently was.

He yanked the phone out of its cradle and barked, "What?"

"Thank God," she said fervently, oblivious to his sour mood. "Nick, I need you at the mall right now!"

"Not in a hundred million years," he said at once. "Are you crazy?"

Just because her duties as a mall events coordinator required Trish to be at a shopping mall on Christmas Eve didn't mean he intended to get within ten miles of the place. He wouldn't have done it when he was in a good mood. Today, it would border on turning him homicidal.

"I'm not crazy," she insisted. "I'm desperate. Santa called in sick. If you ask me he took one look outside at the lousy weather and decided to stay home in front of a warm fire, but the bottom line is it's Christmas Eve and I don't have a Santa."

"Hire another one," he said without sympathy. "Gotta go."

"Don't you dare hang up on me, Nicholas DiCaprio. If you do, I swear I will tell Mom and Dad all about this burnout thing."

Nick hesitated. The only thing worse than having Trish nagging him to death would be to have his parents all over his case. They weren't that happy about his decision to become a cop in the first place. They'd see this so-called burnout thing as the perfect excuse to harangue him about getting off the force for good. If his sister was annoyingly persistent, his protective mother was qualified to drive him right over the brink into insanity.

"What about Rob?" he suggested, referring to their older brother. "He'd make an excellent Santa. He loves the holidays."

"Rob and Susan are taking the kids to cut down a tree today. It's their Christmas Eve tradition, remember?"

Nick groaned. How could he have forgotten that? Last year he'd gone along. It had taken the entire day, because everyone in the family, including one-year-old Annie, had a vote and there hadn't been a single tree on which they could all agree. How they could gauge Annie's vote, when she only knew one discernible word—mama—was beyond him. By three in the afternoon, he'd vowed not only to never begin any Christmas traditions, but to never have a family.

"And Stephen?" he asked hopefully. His younger brother had no traditions that Nick had ever noticed. No family, either. In fact, he was the DiCaprio black sheep, but surely Trish could corral him for the day. She was the only one in the family who seemed to understand his need for rebellion. In return Stephen did things for her that no one else could persuade him to do. She could even coerce him into showing up for holiday meals and tolerating their mother fussing over him.

"I actually spoke to Stephen. He's a little hung over," she admitted. "I don't think that's a good quality for a Santa."

Nick regretted not getting drunk when he'd had the chance. "Okay, fine," he said, his tone grim. "What exactly do you need from me?"

"Isn't that obvious? I need you to substitute for Santa," Trish said sweetly, obviously sensing victory. "It won't be hard. Just a few ho-ho-ho's for the kids. Listen to their gift lists. Don't make any promises. Get your picture taken. That's all."

"How long?"

"I need you here ASAP and the mall's open till six. It's a few hours, Nick. How bad can it be?"

It sounded like hell. "Come on, Trish. This is so not me. There has to be someone else," he pleaded. "Don't they have agencies for this kind of thing? Rent-a-Santa or something?"

"Are you nuts? It's Christmas Eve. All the good Santas are already working. I don't have time to hunt down the last remaining qualified Santa in all of North Carolina. And why should I, when you have absolutely nothing to do today? Please, Nick. You're good with kids."

Once upon a time he had considered himself to be good with kids. He'd been a doting uncle to Rob's kids, taking the older boys to ball games, even babysitting Annie a time or two. But after what had happened with freckle-faced Tyler Hamilton less than a month ago,

Nick didn't trust himself to be within a hundred miles of a child. He didn't even want to be anywhere near Rob's kids this Christmas, at least not without backup.

Still, despite his reservations, somewhere deep down inside—very deep down—he wondered if this wouldn't be a chance for some sort of redemption. He hadn't been able to do much to help Tyler, so he could spend all day today making up for it.

No, he thought wearily, this was more like payback. Like some sort of giant cosmic joke, asking a man with his complete and total lack of holiday cheer to spend a whole day faking it for the sake of a bunch of greedy little brats.

"You'll owe me," he told his sister eventually.

"No question about it," she agreed. "Won't that be a nice change?"

"I beg your pardon."

"I have a list of the favors I've done for you, big brother, beginning with getting you your dream date with Jenny Davis."

"You did not get me a date with Jenny," he snapped, thinking of the redheaded teenager who'd been able to twist his insides into knots at seventeen.

"Did, too. She wouldn't give you the time of day, till I told her what a terrific guy you are. I also offered to loan her my cashmere sweater and to give her my new Kenny Chesney CD."

"You bribed her?" he demanded incredulously. If that wasn't the most humiliating piece of news he'd heard lately, he thought with a shake of his head.

"It was the least I could do for my favorite brother," she said.

"Well, given how badly that relationship turned out, I wouldn't be bringing it up now, if I were you," he muttered. Jenny, whom he'd dated all through his senior year in high school only to be dumped by her the day before prom, had been the first in a long string of disastrous mistakes he'd made when it came to women. At least Trish hadn't had a hand in any of the rest. He'd made those absurd choices all on his own.

"Not to worry, Nicky. My list of the favors I've done for you goes on and on. I keep it posted right beside my desk for times like this," she said cheerfully. "See you in an hour. Come to my office. I have Santa's costume here. This is going to be fun."

"Torture," he mumbled. "It's going to be torture."

"What?"

"Nothing. I'll see you in an hour."

"Love you, Nicky."

Normally he would have echoed his sister's sentiment, but at the moment he was more inclined to throttle her.

## CHAPTER TWO

THE PARKING LOT at King's Mall was already a zoo by the time Amy had showered, dried her hair, packed up the kids and found it after taking several wrong turns. A line of cars waited at the entrance and more inched up and down each aisle looking fruitlessly for someone who might be about to leave. Heavy, dark clouds were looming overhead, almost completely blocking the sun. She couldn't be sure if they were threatening rain or even snow. Though snowfall here was rare, it certainly felt cold and raw enough for it to Amy.

Just a year ago, when she'd been eight months pregnant with Emma and totally exhausted, she'd still felt the excitement of the last-minute holiday crush. Today, all she felt was tired, and the gloomy sky wasn't helping.

"Over there," Josh shouted from the backseat. "Mom, see that lady with all the bags? She's gonna leave. You can get there."

Amy spotted the woman two aisles over. "Sweetie, there are already half a dozen cars waiting for that space. Don't worry. We'll find one. It's always like this on Christmas Eve. We just have to be patient."

"What if Santa's not even here?" Josh asked worriedly. "I mean, he's in Michigan, right? How can he be in two places at once?"

"He's here. I called."

"Maybe he gets off early on Christmas Eve, you know, so he can start flying all over the world. We usually go first thing in the morning back home, then Dad and me shop to buy your presents."

Amy bit back a grin at her pint-size worrier. That, at least, was a trait he'd gotten from her. It probably wasn't the best one she could have shared. "I checked on that, too," she told him. "Santa will be here till the mall closes at six."

"What time is it now?"

"Two-thirty. We have lots of time."

"Not if we don't find a parking place *soon,*" Josh warned grimly.

Amy was forced to admit, she was beginning to have her doubts about that ever happening, too. People were nuts. Two cars were currently in a standoff over a space in the next aisle, both so determined to grab it that the poor driver trying to get out couldn't even move.

"People in Michigan were nicer," Josh declared from the back.

"No, they weren't. These people are nice, too. Everyone gets a little stressed out on Christmas Eve." A fat drop of rain splatted on the windshield and her mood deteriorated even further. She envisioned whatever bug she'd had this morning turning into pneumonia.

"I'll bet Santa won't come see them," Josh predicted direly. "Not when they say bad words and stuff. Look at that guy over there. He said something bad and he did that thing with his finger that you told me never, ever to do."

Amy regretted that her five-year-old had ever seen that gesture, but unfortunately it had been one of his father's routine actions behind the wheel. She'd been forced to discuss its inappropriateness on numerous occasions.

"I think that's enough play-by-play commentary on the parking lot," she told Josh just as a space right in front of her opened up. The driver even backed up in a way that guaranteed Amy would be the one to get it, then waved cheerfully as she drove off.

"See, she was nice," she told her cynical son. "Now let's get your sister into her stroller and go see Santa before it really starts raining."

Unloading the stroller, then getting Emma settled into it took time. Emma liked being carried. She hated the stroller…or thought she did. She kicked and screamed until Amy thought her head would split. Once she was in, though, and they were moving, Emma beamed up at Amy with the sort of angelic smile that made Amy wonder if she'd imagined all those heart-wrenching sobs only moments before. That was the joy of Emma. She could switch moods in a heartbeat.

As they reached the mall entrance, Amy gazed directly into Josh's eyes. "No running off, okay?" she said sternly. "You don't know this mall, so you have to stay with me and hold on to my hand."

"Mom!" he protested. "I'm not a baby."

"It's either that or we go right back home," she said in her most authoritative, no-nonsense tone. "I don't want you getting lost on Christmas Eve."

He rolled his eyes, but he took her hand. As soon as they were inside, he began to hurry her along past the shoe stores, lingerie shop, dress boutiques, cell phone kiosks and jewelry stores. Amy thought it was ironic that with all the big-name chain stores in the mall, it seemed every bit as familiar as anyplace they'd shopped back home. Maybe that's why Josh thought he knew where he was going.

When she was tempted to linger in front of a toy store, Josh barely spared a glance at the games in the window, then tugged her back into motion.

"Mom, come on," he urged. "Santa's gotta be right up here. See all those people? He's there. I know it! Hurry."

"Sweetie, he's not going anywhere. Slow down."

"We gotta get in line, Mom," he countered. "I'll bet it's really, really long."

Before Amy could argue with that, with some sort of child's radar, Josh spotted Santa.

"There he is," he shouted. "See, Mom. He's right there in the middle of all those Christmas trees! It's like a whole Santa's workshop around him." His eyes lit up. "Wow! That is totally awesome! It's better than anything I ever saw in Michigan! Did you bring the camera? We gotta send pictures to Dad."

His excitement was contagious. Even Emma seemed captivated by the glittering sea of lights ahead.

"I gotta see," Josh declared.

And with that he let go of Amy's hand and bolted into the frenzied crowd that was swirling all around between Amy and Santa.

It took less than a second for him to disappear in the

crush of people. Excitement and anticipation died. Panic clawed its way up the back of Amy's throat. Instinctively, she gathered Emma out of her stroller and clung to her as she shouted over and over for Josh, pushing her way through the crowd, the stroller abandoned.

Most people were oblivious to her cries, but finally a young woman stopped, alarm on her face.

"What's happened?" she asked, placing a comforting hand on Amy's arm. "Can I help?"

Amy was shaking so hard, she couldn't seem to form a coherent sentence.

"It's okay," the young woman soothed. "Take a deep breath and tell me. I'm Trish DiCaprio." She gestured toward her name tag. "I work for the mall. What can I do to help?"

"My son," Amy whispered. "He spotted Santa and took off and now I can't find him. There are so many people and we don't know anyone here and he's never been in this mall before." She was babbling now, but she couldn't seem to stop.

"When did you lose track of him?"

"A minute ago at the most."

"Then he can't have gone far. It's going to be okay," Trish reassured her. "My brother is playing Santa. In real life he's a cop. He'll know exactly what to do. I'll talk to him and we'll find your son in no time. Will you be okay right here for a minute till I can get to him?"

Amy nodded. She was clinging so tightly to Emma that the baby began to whimper. Someone appeared at her side just then with the stroller. Dazed, Amy stared at it, wondering where on earth she'd left it.

"I saw your boy take off and then you ran after him and left this behind," the woman said, her voice gentle. Her blue eyes were filled with concern. "Are you okay? Shall I stay with you till that young woman comes back?"

Tears stung Amy's eyes at the kindness in the woman's expression. "Thank you for rescuing the stroller. I don't know what I was thinking."

"You were just trying to catch up with your boy. What's his name?"

"Josh."

"Oh, my," the woman said with a smile. "I have a Josh, too. Of course, he's all grown-up now." She gave a rueful shake of her head. "My kids used to pull this kind of stunt on me all the time when they were small. Trust me, they all turned up. Now they have children of their own putting them through the same thing. What do they call that? Karma, isn't it?" She patted Amy's shoulder. "Don't you worry. Your boy will be back any minute. He'll probably find you before they can even get a search going."

She spoke with such conviction that Amy felt her panic slowly ease. "You're very kind. I really appreciate it. If you need to get your shopping finished, I'll be okay now."

"I have time," she said. "I'm Maylene Kinney, by the way. I'll just wait with you till that nice young woman comes back with help. I heard you say that you're new to Charlotte. Is that right?"

Amy nodded.

"What's your name?"

"Amy. Amy Riley."

"Well, welcome, Amy. I know this isn't the way to get off to a good start in a new place, but you will laugh about it someday, I promise you that." She smiled. "Maybe not till that boy of yours is grown and his son is doing something just as bad, but you will laugh."

Maylene's soft, Southern voice and friendly chitchat kept the panic at bay, at least for now, but Amy couldn't seem to stop searching the crowd for some sign of Josh. She ought to be looking for him, not just standing around waiting. She was always so careful to make sure he stayed in sight, to hold tight to his hand in unfamiliar surroundings. Now he could be anywhere, with anyone. This was her worst nightmare come true.

Her imagination immediately went into overdrive, envisioning every dire fate she'd ever read about. This time when the tears started, she couldn't seem to stop. Apparently sensing her mother's despair, Emma began to howl, too. Maylene put an arm around Amy's shoulder and murmured reassurances.

"I can't do this," Amy said finally. "I shouldn't be standing around crying. I have to do something constructive. I should be looking for Josh."

"You will," Maylene said. "Help will be here any second. They'll know exactly what to do. If you go running around every which way and getting lost yourself, what good will that do?"

Amy knew she was right. She drew in a deep breath and accepted the wad of tissues Maylene handed her. "You're right. I have to be smart about this."

But she'd never felt so helpless in her life.

IF NICK HAD TO UTTER one more ho-ho-ho, he was going to scream. It had been 9:00 a.m. by the time he was decked out in this ridiculous red suit with all the fat man pillows stuffed into it. The stupid beard itched like crazy and the too-big hat kept sliding down over his eyes. If he was fooling one single person in this mall into thinking he was Santa Claus, he'd eat the oversize hat. Even the littlest kids were eyeing him with skepticism.

Even so, the line waiting to see him was endless. It had been nonstop since he'd settled onto Santa's red velvet throne, which he intended to tell his sister was uncomfortable as hell. No wonder Santa hadn't reported for duty.

He'd managed to eat two cookies and sneak a sip of a soda for lunch before Trish had snatched them out of his hands to have his picture taken with a dad and three teenage boys. He was so hungry he was about to snatch a candy cane out of the pile being handed out to the kids. And he was just about blind from the flashbulbs going off in his eyes. Every parent clearly wanted to record the scene.

At least the job didn't require much acting on his part. Aside from trying to inject an unaccustomed note of cheer into his voice, his dialogue was pretty much limited to the ho-ho-ho's and asking what the tiny monsters wanted Santa to bring them. He'd done okay with that, he thought. None of them had run off screaming that he was an impostor. Not yet, anyway.

"You go on being a good girl," he told the shy imp sitting rigidly on his knee. "If you do everything your mommy and daddy tell you to do, Santa will bring you that doll you've been asking for."

Her sky-blue eyes went wide. "Really?" she asked with such amazement that Nick wondered if he'd made a serious blunder. Never promise anything, Trish had warned him. Why hadn't he listened? He cast an anxious glance toward her mother, who gave him a surreptitious wink. He sighed with relief. Thank goodness he hadn't set the kid up for disappointment.

Just then his sister, who'd been suspiciously absent since she'd parked him here in Santa's workshop, except for the photo-op with some contest winners, appeared at his side. He immediately noted the complete lack of Christmas cheer in her expression. She looked pale and even more harried than she had earlier.

"Something up?" he asked.

She leaned down and whispered, "We have a problem, Nicky. I've got a panicky mom back there who can't find her little boy."

Nick's gut began to churn. "Call security and the cops."

"I've already called security," Trish told him. "But I'm worried she's going to pass out or something. She just needs some reassurance that everything possible is being done. Can't you help? It would make me feel a lot better if you would. You're trained to deal with situations like this. And I'd rather not call the police in unless it's absolutely necessary."

"Why the hell not?"

"I'd just rather not, okay?"

He gave her a hard look. "Are you worried about how this would play out on TV or something?"

She frowned at his scathing tone. "Don't look at me

like that, Nicky. It's part of my job to worry about things like that."

A missing child scenario barely a month in the past played itself out in Nick's mind. That one hadn't come to a good end. He didn't want to be in the middle of another one with a tragic outcome. And, goodness knows, he knew how stories like that played in the media. He'd seen his face on the front page of the papers and on the six o'clock news too damn many times.

"Then let security deal with it. Let them be heroes," he repeated firmly, not even trying to hide his reluctance to be involved in any capacity. Trish had to know what she was asking of him was too much. He didn't give a hoot how many favors he owed her.

"But I already told her you're a policeman," Trish pressed. "I know you're not on duty right now, but she's so scared, Nicky. Put yourself in her place. It's Christmas Eve and her little boy is lost. They just moved here, so she's all alone. It's no wonder she's freaking out. Please, you have to do something. Go into your professional mode. Ask the right questions, organize the search. That will calm her down until security can find her son. I'm sure it won't take that long."

Nick wasn't nearly as optimistic as his sister. In a crowd like this, with everyone focused on last-minute shopping, how many people would even notice a little boy on his own? His stomach continued to churn. He poked a hand in his pocket in search of the antacids he usually had with him. Unfortunately, he hadn't transferred them to Santa's costume.

"What about the line?" he asked, preferring even

another hundred kids to one desperate mom whose child had gone missing in this mob scene.

"I'll tell them Santa has to take a break," Trish said at once. "It happens. They won't freak out or anything."

She regarded him with that same imploring look that had lured him into doing whatever she wanted when they were kids. It might work a hundred percent of the time on Stephen, but Nick was pretty much a sucker for that look, too.

Even in the face of his continued silence, Trish didn't let up.

"Security will be here any minute, but I need a real cop in charge, Nicky. You said it yourself. Please," Trish begged.

He compared his own credentials with those of the average mall security staffer and resigned himself to the inevitable. Even if it weren't his sister's neck on the line, he only had one choice. He'd been brought up to help anyone in need. His police training had ingrained the concept. Just because he was a burned-out mess, that hadn't changed.

"You get me out of here without all hell breaking loose and I'll calm this woman down and help her look for her kid." He gave Trish a fierce look. "If we don't have any luck in the next half hour, I want every cop in Charlotte combing this place, okay? I don't care what kind of PR nightmare it creates."

Trish threw her arms around him and kissed his cheek. "Thank you, Nicky. I'll make the announcement about your break right now, then I'll take you to her."

Nick figured his good deeds for the day ought to be racking up big points by now. Maybe his debt to Trish was paid. Maybe with any luck, as soon as he'd located the boy, he could scamper right on out the back door of the mall without one more ho-ho-ho.

Just as that cheerful prospect occurred to him, he caught a glimpse of the restless parents and disappointed kids as they were greeted with the news that Santa was taking a break and knew that plan was out the window.

He might be the lousiest Santa in the history of Christmas, but he was all these kids had. Heaven help them.

# CHAPTER THREE

WHILE SHE WAS WAITING for that woman—Trish something-or-other—Amy called for Josh until she was nearly hoarse, even though Maylene Kinney told her she was only hurting her vocal cords.

"Kids only hear what they want to hear," Maylene admonished. "You save your voice so you can tell him how much you love him the second he turns up."

"Right now I just want to kill him," Amy said, though she knew the older woman was right. No matter how terrified and furious she was, she could hardly wait to hold Josh in her arms again.

How could she have lost him so quickly? She'd known precisely where he was headed—to see Santa. He had to be somewhere in this mob scene of frantic shoppers and impatient children right around Santa's village, but there'd been no sign of him for what seemed like an eternity.

Finally the harried-looking young woman who'd spoken to her a few minutes earlier returned with Santa in tow. He was tall, at least six feet, and well rounded, thanks to plenty of fake padding. She couldn't guess his age, because of the fake white hair and beard, but if he and Trish were brother and sister, then surely he wasn't that old, late twenties or early thirties, maybe. Right around her age. Maybe he even had children of his own and would be able to empathize with her distress.

"Ma'am, this is my brother," Trish told Amy. "Don't be put off by the costume. He's really a terrific detective. He'll help you find your son. You'll be back together in no time."

Amy gazed into Santa's dark blue eyes behind their fake, round little glasses and felt an odd *zing* that was totally inappropriate under the circumstances. She had the oddest desire to fling her arms around this man who was offering to help her find Josh and hold on for dear life. After all, Santa Claus represented all that was good and hopeful in the world. Add to that the fact that *this* Santa was an experienced detective and he was everything she needed in this particular crisis.

"I'm Nick DiCaprio," he told her, his somber expression far from the jolly persona usually expected from Santa.

Her mouth dropped as the irony struck her. "St. Nick?"

His face relaxed and a faint smile touched his lips, then vanished. "Hardly. Trish had a last-minute emergency and, after a lot of sisterly persuasion and blackmail, I agreed to fill in for Santa. Trust me, no one would confuse me with any kind of saint."

The young woman beside him nudged him in the ribs. "Don't be modest, Nicky. You have a few saintly traits." She smiled at Amy, then gave her an oddly speculative look. "For one thing, Nicky is one of the last genuine good guys. You can't tell it now, but he's really handsome. Hot, even. And he stays in great shape."

Santa—rather Nick—frowned and cut her off before she could cover any more of his masculine attributes. "I think maybe she's more interested in my professional qualifications, Trish."

"I already told her you're an excellent policeman," she said quickly, then turned to Amy. "He has lots of commendations. If anyone can find your son—"

"Why don't you tell me about your son," he interrupted, his tone gruff. He still seemed uncomfortable, even though his sister's unsolicited praise had turned professional. "Trish, let me borrow your clipboard and notepad." He glanced back at Amy. "What's your name?"

"Amy Riley."

"And the boy's name?"

"Josh Riley."

"Age?"

"He's five."

"Height? Hair color?"

Amy rattled off the statistics, growing more impatient by the second. She knew he needed the basic information but why weren't they looking already? By now Josh could have been swept along to the other end of the mall.

"What's he wearing?"

Increasingly exasperated, she tersely described the bright red jacket, jeans and Spiderman T-shirt Josh had put on that morning and the red and green scarf he had around his neck.

"I know you think we're wasting time, Mrs. Riley," Nick said as if he'd read her mind. "But with thousands of kids running around the mall today, it's best to know exactly what your son looks like. Giving a good description to the security staff will save a lot of time in the long run."

"I have a picture," Amy said, hurriedly pulling his last school picture from her purse. It had been taken just a couple of months before they'd left Michigan. She choked up at the sight of Josh's precious gaping smile and that untamed cowlick of brown hair that refused to stay put no matter how much gel she used to slick it down.

Handing the picture to Nick, she said, "He needs a haircut now, but this was taken not too long ago."

"Cute kid," Nick said, then turned to his sister. "Trish, how far does the sound from that PA system travel?"

"It's just for the immediate vicinity," she told him. "Some of the department stores have their own. I could write up an announcement and ask them to make it ASAP."

"Do that, and we'll give this one a try, in the meantime. Keep it simple, Trish. Ask Josh Riley to come to see Santa." He glanced at Amy. "Think that would get his attention?"

"Oh, yes," Amy said eagerly. "He was so anxious to see you, I mean Santa. That's why he took off in the first place. I wasn't moving fast enough to suit him. He wanted to see you up close, then get in line."

"Have you checked the line?" he asked.

"Front to back," Amy confirmed. "He's not in it. I just don't understand why he would have wandered away."

"Because that's what little boys do," Nick offered.

"They're easily distracted and often far too fearless for their own good. Trish, let's try the PA and see what happens, then do whatever you have to do to get the co-operation of the stores."

But even after several announcements, there was still no sign of Josh. Amy gazed up at Santa. Despite the beard and makeup designed to give him a jolly look, there was no mistaking the fact that his expression was troubled.

"He really is lost, isn't he?" she whispered, her voice choked.

Nick nodded, but he took her hand in his and gave it a squeeze. "Don't you dare lose it on me now, Mrs. Riley."

"Amy," she told him.

"Okay, Amy. Hang in there. We're going to find your boy."

"Of course, you will," Maylene added.

It was the first time she'd spoken since Nick's arrival. Amy knew she'd stayed close by in case she was needed, but she hadn't intruded. Amy was grateful for her presence. With Maylene around, she didn't feel quite so alone.

"I believe I know your mother, Nick," Maylene continued. "We belong to the same Red Hat Society." She beamed at Amy. "Laura DiCaprio is always bragging about her son the policeman." She smiled at Nick. "Your mother is very proud of you."

Nick seemed as surprised by that as he'd been put off by his sister's glowing comments.

"Weren't you involved in a high-profile case just recently?" Maylene asked, her brow furrowing as she apparently tried to recall the details.

"Let's not get into that," Nick said curtly.

Maylene looked taken aback by his sharp tone, but then something must have come to her because she nodded. "I'm sorry. You're absolutely right," she said hurriedly. "I don't know what I was thinking. You need to be concentrating on finding Josh."

"That's exactly right," Nick said, his sympathetic gaze pinned on Amy. "You okay?"

"I'll be a lot better when we find Josh."

"It won't be much longer," Nick reassured her. "I can see some of the security guys coming now. We want to get this search organized the right way. Once security fans out through the mall, it shouldn't take any time at all."

Oddly enough, Amy believed him. There was something solid and reassuring about a detective who would be willing to take the time to play Santa in a mall filled with last-minute shoppers and hyperactive children. It said a lot about his character that he'd helped out his sister, when most men wouldn't have wanted to be within a hundred miles of the mall today. Of course, he had mentioned something about Trish needing to blackmail him to get his cooperation, but still...

With his warm, comforting hand wrapped around hers, Amy finally let herself start to relax. Nick might be a reluctant substitute for the real Santa Claus, but perhaps he was capable of performing at least one minor miracle and reuniting her with her little boy.

BY THE TIME NICK ACCEPTED the fact that Josh Riley was nowhere near Santa's village, a dozen mall security officers including the less experienced extras hired during the holidays, had arrived. Familiar with the mall's various wings, Nick hastily organized them into an efficient search party, showed them the picture of the boy, gave them a description of his clothes, and sent them to the areas of the mall most likely to draw an adventurous five-year-old.

All the while, he was aware of Amy regarding him with her big, soulful eyes that were shadowed by fear. Tyler Hamilton's mom had looked at him exactly like that, trusted him to bring back her boy. Nick shuddered at the memory of those harrowing hours, which Maylene Kinney had almost revealed at a most inopportune moment. Thank goodness the woman's memory had temporarily failed her. When the incident had come back to her, she'd covered well. Meanwhile, Amy seemed too distracted to notice the byplay between them. He didn't want her to start asking a lot of questions about why Nick had been in the news recently.

None of them could afford to go back and think about that tragedy right now. Amy needed to believe in him. And he had to stay focused on this mom and this boy. He refused to consider the possibility that this was anything more than a missing child. Anything else took him down a road he couldn't bring himself to travel.

That didn't mean that he didn't understand the urgency of finding Josh before his mom freaked out completely or before the situation turned into something worse. Any location that attracted a lot of children also had the potential to draw those who preyed on them.

With the security staff fanning out, he turned back to Amy.

"Let me take the baby, okay? Then we can leave the stroller here with Trish," he said lightly. The little sweetheart with her blond curls and pink bow in her hair immediately beamed at him in a way that made his heart ache.

"Who's this angel?" he asked, responding to that smile with one of his own.

"Her name's Emma," Amy said. "She's eleven months old. Are you sure you want to hold her? I can keep her."

"I don't mind. I have a niece who's not much older," he told her.

He gently patted the baby's back till she settled down again. She felt good in his arms. There was something about holding an innocent baby, smelling that powdery scent, feeling that weight relax against his chest, that always affected him and made him yearn for something that he rarely acknowledged was missing from his life.

Feeling the start of that yearning somewhere deep inside, he snapped his attention back to the current crisis.

"Is there any store in the mall that your son especially likes?" he asked.

She shook her head. "We've never been here before. We just moved to town a couple of weeks ago and we're getting settled. I wasn't even sure exactly where the mall was. I got lost getting here. We probably shouldn't have come, but it's been a family tradition to see Santa on Christmas Eve and I didn't want to disappoint Josh. It's hard enough on him since his dad's back in Michigan."

"You're divorced?" A glance at her ring finger confirmed the absence of a wedding band.

She nodded and Nick's sense of dread magnified.

"You're absolutely sure your husband's in Michigan?" he asked, his voice filled with tension.

Amy regarded him with confusion. "Of course. Why?"

"What were the terms of custody?"

"I have full custody. Josh will spend summers with his dad. What does that have to do with anything?"

"And your husband agreed to that willingly?"

"He was eager to have us leave," Amy explained. "Why are you asking all these questions about my ex-husband? He has nothing to do with this."

Nick regarded her with a penetrating look. "Are you sure about that? He wouldn't try to snatch Josh away from you?"

"No. Never," she said fiercely. "I told you, he was glad we were leaving, so he could move on with his new wife. I don't understand what you're trying to get at."

Nick recalled that Mitzi Hamilton hadn't believed her ex-husband was capable of taking their son, either. They'd wasted precious time searching for a stranger, only to determine that Tyler had been taken by his own dad, a man intent on revenge. How the hell was Nick supposed to know if Amy Riley was telling him the truth about this situation?

He looked into her eyes and tried to read her expression. She looked a bit confused, maybe even troubled by his questions, but she seemed totally sincere.

"You're absolutely certain your ex-husband wouldn't change his mind, come looking for Josh?"

"Not a chance," Amy said. She pulled a cell phone from her purse. "I could call him, if you want."

"Do it," Nick commanded. "At home, not on his cell phone."

"Why?"

"If you call his cell phone, he could be anywhere. I want to know for a fact he's in Michigan."

She looked shaken by his persistence, but she dialed. "Ned," she said eventually. "It's Amy." Her gaze locked with Nick's. "I…" Her voice trailed off, as if she'd suddenly realized that she needed an excuse for calling. Clearly she wasn't anxious to tell her ex-husband the truth, that their son was missing. After a noticeable hesitation, she said, "I was just wondering if you'd sent a gift for Josh. Nothing's come yet."

Nick sagged with relief at the evidence that Josh's dad wasn't involved in his disappearance. He barely listened to the rest of Amy's brief conversation.

When she'd hung up, she frowned at him. "Satisfied?"

He nodded. "Sorry. I had to be sure, Amy."

"Something tells me I need to know why all of this mattered so much."

He shook his head. "Just covering all the bases."

"I'm not sure I believe that," she said, studying him intently.

Nick hated seeing the doubts in her eyes, but he knew there would only be more if he explained. "Just trust me, okay?"

"I don't have much choice, do I?" she muttered wearily. She met his gaze. "Now what?"

Nick tried to think like a five-year-old boy on the day

before Christmas. "Would Josh go to a store to buy a present for his dad?"

Amy frowned. "I don't think so. We sent a present last week."

"What about you? Would he want to find a last-minute gift for you?"

Her eyes, an unusual shade of amber, shimmered with unshed tears. "I don't think so. I don't think he has any money. All he wanted to do today was see Santa. He didn't even want to waste time looking in the windows at the toy store. He was so upset this morning when I didn't feel well and said we couldn't come. I felt so awful about letting him down that I got dressed and came anyway." The tears spilled over and ran down her cheeks. "We should have stayed at home. I should have known something bad would happen."

"Come on now, Amy. You couldn't predict something like that. Stop beating yourself up. This isn't your fault."

"I just don't understand why he didn't come straight here. I swear to you that he's never done anything like this before."

"With kids, it seems as if there's a first time for everything," Nick said. "My nieces and nephews are always catching their parents off guard."

"That's what Maylene said." She glanced around. "Where is she?" Regret clouded her eyes. "She must have left. I should have wished her a merry Christmas. She was so kind to me."

Nick regarded her with wonder. What kind of woman worried about wishing someone a merry Christmas in the middle of her own crisis? "I imagine she knew you had other things on your mind. And you know her name. You can always give her a call tonight and let her know Josh is home safe and sound."

"Do you think he will be?" she asked.

"I know it," he assured her, because he couldn't very well tell her anything else. There would be time enough for a reality check if the boy didn't turn up in the next few minutes.

Suddenly her expression turned frantic again. "You don't think he'd go outside and try to find the car, do you?"

Nick sure as hell hoped not. The parking lot would make a kidnapping a thousand times easier, to say nothing of the other dangers from careless drivers trying to snag a parking place in their rush to finish up last-minute shopping. "What do you think?" he countered.

"No," she admitted. "He was totally focused on Santa, but where on earth could he be? He saw where you were."

"It's one thing to see the whole Santa's workshop thing from a distance," Nick explained. "But the closer he got, probably all he could really see were people. That's what happens with kids. They're intrepid. They rush off and the next thing you know they're lost in a sea of legs."

"I should have held on to him," she lamented, looking miserable. "I tried. I told him not to let go of my hand."

"I'm sure you did," he soothed. "Tell you what. Why don't you and I take a walk?"

She regarded him with bemusement. "A walk? Why?

He'll come here first. I told you all he cares about is seeing Santa."

"Which is why we're going for a walk," Nick told her. "We'll see if we can help him spot Santa a little more easily. When I came out here this morning, I was like some sort of kid-magnet walking through the mall. If Josh is anxious to see Santa, maybe he'll see the commotion and find us."

"But what if he comes back here, thinking you'll be in the workshop seeing kids?" she asked worriedly. "He was in such a rush to get in line."

"But he didn't, did he? Which means something else caught his attention," Nick suggested, then turned to his sister who'd rejoined them after making her announcements and contacting the stores in the mall to get them to make the same announcement. "Trish will watch for him, just in case, though, right Trish?"

"Of course, I will," Trish said at once. "I'll keep his picture with me, so he won't be scared if I approach him. Nicky, you have your cell phone?"

He nodded.

"Then I'll call you the second he shows up here," Trish volunteered, giving Amy a sympathetic look.

Nick studied his sister. She was a warm and generous woman and she seemed okay with his plan, but it had to be throwing her whole Santa photo-op thing off-kilter. As frantic as she'd been this morning over finding a Santa replacement, he couldn't help wondering if she was holding back her own emotions over this turn of events.

"Is me taking off for a little while longer going to be a problem?" he asked her.

She looked at Amy's pale face and immediately shook her head. "This is more important. I'll manage. If anyone complains I'll tell 'em Santa got stuck in the workshop elevator."

Nick grinned at her quick thinking. Her inventiveness was one of the traits that had made her perfect for this job.

"That'll work," he said just as Emma gave his beard a hard tug. "Hey there, sweet thing," he said, extricating her tiny fist from his beard. "Don't be giving away my disguise right here. We're likely to be mobbed by angry kids if they figure out they're being duped by a fake Santa."

A faint smile crossed Amy's lips, but it didn't take the worry from her eyes. She was trying so hard to hold it all together, but she had to be close to the edge. She was in a strange city, recently divorced, her kid had wandered off on Christmas Eve and a cop had been asking her all sorts of uncomfortable questions. Nick had to admire the strength it must be taking for her not to come unglued.

She gazed up at him just then, her heart in her eyes. There was no mistaking the fact that she was counting on him, that she trusted him to find her boy.

Seeing that expression on her face made Nick want to thrust Emma back in her mother's arms and take off, but he knew he couldn't. Trish had dragged him into this and now he had to see it through, for Amy's sake and maybe even for his own.

Something told him, as well, that Amy Riley could get under his skin if he gave her half a chance. He immediately sent that errant thought right back to wherever it had come from. His sense of timing obviously sucked. He could hardly hit on a woman, when he was supposed to be finding her child.

"Where are we going?" she asked him as they set off, their pace slow because of the wall-to-wall throng of people.

"Everyplace and no place," he explained. "The goal is just to draw lots and lots of attention, so maybe Josh will find us."

As a plan, it lacked finesse, but Nick was a pro at using whatever unorthodox tactics were handed him. And finding a kid who wanted to see Santa by putting Santa directly into his path seemed to be as smart a strategy as any.

## CHAPTER FOUR

SANTA WAS DEFINITELY a kid-magnet, just as Nick had predicted, Amy concluded with wonder. They were instantly surrounded by children everywhere they went. She couldn't help wondering if Nick himself weren't a babe-magnet under that padded red costume. His sister had certainly hinted at as much and he didn't seem all that put off by being the center of attention.

Nor did the throngs of children seem to rattle him any more than Emma's attempt to unmask him had. Despite his grumblings about being coerced into taking the Santa job, he handled their awestruck silences or chattered barrage of questions with equal aplomb. He hunkered down to speak with them, listening carefully as if each child was the most important one in the world. Amy couldn't miss their childish delight after getting a private moment with Santa on Christmas Eve. Despite his patience with each child, they made good progress. Nick's gaze was watchful every second.

"Do you have kids?" she asked curiously, during a rare moment when Nick wasn't being besieged.

He seemed to freeze at the question. "No. Why?"

"You're wonderful with Emma and with all these

kids who keep stopping you," Amy told him. "I'm impressed. You never seem to lose patience."

"Just playing a role," he said tersely. "What would it do for Santa's reputation if I were a grouch? Just because I'm not into the holiday thing this year, why ruin some poor kid's Christmas?"

Amy didn't entirely buy the explanation. She had a hunch he was trying to hide a tender heart, though she couldn't imagine why he would want to.

"You said you have nieces and nephews, though. Trish's kids?"

"No, our older brother's. He has three boys and a girl."

"And she's the one who's about Emma's age?"

"A little older." He gave her a penetrating look. "Why all the questions?"

Amy shrugged. "Just making small talk, I suppose, anything to keep my mind off the fact that we haven't found Josh yet." She'd strained her eyes scanning the crowds, but so far she hadn't even caught a glimpse of any boy who looked like Josh wandering around lost and alone.

"I have to admit it's getting to me, Nick," she confessed, then voiced her greatest fear, "What if we don't find him?"

Nick's expression immediately turned sympathetic. She was growing to hate that look, the pity that couldn't quite cover his own worry. And he was worried. She could see it in his strained expression whenever he thought she wasn't looking.

"Don't tell me he'll turn up any minute," she snapped before he could respond. "He hasn't yet."

"Come on, Amy," he chided. "Don't give up so easily. We haven't been looking that long."

She glanced at her watch and realized it really had been little more than a half hour since this nightmare had begun. She felt as if her whole life—and Josh's—had played out in her mind since she'd last seen him. She'd formed some sort of bond with this man in the Santa suit, a closer bond of trust than she'd had with her husband toward the end. Maybe that just proved that all kinds of emotions were heightened in a crisis.

"You're right, but it seems like an eternity. Don't worry, though, I'll never give up," she said fiercely. "In the meantime, you placating and patronizing me is getting on my nerves."

"I'm sorry," he apologized, his eyes filled with un-mistakable regret.

She drew in a deep breath. "No, I'm sorry. I know you're doing everything you can. I'm just scared."

"Of course you are. You have every right to be, but we are going to find him, Amy."

She heard a giggle just then and glanced up to see Emma trying to snatch Santa's hat off. Nick grabbed it just in time, but not before she caught a glimpse of black curly hair under the white wig Emma had tugged askew along with the red velvet hat.

"Are you sure you don't want me to take her?" she asked Nick. "She has to be distracting you."

"Emma's fine right where she is," he assured her. "Besides, she's actually part of the bait."

"Bait?"

"With me holding her, she's high enough in the air

for Josh to spot her. If I know anything about kids, he will not be happy that baby sister got to Santa first."

Amy recognized the truth in that. "You really must be a terrific detective."

He seemed taken aback by the comment. It wasn't the first time he'd seemed surprised or embarrassed when his expertise as a cop was touted. Amy couldn't imagine why it seemed to throw him. Was he just naturally modest or had something happened to make him question himself? Did it have something to do with that high-profile case Maylene had mentioned? Nick had gotten very uptight when she'd brought it up.

"Why do you say that?" he asked. "We haven't found your son yet."

The question only confirmed her reading that he was thrown by any praise of his professional skills. She was tempted to ask him why, but instead she merely answered the question.

"Maybe not, but you're obviously clever and intuitive about people," she told him. "At least you have my son pretty well nailed down. You seem to know how he thinks."

For an instant, the somber expression faded and his eyes twinkled behind his wire-rimmed glasses. "You met Trish. I'll bet there's the same age difference between her and me as there is between Josh and little Emma here. I was not happy when she came along. Having two brothers was bad enough, but a girl? I was not ready for that."

"But Josh loves Emma," Amy countered. "He's a terrific big brother."

"On the surface," Nick responded. "Underneath

there are bound to be a few minor insecurities about having the whole order of his universe disrupted."

"Somehow I can't imagine you being insecure about the arrival of a baby sister," she scoffed.

"I was five," he said with a shrug. "It didn't take much to shake my world. The fact that my folks wanted a girl so badly was very apparent to me. After three boys and a whole lot of trucks and sports equipment, suddenly the house was filled up with dolls and frilly dresses and way too much pink."

She smiled at the image and at his exaggerated shudder of disdain. "How did your brothers react? Were you the only one green with envy?"

"Rob—he's the oldest—was okay. He was nine and already into sports and barely noticed a new baby in the house. Stephen, who's between me and Trish in age, seemed to take it in stride, too. He just ignored her, though I have to wonder in retrospect if that wasn't the moment he started to rebel to get attention."

"What did you do?"

"I alternated between being fascinated by this tiny creature with all her pink ruffles and bows and hating her guts because she was taking up all of my mom's time. I hadn't felt that way when Stephen came along. He seemed to fit right in." He gave her a wry grin. "Must have been all that girlie-girl stuff."

Amy regarded him with amusement. "And now? Do you still have mixed feelings?"

"Yes, but the princess back there rules the world. Otherwise, can you think of any reason a sane man would agree to step in as Santa on Christmas Eve?"

"Not many," Amy agreed. "Unless the pay was very, very good."

"No pay. I'm here as a favor," he said, then added, "At least it's a favor if you don't take into account her particular techniques."

"Blackmail?"

Nick nodded. "Afraid so."

"Care to explain?"

"Not at the moment."

"Then I think I'll just go on believing that Trish has you wrapped around her finger," Amy replied. "I like what that says about you."

"That I'm a wuss?" he asked, clearly amused.

"No, that you love your sister. What about the rest of your family? Are you close to all of them, too?"

"Yeah, I guess so," he admitted. "I spend a lot of time with my folks, just so my mom can nag me about being a policeman. It bothers her a lot, so I make sure she sees me enough to know that I'm still all in one piece, but not so much that her commenting drives me insane."

"That's why you were so surprised when Maylene said your mom brags about you being a cop," she concluded.

"Exactly. I never wanted to be anything else, but she and my dad did everything they could to dissuade me. I've been on the force for nearly ten years now and they still take every opportunity to suggest other career options. If I complain about anything work related, they're all over it. My charming sister used that to get me here today."

Amy studied him curiously. "How? Are we back to the blackmail?"

He smiled, though he looked as if he regretted saying anything about it. "Maybe I'll tell you sometime, but not today. We need to concentrate on finding Josh."

Amy could hardly argue with that. The whole time they moved slowly through the mall, she was scanning the faces of the children who were staring in wide-eyed wonder at Santa. Where was Josh? Why hadn't someone found him by now or why hadn't he found them?

Just then Nick's cell phone rang. He answered it, then glanced around as if to get his bearings. "Got it," he said eventually. He explained exactly where they were located. "We'll start in that direction."

"What?" Amy demanded, her heart in her throat.

"Security found a boy wandering around by himself. He says his name is Josh."

Amy's heart turned over. "He's okay?"

"He's scared and crying, but otherwise he's just fine."

"Where is he?"

"All the way down at the other end of the mall. Security's going to pick us up in a golf cart and take us to him. In the meantime, let's start heading that way."

Amy took off at a run in the direction he'd pointed.

"Hey," he said, catching up to her. "Stick with me. I'm the one the guard's watching for, remember?"

"Of course," she said. "I'm sorry."

He touched her shoulder. "It's okay. Here he comes now."

The golf cart cruised to a stop beside them and Amy climbed in. Still holding Emma, Nick sat on the seat in back.

"Were you there when they found him?" Nick asked the security officer.

"No. I just got a call to come pick you up."

The golf cart made slow progress, especially when kids spotted Santa riding in it. In fact, at times Amy wanted to leap out and run ahead to get there faster, but she restrained herself. As Nick had pointed out, the driver knew where they were going. She didn't. She'd only waste precious time if she got lost herself.

Her heart was pounding so hard in anticipation of seeing her son, she thought it would burst. Apparently Nick sensed her restlessness.

"We're almost there," he told her, his gaze locked with hers.

The golf cart made a sharp turn to the left down another corridor, then slowed.

Amy glanced around frantically looking for Josh, but rather than spotting him, she saw only a very young security officer walking their way, his expression chagrined.

"I'm so sorry," he said, barely able to look her in the eye.

"What?" Amy demanded, her heart sinking. "He ran away again?"

"What happened?" Nick demanded.

The officer shook his head. "It was the wrong boy," he admitted, looking miserable. "His name *was* Josh, but not two seconds after I called you, his folks turned up." His gaze met Amy's, then shifted away. "I'm so sorry, ma'am. I've already put out a call. Everyone's searching again. We didn't lose more than a couple of minutes."

The last faint shred of strength Amy possessed seemed to snap in that instant. Tears tracked down her cheeks and her chest heaved with sobs. She was barely aware of Nick shoving Emma unceremoniously into the arms of the startled security guard. Then he was gathering her close.

"Come on, Amy," he murmured. "I know how strong you are. Don't fall apart now. It's going to be okay. This was just a small setback."

"I know," she whispered in a choked voice, but she couldn't seem to stop the tears or to let go of him. Nick might think she was strong, but he was wrong. She needed to absorb some of his strength before they went back to search some more. "I'll be fine in a minute, okay?"

"Okay," he said gently. He rubbed her back as he had Emma's earlier. There was nothing sensual about the gesture. It was meant only to calm, but it had been so long since anyone had touched her so tenderly that she wanted the contact to go on forever.

Not once during her divorce had she let herself lean on anyone, not her family, not her friends. She'd wanted all of them to see that she was handling it all right. But this…this was too much to expect. She didn't have any reserves of strength left. She needed someone else to share the burden. Nick, a virtual stranger to whom she owed no apologies, filled a terrible void in her life. So what if she held on for just a short while?

With her face buried against his padded chest, she could smell the faint scent of mothballs—the costume, no doubt—and a mix of clean aftershave and mint mouthwash. The velvet texture of the Santa suit felt good against her cheek, though she couldn't help wondering how his fake beard would feel. The lyrics of an old Christmas song about mommy kissing Santa Claus came to mind and made her smile.

"What's that for?" Nick asked, tucking a finger under a chin and looking into her eyes.

Amy blushed. "What?"

"The smile," he reminded her. "Not two minutes ago you were soaking my costume with your tears."

"I just remembered something," she said evasively. "It isn't important."

His gaze locked with hers and something simmered in the air between them. "It is if it put a smile back on your lips," he said quietly.

She didn't want him talking about her lips or looking at them or thinking about them. Frantically she searched for something to throw him off track. "I was just thinking about how mad Josh will be that he didn't get to ride in the golf cart."

Nick didn't look as if he believed her, but he didn't press her on it. "Then we'll see that he gets a ride. You ready to go for another stroll through the mall?"

Amy blotted up her tears with the last of the tissues Maylene had given her and forced a bright smile. "Absolutely," she said. She looked at the damp spots on Nick's costume and winced. "Sorry about that."

"No big deal." He shrugged. "It'll dry out."

When he would have taken Emma back from the security officer, Amy put her hand on his arm and felt the muscle clench. "I'm sorry we've caused such an uproar."

"You have nothing to be sorry for," he said tersely,

his expression suddenly distant. "But let's not waste any more time, okay?"

Startled by his abrupt change in mood, she merely nodded, then set out to keep pace with him when he strode off with Emma back in his arms. One of these days she might not mind trying to unravel the many contradictions in Nick DiCaprio, but now certainly wasn't the time. With his quick withdrawal still fresh in her mind, she couldn't help wondering if the timing would ever be right.

NICK HAD JUST DESCENDED straight into hell. He'd had a woman in his arms who'd felt exactly right there, but unless he found her son and did it soon, she would wind up hating him. He imagined Tyler Hamilton's mother didn't have a lot of nice things to say about him these days and for good reason. He'd failed her—and her boy—and this whole episode with Amy Riley was beginning to feel the same way…as if it were skidding downhill at a breakneck pace.

The emotional roller coaster of thinking her son had been found, only to realize it had been another lost child had to have been devastating. It had nearly torn him apart watching the hope in her eyes fade and the despair return.

"Let's stop back at Santa's village," he said, praying that maybe there would be news there. Of course Trish had promised to call if Josh turned up, but Nick was starting to run out of ideas except for the kind that didn't bear thinking about. He'd have to start considering those possibilities soon enough.

"Sure, whatever you think," Amy agreed, once again sounding defeated.

Nick didn't even try to dream up some lie just to bolster her spirits. She obviously knew as well as he did that the longer Josh was missing, the more danger he might be in. Besides, he was fresh out of good cheer and he wasn't sure he could fake it. He was almost as worried as Amy must be by now.

A minute later as they approached Santa's workshop, Trish spotted them and met them before they could get too close and cause a stir. Her worried gaze shifted from him to Amy, then back again.

"Nothing?" Trish asked.

"Not yet," Nick admitted.

Trish turned to Amy. "I am so sorry about the false alarm. You must have been heartbroken. Would you like to go freshen up or anything? Get something to drink or eat? You could get off your feet for a few minutes in my office, while Nicky continues the search for Josh."

"I'm okay," Amy insisted. "I have to keep looking." She faced Nick. "But shouldn't you go back to work? Santa's been missing a long time now. The kids must be losing patience and driving their parents nuts."

"I'll go back, but not until we've found your son," he said.

"But all those kids." She gestured toward the line that still snaked down the mall's main corridor. "They're going to be so disappointed."

"They'll survive," he insisted. He gave his sister a speculative look. "But with some extra padding, Trish, you could probably pull off the Santa thing yourself."

Amy chuckled at his outrageous suggestion, which was what he'd hoped for.

The sound made his spirits lift fractionally. He grinned at her. "I wasn't kidding."

Trish frowned at him. "Well, it's not going to happen, big brother, so get over that idea. You're going to find Josh any second, then get right back into Santa mode. If I didn't know for a fact that Amy really does have a son and it's obvious that she's worried sick about him, I'd suspect you of putting her up to this just to help you sneak away from Santa duty."

Amy's eyes widened. "Would he do that?"

"In a heartbeat," Trish confirmed. "I could tell you stories about my brother—"

Nick decided these two had bonded enough. "Amy doesn't have time to listen to you go on and on about how badly I've mistreated you and how I've misbehaved through the years," he said. "Her son's missing, remember?"

Amy's intrigued expression immediately faded, but she cast a last glance over her shoulder as Nick led her away. "Later," she told Trish. "I want to hear everything."

"That's a promise," his traitorous sister replied.

Nick shook his head. If he had his way, these two wouldn't spend five minutes alone together. It was a toss-up whether his sister would sell him out...or just try to sell him. He'd seen that matchmaking glint in her eyes a few other times over the years, beginning way back with Jenny Davis. It never boded well.

# CHAPTER FIVE

NICK TUCKED HIS HAND under Amy's elbow and started away from Santa's village, then hesitated. As much as he hated it, there was something that had to be done. He'd waited too long as it was. To wait any longer would be totally irresponsible. He could only imagine what his bosses would have to say if this whole search blew up in his face because he'd been trying to prove something to himself. He had to stop thinking about his shattered ego and do what was best for the boy.

"Wait here a sec, okay?" he told Amy, as he held Emma out to Amy. "There's something I forgot to tell Trish."

"Sure," she said, taking the protesting Emma from him.

Warmed by the baby's reaction to parting with him, he slipped back through the crowd and found his sister. En route, his good spirits had given way to grim reality. Trish apparently sensed his mood.

"What's up?" she asked, regarding him with concern.

"I didn't want to say this in front of Amy, but I think it's time to call in the police," he told her. "I don't like the fact that we haven't had any sightings of the boy at all. I'd think even on a day as crazy as today someone would have noticed a kid alone and stopped a security guard."

Trish's worry turned to dismay. "You don't think…?"

Nick cut her off before she could voice the thought. "I'm trying not to jump to any conclusions. Maybe Josh is just a self-possessed kid who isn't the least bit afraid to wander around in a strange place alone, but it's not likely. Most kids start to worry when their mom's been out of sight for this long. I don't want to upset Amy any more than she is already, but I'd feel better if there were some more professional cops on the scene or at least watching things in the parking lot to see if anything looks suspicious out there."

"You're absolutely right. I'll call nine-one-one," Trish said at once, clearly grasping the urgency.

"Tell the dispatcher I'm on the scene in an unofficial capacity and that I need some backup over here."

His sister nodded and pulled her cell phone out of her pocket.

Nick felt awful for Trish. He knew how important this job was to her and that a Christmas Eve story with an unhappy ending was the last thing she needed, but he didn't have a choice. Josh's safety came first. If they did everything right, there was still hope that the ending would be the happy one they all wished for.

"I know this is exactly what you were hoping to avoid, Trish, but I don't want to take chances. I hope you understand that."

"Of course I do," she said readily. "Without a doubt, finding Josh is far more important than the mall's PR.

I'd never forgive myself if something were to happen to that boy and we hadn't done everything we could to find him."

"Tell me about it," Nick agreed grimly.

She gave him a penetrating look. "You holding up okay, Nicky? I know this can't be easy for you and I'm sorry I put you in this position. Maybe when your backup gets here, you can walk away and let them handle this."

"No way," he said tersely. "Amy's counting on me."

"That's what worries me," Trish said gently. "I know how you'll react if you think you've let her down."

"I'll be fine," Nick insisted. "Or I will be, as long as we find that boy safe and sound."

AMY BOUNCED EMMA in her arms and tried not to lose her patience as she waited for Nick to return. She kept consoling herself that they weren't the only ones searching for Josh, but she needed to be doing *something*, not just standing idly by while others looked for her son.

"Sorry that took so long," Nick apologized as he joined her. "Let's try this corridor over here on the left. We didn't go this way earlier."

"Your sister must be tearing her hair out over having Santa disappear on the busiest day of the season," Amy said. "I could look by myself."

"I thought we'd settled that. I still think we'll have a better chance of finding him if I'm with you. Do you have another picture of Josh in your wallet? I think we should start showing it to some of the shop employees. Maybe they've spotted him if he's been doing some shopping. A kid that age on his own would definitely leave an impression."

"I really don't think he has the money to shop," she said, though Nick's plan was probably as good as anything else they'd tried.

"No telling what a kid might have saved up for Christmas," Nick countered. "Is he a thoughtful boy?"

Amy recalled the breakfast he'd tried to make her for Mother's Day and the brightly painted lump of clay with an imprint of his hand he'd given her for her birthday. "He tries to be."

"Then he might have spotted something he wanted to buy for you," Nick said. "Have you mentioned anything in particular you want?"

Amy shook her head.

"Nothing?" he asked as if it were impossible for a woman not to want something.

"I've been totally focused on getting settled in our new place," she said with a shrug. "And I've never much cared about accumulating things."

"You haven't spotted a sweater in a newspaper ad or some earrings you might have mentioned around Josh?"

She glanced down at her comfortable, well-worn jeans and the warm red sweater she'd owned for four years at least. "I've never exactly been a fashion plate," she told Nick. "I dress better than this for work, but my wardrobe's not fancy. Just some suits and blouses. I can't imagine Josh shopping for those."

Nick surveyed her with an appreciative once-over that heated her cheeks. "You look good to me," he said, his gaze lingering on the soft red wool clinging to her chest. Then he jerked his gaze away. "Okay, then," he said, his voice a little choked. "If not clothes, what about candy? Do you have a weakness for chocolate?"

Amy laughed. "Do you know a woman who doesn't? But I'm happy with a bag of mini candy bars from the grocery store. I don't crave the gourmet stuff. It's definitely not in our budget."

"Still, a kid might spot those big gold boxes of chocolates and check them out," he said, turning into a candy boutique.

Amy reluctantly followed him inside, where she was immediately assailed by the rich scent of fine chocolate. She couldn't help staring at the selection of truffles in the glass case, the piles of elegantly wrapped holiday boxes on the display tables. Her mouth watered despite her claim that ordinary candy satisfied her cravings. The last time she'd indulged in anything this decadent had been before her marriage when Ned brought one of the small boxes for her as a Valentine's Day gift. It was one of those rare thoughtful gestures that had convinced her he was the right one for her.

She was so absorbed in reading the labels on the trays of individual candies that she was barely aware of Nick chatting with the salesclerk, then showing the woman a picture of Josh. Only when they were back outside did she notice the small gold bag in his hand.

"Here," he said. "You need to keep your strength up."

Startled, she met his gaze. "But I told you I don't have to have the decadent kind of chocolate."

He grinned. "Maybe not, but you were practically drooling all over the case. I had to buy something."

She was too tempted by the decadent scent of that

chocolate to turn him down. She opened the bag and found four different candies inside. She took a deep breath just to savor the aroma.

He watched her with amusement. "I hear they're even better when you actually eat them."

She held out the bag. "Would you like one?" she asked politely.

Chuckling, he replied, "I am not risking life and limb by trying to take one of those away from you."

"I offered," she said, though she drew the bag back.

"But the look in your eyes is daring me to accept," he teased.

Embarrassed, she held out the bag again. "No, really. Have one."

"Watching you enjoy them will be treat enough for me," he said.

She couldn't totally hide her relief. She reached in the bag, drew out one with a dark chocolate coating. If she remembered correctly, it had a chocolate raspberry filling. Very slowly she bit into it, then closed her eyes as the flavors burst on her tongue.

"Oh, my," she murmured.

When she opened her eyes again, Nick was regarding her with an odd expression. In fact, he looked a little dazed.

"What?" she asked.

"Just thinking what it would be like," he began, then cut himself off. "Never mind. We need to keep looking for Josh."

"Nick?"

He grabbed her hand. "Come on, Amy. There are a lot of stores left to cover."

He moved so quickly, she practically had to run to keep up with him. Emma jiggled in his arms, giggling happily at the unexpected adventure. He whipped in and out of half a dozen stores before he finally slowed down again.

Amy regarded him wearily. "I feel as if we're just spinning our wheels. Josh could be anywhere."

"What have you told him to do if he ever gets lost like this?" Nick asked.

"To look for a security guard or policeman, then stay put and wait for me to find him."

"Do you think the lesson took? Has he ever gotten lost before?"

"No, he's usually very good about sticking close to me."

"Would he talk to strangers?"

"Not unless it's a policeman or somebody like that. I know he's listened to me and his dad about that. He never answers the door unless he knows who it is. And he absolutely wouldn't get in a car with anyone he doesn't know. He even asks for permission before he'll accept a ride home with a friend's parent."

Nick nodded. "That's good. Would he kick up a fuss if someone approached him that he didn't know?"

"Absolutely," she said with confidence. It was the one thing she was sure of. No one would snatch Josh from the mall without someone noticing a struggle of some kind. Outlining all the safety measures they'd taught Josh reassured her.

"You know, I'm beginning to think you're right about him shopping," she told Nick, clinging to her newfound conviction. "He probably doesn't even think he's lost and he's probably completely forgotten about the time. I'll bet something in some store caught his attention and off he went without a second thought. Maybe it's not even me he's shopping for, but Emma. I saw a baby store somewhere. And there was a toy store when we first came in the mall."

Nick gave her an encouraging smile. "Let's hope you're right. We'll work our way back to those. If what you say is true, if he's just gotten distracted, he could still find his way over to Santa's village very soon."

"Yes," she said eagerly, ready to seize on the slim hope. "I'll bet that's exactly what will happen."

They went into another half-dozen stores with no luck, then started down the other side of the corridor. The canned Christmas music, barely discernible over the hum of conversation, seemed to mock their somber mission.

"How did you end up in Charlotte?" Nick asked as they walked past a wall of display windows for a department store.

Amy regretted more than ever that Josh wasn't with them as she glimpsed the elaborate displays of snow-covered villages and mechanical elves and reindeer. She dragged her gaze away and concentrated on answering Nick.

"Things were pretty bad after my divorce," she told him. "I'd been working for a bank that has headquarters here. My boss knew what I'd been going through and asked if I'd be interested in a transfer. I grabbed at the chance."

"Was Josh happy about the move?"

"No," she admitted. "He misses his dad. I've tried

not to let him know how I feel about my ex, because I don't think it's fair for a kid to be caught in the middle between parents."

"I couldn't agree more," Nick said with feeling. "You'd be surprised how many times I see parents using their children as weapons in their grown-up wars. It's always the kids who suffer most." He studied her intently. "I'm a little surprised, though, that your ex-husband agreed to let you bring the kids this far away."

"I never said he deserved the love Josh has for him," she said wryly. "He was reasonably attentive when Josh was underfoot. The same with Emma. But he's remarried and he has another baby on the way. Our kids are extraneous to his new life. I figured in the long run Josh and Emma would be better off in North Carolina, than they would be in Michigan where they'd experience their dad's growing disinterest on a daily basis."

"He sounds like a real jewel, this ex of yours," Nick said with evident disgust.

"He was that and worse," Amy confirmed. "But he gave me two great kids, so I can't hate him completely." She met his gaze. "Why were you so worried earlier that my ex-husband might be involved in Josh's disappearance?"

"It happens sometimes in divorces," he said. "Custody might be settled in a courtroom, but parents don't always agree with the decision. Then the noncustodial parent decides to do something about it."

His answer was too pat and the way he avoided meeting Amy's gaze told her there was more to it. "Have you handled some of these custody battles?"

"From time to time," he affirmed, his expression more strained than ever.

"How ugly have they gotten?" she pressed.

"Pretty damn ugly," he said. "Let's not go there, okay? Your ex is back in Michigan, so that's one less thing for us to worry about."

Amy recognized that he'd closed down the subject, but that only made her want to pursue it more. Before she could, Nick deftly changed the subject.

"It must be hard being in a new place at Christmas," he suggested. "Especially with kids."

Amy gave him a knowing look, but decided to let him get away with it.

"I don't think I realized until today how hard it would be," she admitted. "The Santa thing was a big tradition with us, at least for Josh. And we always went to church on Christmas Eve to the children's service, then went home and had hot chocolate, put out cookies and milk for Santa, and watched Christmas movies till Josh fell asleep. Then Ned would carry him upstairs and we'd put all the presents under the tree, then eat the cookies."

Nick smiled. "You didn't drink the milk?"

Amy wrinkled her nose. "Warm milk? Yuck. We dumped it out and left the glass sitting there with the empty cookie plate." She sighed suddenly. "I wonder what traditions we'll have now."

"You'll make new ones," Nick said. "And keep the old ones that work, just like coming to the mall today to see Santa." He hesitated, then said, "You know, you could come to church with my family tonight if you wanted to. I wasn't going to go, but I will if you think

Josh would enjoy going and keeping another tradition alive."

Amy's eyes turned misty at the suggestion, as well as at his confidence that Josh would be safely back with her before long. "You'd do that? You don't even know Josh and you can't have a very good impression of him—or me—after what's happened today."

"He got lost. He didn't commit a crime," Nick told her. "As for you, there's no mistaking the fact that you're a loving mom. Even the best mothers can't stop kids from slipping away in the blink of an eye."

"Thank you, but I'd hate to have you change your plans for us. You said you hadn't planned on going. What were you going to do?"

"Nothing in particular," he revealed.

Amy regarded him with surprise. "You were going to spend Christmas Eve alone?"

"People do," he said gruffly. "It's no big deal."

"Of course, it is. Surely you'd rather be with your family."

"Thus the invitation to church," he said wryly. "I'd definitely get points with my folks. Besides, I think maybe going to church would be as good for me as it would be for Josh. Maybe I need to stick with tradition, too."

She studied him curiously. "Why is that?"

"Just some demons that need to be laid to rest," he said evasively.

Amy sensed they were finally cutting close to whatever Nick was struggling with. He'd been so kind to her today, she wanted to return the favor. "I don't want to pry, Nick, but is it anything you want to talk about? You've been dancing around something ever since we started searching for Josh."

For an instant it looked as if he might open up and tell her, but just then the color washed out of his face and he abruptly whirled around as if he were trying to avoid someone.

"Nick?" she said, startled by his behavior. "What is it? Did you see someone you know? Someone you'd rather not see?"

"Let's check out this place," he said brusquely, dragging her inside a men's shoe store.

Amy scanned the faces outside to see if she could figure out who had sent Nick fleeing. All she noticed were families, some laughing, some obviously stressed by the mad rush. A few men hurried by looking thoroughly harried. And a few women—young and old—passed, laden down with packages. There was even one group of teenage girls who seemed more intent on looking for boys than shopping. They preened and pretended nonchalance whenever a boy passed by. No one jumped out at Amy as the possible cause of Nick's sudden panic, and that's what it had been, she realized. He'd been thoroughly spooked by whomever he'd spotted.

She turned back to Nick, who was chatting with the clerk behind the counter, his actions now briskly professional again.

Only after they were outside and walking toward the next store did she meet his gaze. "What happened back there, Nick?"

He regarded her with a neutral expression. "I don't know what you mean."

"You're not a good liar," she accused. "Was it an old girlfriend? A current one?"

"Not that it's any of your business, but it was nothing like that," he snapped.

His tone was like a slap. She felt oddly saddened by his refusal to confide in her, but what had she expected? He was right. She hardly knew him. He was a policeman helping her out in a crisis. She had no right to pry into his personal life.

And what about his questions, she asked herself. Were all of those strictly professional, the mark of a thorough detective? She didn't think so.

Nor was the invitation to church. No, there was something between them, some spark that might be explored sometime in the future. That spark went beyond the intensity of the situation. It was definitely personal. The surprise was that after all her vows to concentrate on her new job and her kids, she'd wanted to see where that spark led.

Or, she amended, she'd wanted to until the moment when Nick had deliberately lied and shut her out. She'd already been with a man who'd been a master at keeping her in the dark. She wouldn't knowingly get involved with another one who was capable of the same kind of deceit. It hurt to think that there might be any comparison whatsoever between her ex-husband and this man who'd been only decent and kind to her, but she couldn't take the chance.

Not that she could spend even one more second worrying about such things when Josh was still missing. Nick was her best hope for finding her son. She needed his help. And when Josh was safely with her, then she and Nick DiCaprio would go their separate ways.

Even with her mind made up, though, she couldn't help feeling as if she'd just lost something important, something good that had almost been within her grasp.

# CHAPTER SIX

NICK KNEW HE'D BEEN too abrupt and sharp with Amy.
He'd immediately recognized the hurt in her eyes when
he'd dismissed her well-meaning questions, but what
other choice had he had? How could he explain to her
that he'd just seen the mother of a child who'd died
while he was supposed to be rescuing him? Not only
was it something he could barely stand to remember,
but it would be the worst possible testimonial to his
skills as a police officer. Amy would be justified in de-
manding that someone else take over the search for her
son.

For reasons he didn't care to examine too closely,
Nick didn't want that to happen. As he'd told his sister,
he wanted to see this through. Not only did he want to
spend more time with Amy, but he needed redemption
and this seemed like fate's way of giving him a chance
for it. He needed to prove to himself that he could find
this boy and return him safely to his mother, that the
tragedy with Tyler Hamilton hadn't destroyed him.
Otherwise he'd never be able to go back on active duty
on the force. And if he wasn't a cop, who the hell was
he?

Okay, so his motives were partly selfish. He admitted

that without shame. He didn't want his career going up in flames. He knew in his gut he was *still* one of the best cops in the department. All modesty aside, his skills were superior. He had the citations and job performance reviews to prove it. He just had to tamp down his anger and get his confidence back. The shrink was right about that much. But finding Josh—not endless hours baring his soul—was the answer.

Although he believed wearing this hot and bulky Santa outfit would work to their advantage eventually, he had to admit that right this second he would have preferred being in street clothes so he could blend in and move more quickly. Then, again, the costume may have been the only thing that had kept Tyler Hamilton's mom from recognizing him and for that he was grateful. A confrontation with Mitzi Hamilton was the last thing he needed. He still had nightmares about the bleak expression on her face when he'd had to tell her that Tyler was dead.

"Nick?"

He gazed down into Amy's troubled eyes. "What?"

"Are you okay?"

He forced a reassuring smile. "Fine. Let's get back to work."

Once again, she looked disappointed by his response, as if she'd been expecting—or hoping for—something more. Unfortunately, until they found Josh, he was fresh out of revelations he could make without having her doubt him and scaring her to death.

AMY REEVALUATED her earlier dismay over Nick's reticence. It was evident he was genuinely troubled by something, something more than their unproductive search. Maybe she should force the issue, no matter how reluctant he seemed. Maybe it would do them both good to think about something other than her son. Whatever those demons were that Nick had mentioned, maybe she could help him deal with them.

"You know, Nick," she began casually. "You can talk to me."

He glanced at her with a questioning look. "We've been talking."

"Not about anything significant," she said.

"Oh, I don't know about that," he protested. "You've told me all about your son and about your divorce. I know about how hard it is being away from your family for the holidays. I'd say we've scratched below the surface."

"Up to a point, that's right," she agreed. "You know all that about me, but I know very little about you, other than how many siblings you have and that your folks don't like you being a cop."

"That's my life in a nutshell," he said glibly.

She looked away and thought back over their conversation. One comment stood out. She was pretty sure it held the key to understanding Nick.

"I don't think your life can be summed up so easily," she said quietly. "For instance, I think there's a very specific reason you planned to stay away from church tonight." She stared directly into his eyes. "Are you mad at God? Has something happened to make you question your faith?"

He turned away, but not before she saw that her questions had struck home.

"What was it?" she prodded. She connected the dots and realized that whatever it was that had happened was somehow work related. "Did something go wrong on a case you were handling?"

His hard expression, a stark contrast to the rosy tint of his cheeks and thick white beard of his Santa costume, told her she'd hit on it. Somehow, though, she didn't have the sense that Nick admired her detecting skills.

"Leave it alone," he commanded, his tone like ice. "I'm not discussing it with you or anyone else, especially not when we're in the middle of a search for your son."

"Something tells me this is exactly the time you should talk about it," she countered. "It's weighing on you now. Is it interfering with your ability to help me find Josh?"

"Absolutely not. I don't let anything interfere with my job, not even a woman asking too many pesky questions about things that are none of her business. Now will you get your priorities in order? Stop trying to dig around in my psyche and pay attention to the people around us. You could walk right on by Josh and never see him."

The harsh accusation stung, but unfortunately Amy couldn't deny it. She'd needed a temporary distraction and she'd seized on fixing Nick, whether he needed it or not. She still believed he did, but that wasn't the point and it wasn't her job, particularly not this afternoon.

"Okay," she said softly. "I apologize for prying."

"Whatever," he said, avoiding her gaze.

Nick's attention was deliberately focused on scanning the crowds around them. Amy sighed, then followed suit, looking into the face of every child they passed. With each one that wasn't Josh, she grew more and more discouraged. With each second that passed without a call from one of the security guards or Trish, her heart ached a little more.

Then, just when she was losing all hope, she spotted a familiar-looking shock of brown hair sticking up on the back of a boy's head. He was too far away for even a glimpse of his face. Even so, a faint spark of recognition made her spirits soar. She tried to tamp down her excitement. Too many times before her hopes had been dashed seconds later.

Then her eyes locked on a red and green scarf that had come unwound from around the boy's neck. It was dragging on the ground behind him. There was no mistaking that scarf. She'd knit it for Josh herself just last Christmas.

"There!" she screamed, seizing Nick's arm and pointing across the mall. "I see him, Nick. He's right over there, going into that store. You were right all along. He is shopping."

Nick stared in the direction she was pointing. "Where did you see him, Amy? Are you sure it was Josh?"

By then Josh had disappeared into the store, so rather than answer she started to dash across the mall, dragging Nick with her. Trying to cut through the crowd bordered on impossible until Nick cupped a hand under her arm and guided her through. Whether it was his size, his determination or the Santa costume, the crowd gave him room to pass.

"Which shop?" he asked when they reached the other side. "I still don't see him."

"Right here," Amy said, her cheeks burning as she stopped in front of a display window filled with mannequins clad only in lacy underwear. "He went into the lingerie shop."

Nick gave her an odd look. "Your five-year-old son went into a lingerie shop?"

"Hey, you asked what he might buy me for Christmas. His dad used to give me fancy lingerie. It never occurred to me when you asked, but I suppose Josh got the idea from that."

Nick still looked vaguely disconcerted. "I see."

As they reached the store's entrance, she sensed Nick's hesitance and thought she knew the cause. Most men loved to see women in sexy, lacy undergarments, but they'd rather be caught dead than be seen shopping for them. Amused, she looked into his eyes. "You're not scared of a few bras and panties, are you?"

He frowned at the question. "Nope, just the women swarming around in there buying them."

"It's Christmas Eve," she reminded him. "Take another look inside. Most of the shoppers today are desperate men. I'm the one who ought to be embarrassed."

"You're absolutely sure Josh went in there?" he asked, still hanging back, though his alert gaze continued to scan the customers.

Even amidst the crush of much taller men inside the shop, she could see Josh…or at least the tail end of that dragging scarf. Filled with relief at the realization that her boy was safe and sound, she nodded. Then the crowd parted and she saw him clearly, head to toe, totally absorbed by a table full of sale items.

"I can see him from here," she said excitedly. "Right there, Nick! He has a pair of red thong panties in his hand."

At her claim, rather than looking into the store, Nick's gaze sought hers and never left her face. His eyes darkened with unmistakable heat. "Red, huh?"

Amy couldn't help it. She laughed. "It's not becoming for Santa to drool. You look a little like I must have looked in the candy store. Will you come on? Let's not let him slip away from us."

"It's probably not a good idea for Santa to be seen ogling ladies' lingerie, either," he commented. "Why don't I just stand right here blocking the doorway with Miss Emma, while you retrieve your son? I'll be backup in case he tries to scoot off again."

"Chicken," she accused lightly, able to tease because the nightmare was almost over.

"Damn straight," he agreed without apology.

Amy didn't waste another second arguing. She made her way through the mobbed store till she was right beside Josh. For a second she simply stood there, drinking in the precious sight of him. Finally she spoke.

"Young man, you are in so much trouble," she said, hunkering down to draw him into her arms in a fierce embrace. She was so relieved, she wanted to never let go.

"Mom!" he protested, pulling away. "You're not supposed to see me."

She shook her head. He was oblivious to her distress and to the relief that was now spilling through her.

"And why shouldn't I see you?"

"'Cause I'm buying your present," he said reasonably. "It's supposed to be a surprise."

As desperately as she wanted to hug him and hold on forever, she had to make him understand that what he'd done was not acceptable.

Keeping her expression stern, she demanded, "Present or no present, Joshua Riley, did you stop to think for one second that you might scare the living daylights out of me by running off to go shopping?"

He blinked hard. "You were scared?"

"Well, of course, I was," she said, giving him a gentle shake. "When have I ever let you go off shopping all by yourself? More than that, you've never been to this mall before. When you let go of my hand, I thought you were going straight to see Santa, but you never showed up. I had no idea where you were. You've been missing for a very long time."

He regarded her earnestly. "I did go to see Santa, but the line was really, really long and I wanted to get you a surprise, you know, something like Dad would get you so you wouldn't be sad."

Touched more than she wanted to admit, she asked, "How did you know where to look?"

"I knew the kind of store, 'cause I went with Dad last year," he explained. "First I had to find the directory thing, because I knew you'd be mad if I asked a stranger. I looked and looked, but I couldn't find one, so I just kept looking for the store. There are lots of stores and it's hard to move 'cause there are so many people. It took a really long time, but this is just like the one where Dad used to shop."

He sounded so proud of himself, it made Amy want to cry. She blinked back tears. "Oh, sweetie, I don't need a present like that. Besides, where did you get that kind of money? Even on sale, these things are expensive."

"I saved the money Dad gave me before we left Michigan." He held out the red thong panties. "Do you like these?"

In Amy's opinion they looked uncomfortable, just as the ones Ned had given her through the years had been. Those had stayed tucked in her lingerie drawer most of the time. She was not letting her son waste money on another pair that would be consigned to the bottom of her dresser.

"What I think is that you are an amazing boy to want to buy me a present like that, but I want you to save that money for something special for you, just like your dad intended." She regarded him seriously. "Though, it will be a very long time before you get to spend it, because after this stunt you're going to be grounded till you're thirty."

His expression faltered. "But, Mom, I just went shopping for you," he protested. "I thought you'd be happy."

"While buying a present is a thoughtful thing to do, running away to do it is not. A policeman and an entire mall security team have been searching for you for more than an hour," she responded.

For the first time, Josh seemed to grasp the magnitude of what he'd done. "Uh-oh," he whispered. "Are they gonna be mad at me?"

"I think they're going to be relieved that you're

okay," she said. "And I know they'll appreciate it when you apologize to each and every one of them."

"Okay," he said meekly. "I'll tell 'em I'm really sorry. Maybe we could go home and get some Christmas cookies for them."

Her point seemed to have sunk in, at least enough for now. She'd spend the next ten years driving it home. With a boy this precocious, she was sure she'd have lots of opportunities.

"Now that you understand that what you did was wrong, I think there's somebody here you might want to meet. He needs to see for himself that you're safe and then let everyone know we've found you. Put those panties back, and let's go."

Josh parted with the panties reluctantly, then dutifully took the hand she held out.

"Who is it?" he asked as they walked through the store. "Who wants to see me?" His eyes widened. "Is it Dad? Did Dad come for Christmas?"

She was seized by momentary anger at her ex, who hadn't even made a phone call to Josh for over a week now. But what was the point? Ned was Ned. She was tired of covering for his lack of consideration.

"No, sweetie," she consoled Josh, biting back the desire to make excuses. "It's not your father."

"Oh," he said, his tone flat with disappointment.

"Come on now. I think this will be just as good," she told him.

"Grandma and Grandpa?" he asked, but without as much enthusiasm.

Before Amy could reply, Josh spotted Santa holding Emma. His cheeks turned pink and his eyes lit up.

Whatever disappointment he'd felt that it wasn't his dad vanished in a split second of recognition.

"Santa!" he shouted, clearly thrilled. "You brought me Santa!"

For the second time that day he jerked free of Amy's grip and made a dash for it, but this time Santa was right there to scoop him close in a hug.

## CHAPTER SEVEN

NICK'S GAZE HAD LOCKED on Amy as she'd traveled through the store and reunited with her son. Emma had laughed and pointed, clearly recognizing her big brother and delighted to see him. Something inside Nick melted as he watched the reunion.

This was what should have happened with Tyler Hamilton. His mom should have had a joyous moment just like this, but she hadn't. Instead, there had been only the awful news that her boy was dead, news Nick had insisted on delivering himself. He had to stand by helplessly as the color had drained from her face. He'd caught her as her knees gave way and she'd been racked by grief-stricken sobs. He couldn't imagine that memory ever fading, not even with this far happier memory to replace it.

When Josh spotted him, whooped joyously, and let loose of Amy's hand, Nick dropped to his knees so he could catch the boy as he barreled straight into his knees. For at least a fraction of a second, all he felt was relief. *This* search had ended well. *This* boy was back with his mother and Nick had played at least a small part in making it happen.

His gaze stayed on Amy's. She looked as if she'd been given the very best Christmas present ever.

"Thank you," she mouthed.

Before Nick could respond, Josh wiggled free and studied him intently. "I met Santa last year," he said. "You don't look like him."

Nick bit back a smile. "Santa had a rough year. I'm older."

Josh didn't look convinced. "You don't sound like him, either. You sound funny, like you live around here instead of at the North Pole."

"Well, you see, Josh, that's the thing. Santa has to adapt to his environment," Nick improvised as Amy chuckled. "I've been here at this mall for a while now and everyone talks like this. They expect me to sound just like them."

"I guess," Josh said doubtfully. Then his expression brightened. "Can I tell you what I want for Christmas right now? That way I won't have to wait forever in line. That's how come I got lost, 'cause the line was too long and I didn't want to wait in it."

Nick exchanged a glance with Amy, who looked as if she'd give the boy the sun, moon and stars now that he was safely back with her. He wasn't inclined to be as lenient.

"Let's talk about this," he suggested to Josh. "Man to man."

"Okay," Josh said eagerly.

Nick barely contained a grin. "I'm not so sure little boys who run away and scare their moms ought to be getting presents from Santa," he said. "What do you think?"

"You're asking me to decide if I should get presents?" Josh asked incredulously.

"Yep."

Josh's expression turned serious as he pondered Nick's—*Santa's*—question. "Okay, here's what I think," he told Nick earnestly. "I didn't mean to scare Mom. And I only went to buy her a present. That's a good thing, right? Mad as she was, even Mom said I was amazing."

Nick swallowed a laugh. Amy must have her hands full with this one. He had well-developed reasoning powers for a boy his age, or else it was just a strong sense of self-preservation. Nick had been very much like that as a kid, able to fast-talk himself out of most trouble. And his mother had been every bit as tolerant as Amy. His father had been the disciplinarian. Josh didn't have anyone around to fill that role. For today, at least, maybe Nick could do it.

He looked Josh in the eye. "It was a very unselfish thing to want to do," he agreed. "So, yes, that does count as a good thing. But running away, even with the best intentions, is never good. Lots of people have been very worried about you."

The boy regarded him with genuine dismay. "I know. Mom said." Then his expression brightened with hope. "But I'm going to apologize, so it'll be okay."

Nick glanced up at Amy. "I'm sure an apology will be appreciated, but I want to be sure you understand why what you did was wrong."

"Because I scared Mom," Josh said at once.

"That's one reason," Nick confirmed.

He tried to find a way to drive his point home without scaring Josh and robbing him of his astonishing fearlessness. It would be a good trait later in life, though in the meantime it was likely to give Amy frequent anxiety attacks.

He regarded Josh with a somber expression. "But there's another one and it's just as important. It's very dangerous for someone your age to be alone in a crowd like this. All sorts of things can happen to children when there's not an adult around to keep an eye on them."

Josh studied him intently, absorbing his words, but clearly not ready to take them at face value. "Like what?"

Nick debated how specific to get, then decided on another tack. "You believe in Santa, right?"

"Sure."

"Well, Santa sees a lot of things, like when boys and girls are good and bad."

Josh nodded. "That's why I'm really, really good." He glanced at his mom, then amended, "Well, most of the time, anyway. Until today."

Nick hid a grin. "Okay, then, if you understand that Santa knows a lot about what happens all over the world, then could you just take my word for it that it's dangerous for you not to be with an adult in a busy mall like this?"

Josh still looked vaguely skeptical. "But nothing bad happened," he protested.

"This time," Nick emphasized. "You were very lucky today, Josh, but it's not a chance you should ever take again. Do you understand that?"

"I guess so."

"Then here's the deal. If you want Santa to reconsider discussing presents with you, you have to promise never to do anything like this again."

With presents on the line, Josh nodded solemnly. "Okay. I promise." He turned to his mother. "I'm sorry, Mom."

"Santa will know if you go back on your word," Nick warned him. "So you have to keep that promise forever."

Josh gazed at him with dismay. "Like, till I'm a teenager or something?"

"No, forever is even longer than that. It's till you're all grown-up and even then you should never do anything that might make your mom worry. Okay?"

"I guess," Josh said. "I'll try, but that sounds like a long time to be good." He studied Nick closely. "Do you have a mom?"

Nick nodded.

"Does she still worry about you?"

"Oh, yeah," Nick said fervently. And unfortunately he worried her all the time, though he wasn't about to tell Josh that.

"But you're Santa!"

"Moms never stop worrying, no matter who you are or how old you get," Nick told him. "I know forever seems like way too long, but I think you can do it."

"Maybe," Josh said, his voice filled with doubt.

"Why don't you think about it for a while and we'll talk about it again when you come through the line to tell me what you want for Christmas?"

Josh started to break away. "I'll get in line right now," he said, clearly about to make a dash for Santa's village.

Nick snagged his hand. "Hey there, what did we just talk about?"

Josh winced. "Oh, yeah. Mom, can we get in line now?"

Before Amy could reply, Nick glanced at the endless line. He figured if he was going to have to deal with all these kids who'd been waiting patiently to see him for more than an hour, there should be a reward for him at the end of it. Besides, something compelled him to make sure he had a chance to spend more time with this family. He wanted time to persuade Amy to go to church with his family this evening. He sensed that with them beside him tonight, he might start down the path to something special.

"Tell you what," he said to Josh. "Since the line's so long, why don't you, your mom and Emma here, go grab a snack and then come back? Then you can tell me what you want for Christmas."

"Will there still be time?" Josh asked worriedly.

"I won't leave till you've come back," Nick promised. He glanced at Amy. "Is that okay with you? You look as if you could use something to eat. The food court's right across the way. I highly recommend the pizza."

She seemed uncertain for a moment, then her expression brightened. "Actually I'm starving. I had a touch of the flu earlier, but it seems to be gone. To my amazement, pizza sounds great. Can we bring you anything?"

Nick shook his head.

"Then we'll see you in a little while," Amy concluded.

She started away with Emma in one arm and Josh holding her other hand, then turned and came back. Before Nick realized her intention, she stood on tiptoe and pressed a kiss to his cheek.

"Thank you for helping me find Josh," she whispered, her eyes damp with tears. "You have no idea…" Her voice broke.

He touched a finger to her cheek, wiped away a single tear. "I think I do," he responded. "And I'm glad I was able to help."

Her gaze locked with his. "I'll never forget what you did for us." Then her lips slowly curved. "Or all the unanswered questions I asked you."

Nick knew she'd meant it as a mild threat, but he couldn't help chuckling. "You may be the most persistent person I know."

She grinned. "Remember that. Now, are you sure you don't want me to bring something back for you? A soda? A slice of pizza?"

"Nothing," he said again.

Not until she was moving through the crowd did he murmur, "Just yourselves."

He uttered the telling words just in time for Trish to overhear them.

"Find something more than a lost boy, big brother?" she taunted.

"Who knows?" he said, sounding only slightly defensive. "I might have."

"I saw the kiss, by the way. And I couldn't miss the thunderstruck expression on your face." She smiled. "Apparently, it's a season for miracles, after all."

Just then their mother, Laura DiCaprio, rushed through the crowd and joined them. "There you are," she said, sounding slightly winded as if she'd run through the mall. She looked Nick over from head to toe. "Nicky, you make a wonderful Santa," she said approvingly.

His mother's arrival was not a development he'd anticipated. Nor was he particularly overjoyed to see her. He couldn't help wondering what had brought her here, especially since she looked as if she'd interrupted her Christmas baking to come. He frowned at his sister, convinced she was somehow behind this, but Trish merely shrugged.

"Don't look at me," she said. "I haven't spoken to her all day."

He turned back to his mother. "What are you doing here, Mom? Don't tell me it's a coincidence, because I know you finished your Christmas shopping a month ago."

"I finished in September, as a matter of fact," she informed him.

"Not a direct answer," he accused.

"And I'm not some suspect," she retorted.

"Mother!"

"Okay, if you must know, Maylene Kinney called me. She told me about the missing boy…" Her voice trailed off as she studied him intently. "Well, I'm sure you understand why I had to come, Nicky. I wanted to see for myself that you're okay. Your father's outside cruising around looking for a parking place. I imagine he'll be in here eventually." She regarded him hesitantly. "Is it over? Is the boy okay?"

"He's fine," Nick said tersely.

None of this was good, Nick thought wearily. If news of another missing boy, even one that had been found already, got out, the mall was going to be crawling with reporters. He pinned his sister with a look. "If any of the media show up, keep them away from me, okay? Tell them it was a false alarm. Or tell them the truth, that Josh is back with his mom and it's all over, but leave me out of it."

Trish regarded him with dismay. "I'll do my best, but Nicky, there's a reporter here already, doing a story about the last-minute holiday shoppers. I'll talk to her, but you know she may not give up easily. It's a great story. Family reunited by Santa on Christmas Eve."

"If that's all there was to it, it would be one thing, but we both know better," he said.

"But Nicky you'll be a hero," his mom spoke. "Wouldn't that be a good thing after…well, after what happened before?"

"I don't want to be a hero and it would take more than this to turn me into one. Hell, I don't even want to be Santa." He shook his head. "I never should have answered my phone this morning."

Then he thought of meeting Amy and that precocious boy of hers. He remembered how it felt to have sweet Emma in his arms. He wouldn't have missed that for anything.

He caught the expression in his sister's eyes and knew she understood. "I'm going back to work before these kids start a riot," he said grimly.

Then he was struck by another thought. "Trish, maybe you ought to find Amy and warn her about that reporter. I don't know if anyone would recognize her or Josh and point them out, but she ought to be prepared. Tell her to stay in the food court till you come back for her. I promised Josh he could visit with Santa before the mall closes."

His mother's eyes brightened with curiosity. "Amy? Is that the woman whose boy you found? Maylene said she was lovely and that she's new in town and a single mom. And Josh must be her son."

"That's right," Nick said, aware of the matchmaking wheels spinning into action.

"I'll go with you, Trish," his mother declared. "I'd like to meet her. Maybe she'd like to bring her family to Christmas dinner tomorrow."

Trish couldn't seem to hide her amusement. He doubted she'd even tried.

"Any comment, big brother?" she inquired.

He sighed. "What would be the point? You two never listen to a word I say, anyway."

"That is not true, Nicholas DiCaprio," his mother scolded, then winked. "Sometimes we just read between the lines, too. Come, Trish. Let's go find this woman. Nicky, when your father turns up, you tell him where to find me."

Nick watched them go. He swallowed hard. If it weren't for the jostling throng of kids waiting for him, he would have tried to stop his mom and sister, or at least gone with them to protect Amy. He had a hunch she'd be safer with a whole battalion of news-hungry reporters than she would be with his mom and sister when they were on a mission to give him the priceless Christmas gift of a new romance.

AMY BOUGHT SLICES of pizza and soft drinks for herself and Josh, then searched for a place to sit. Every table was jammed with shoppers taking a break from the frenzy. She could barely maneuver Emma's stroller, between the chairs. She watched with her heart in her throat as Josh tried to balance the tray with their food.

"Over here," Trish said, waving and greeting her with a smile. "My mom's holding a table for you."

"Thank you so much," Amy said, relieved. "Did Nick get back on Santa duty okay?"

"He's on the job, but he wanted me to warn you to stay put here till I come back for you."

Amy paused in midstride. "Oh?"

"I'm so sorry," Trish apologized. "We think word may have gotten out about the missing child. Because of Nick's involvement, it could turn into kind of a big story. I'm going to do what I can to fend off any reporters, including the one who's already here on a different assignment, but Nick didn't want you guys to get dragged into the middle of it." She gave Amy a questioning look. "I'm assuming he's right, that you'd prefer not to be interviewed?"

"He's absolutely right," Amy said, filled with dread at the prospect. Now that the incident was over, she didn't even want to think about it again.

Unfortunately Josh overheard them. "But Mom, we could be on TV," he said excitedly. "That would be so awesome! We could tape it and send it to Dad and Grandma and Grandpa."

"You don't get a say in this," Amy said firmly. "Besides, do you really want your dad to know you ran away? You're in trouble, remember? You have a lot of apologies to deliver."

"But I could say I'm sorry on TV and then everyone would know," Josh countered.

Amy merely shook her head as Trish tried to stifle a grin.

"Let's just sit here and eat our pizza, and be grateful

things turned out okay," Amy told him. "And I need to feed Emma."

"My mom will be glad to help with that," Trish offered. "She's great with kids. She's right over here."

Trish led the way to an empty table that was being held by a woman who looked to be in her midfifties, about the same age as Amy's mother. She looked as if she'd run out of the house in the midst of baking. She still wore an apron over her slacks and sweater and there were streaks of flour on her clothes. The coat she'd flung on looked as if it might be her husband's hunting jacket. Her hair was mussed, as if it had curled while she was working around a hot stove. Despite her disheveled appearance, she gave Amy a warm smile.

"You must be Amy," she said as they approached. "Maylene Kinney described you perfectly." She beamed at Josh. "And you must be the little boy who got away."

Josh nodded. "I'm in trouble," he said, awkwardly balancing the tray of pizza and drinks.

"I imagine you are," she said. "But you're safe and that's what counts."

Mrs. DiCaprio rescued the tray of food and set it on the table. "Oh, that looks good. I think I'll run and get a slice for myself. I've been baking all day and haven't had a minute to eat anything. Don't wait for me."

Amy stared after her. She felt as if she'd been caught up in a whirlwind, then set back down in the calm that followed. "Is she always like this?"

Trish chuckled. "Pretty much. Look, is it okay if I leave you in her hands? I need to go and check on Santa. He was a bit surly before."

"Sure," Amy said, then thought of her earlier conviction that something had happened to Nick on the job recently. That fit with what Trish had mentioned about his involvement in Josh's search being newsworthy. "Trish, before you go, can I ask you something?"

Trish's expression turned cautious. "About?"

"Your brother." She moved away from the table and out of Josh's hearing so she wouldn't completely destroy his illusion of Nick as Santa. "Is there some reason reporters would be all over this story, other than it being Christmas Eve and Santa helping to find Josh?"

Trish hesitated a long time before answering. "You'll have to ask Nicky about that," she said finally. "I really do have to go now. He'll be over to get you soon, I'm sure. Or I'll come back myself. In the meantime, Mom will be around if you need anything."

She took off, leaving Amy's question unanswered. But even without Trish's confirmation, she knew she was right. There was something about Nick she needed to know before things went any further between them. Everything pointed to the fact that he was a great guy and he was certainly surrounded by a wonderful family, if Trish and his mom were anyone to judge by. But he had a secret and she'd had her fill of men with secrets.

# CHAPTER EIGHT

IT HAD BEEN A DAY of astonishing ups and downs, Amy thought as she and Mrs. DiCaprio slowly ate their slices of pizza and listened to Josh going on and on about everything he'd seen while he was on his own in the mall. Nick's mom seemed highly amused by his nonstop chatter, which was all Josh needed. He liked nothing more than an appreciative audience. More worrisome to Amy was the fact that he sounded as if he still thought it was all a huge adventure.

"You do remember what you promised Santa, right?" she asked eventually.

"That I won't ever run away from you again," he said at once. "But Mom, I wasn't lost, not really. You were right here."

"But I didn't know where *you* were," she explained. "That's what counts."

"I get it," he said impatiently as he stuffed the last of his pizza into his mouth. "Can we go back now?"

Amy thought of Trish's warning and cast a helpless look toward Mrs. DiCaprio, who immediately grasped her dilemma.

"Josh, I think your mom needs to rest a bit longer," Nick's mother said. "She wasn't feeling well this morning and then she had quite a scare when you disappeared."

His expression turned into a pout that set Amy's teeth on edge.

"Young man, don't give me a look like that or we'll leave this mall and you won't see Santa at all," Amy threatened. "You need to sit here and behave yourself while I feed Emma. Thank goodness I thought to stick some baby food and a bottle in my bag when we left home. I must have had some instinct that seeing Santa wouldn't go as planned."

"Can't I go see Santa while you feed her?" he pleaded. "Mrs. DiCaprio could take me." Apparently he recognized his mother's exasperated expression, because he sighed heavily. "Okay, okay, I'll wait."

"Smart decision," she commended him.

"Josh, what's on your list for Santa?" Mrs. DiCaprio asked him.

"I can't tell," he said. "It's like a birthday wish. If you tell, it won't come true."

She grinned at him. "But I happen to know Santa very well," she confided in him. "Maybe I could put in a good word for you."

Josh's expression turned thoughtful, but then he shook his head. "That's okay. I think me and Santa are pals. I'll just tell him myself."

Mrs. DiCaprio chuckled. "You know something, Josh. You are a very self-possessed, confident young man. You remind me of another boy."

"Your son?" he guessed.

"Exactly." She pointed to the strands of gray in her hair. "You see all this gray hair? He's the reason I have it. Every time I turned around, he was getting into some kind of mischief. I have four children, all grown now, but only one of them threatened to turn me old before my time." She winked at Amy. "He still has that effect on me, thanks to that job of his."

"What kind of job is it?" Josh asked, regarding her with a rapt expression. "Maybe I could do the same thing when I grow up."

"He's a police detective, as a matter of fact," Mrs. DiCaprio said. "And while he's very good at it, I worry about him."

"Santa says all moms worry about their kids, no matter how old they get," Josh told her.

"That's very true," Mrs. DiCaprio confirmed.

"Do you worry about Trish, too?" he asked.

"Sometimes," she told him. "She works too hard and she could use a little more fun in her life, but at least her work isn't dangerous like my son's."

Amy thought of Nick and envisioned him as a mischievous boy a lot like Josh. It gave her a whole other perspective on the man. She considered asking Mrs. DiCaprio about whatever might be troubling him these days, but decided Trish was right. The answers needed to come from Nick himself.

"Amy?"

Startled, she met Mrs. DiCaprio's gaze. "I'm sorry. Did you say something?"

"I asked if you and your children have plans for tomorrow."

"It's Christmas!" Josh said, interrupting. "We're opening presents."

The older woman smiled. "I meant after that, of

course," she assured him, then met Amy's eyes. "Would you like to spend the afternoon at our house and have dinner with us? It'll be a madhouse, but Rob's sons are about Josh's age. I think he'd enjoy meeting them, don't you? And he has a little girl—Annie—who's only a little older than your Emma."

Amy appreciated the woman's kindness, but surely their presence would be an intrusion. "I'm sure Josh would love meeting them sometime, but we wouldn't want to impose on your family's holiday."

"Don't be silly," Mrs. DiCaprio said at once. "It's no imposition at all. I always cook enough for an army. The turkey's huge, so everyone can take home leftovers. And I've been baking for a month now." She cast a chagrined glance at her flour-covered clothes. "I'm still at it, as you can see. I'm hoping to get one more batch of cookies done before church tonight. There's a reception after the early service."

"Then we shouldn't keep you," Amy said. "We'll be fine here till Trish comes back for us."

"A little while longer won't make a bit of difference," Mrs. DiCaprio responded. "The dough's in the refrigerator chilling. All I need to do is slice the cookies and put them in the oven, while I get dressed for church."

"We used to go to church on Christmas Eve," Josh said.

"Aren't you going to a service tonight?" Mrs. DiCaprio asked.

"Actually we haven't had a chance to find a church since we moved here," Amy admitted. "Nick mentioned something about us coming with you."

"Really?" she said, a speculative glint in her eyes.

"What a wonderful idea! Then you'll get to meet everyone before tomorrow, so you'll have no excuse not to join us for Christmas dinner."

"Can we, Mom? Please!" Josh begged.

Amy recognized that Mrs. DiCaprio had an agenda, but Josh looked so excited that she couldn't bring herself to say no. "If you're sure it's no trouble, we'd love to. The prospect of just the three of us for Christmas dinner didn't hold a lot of appeal."

"I'm sure it didn't," Mrs. DiCaprio sympathized. "The holidays are meant for families to celebrate together." She glanced up. "Ah, here comes Trish now." She stood up. "I'll leave you in her hands and see you this evening. If my husband's still circling around in the parking lot after all this time, he may never bring me here again."

To Amy's surprise, she leaned down and gave her a warm hug. "It was wonderful to meet you, Amy. I think fate had a hand in everything that happened today."

With that, she gathered up their trash, tossed it away, then rushed off with a merry wave in their direction.

Trish gave Amy a speculative look. "I imagine we'll be seeing you at her house tomorrow."

Amy nodded. "She doesn't take no for an answer."

"Not when it's for the greater good," Trish agreed.

"Which is?"

"Giving my brother exactly what he needs for Christmas."

Amy blushed when she realized that Trish was referring to her. To change the subject, she asked, "How did it go with the reporter?"

"She understands," Trish said. "Everything should be fine."

Amy smiled. "Is it okay for Josh to visit with Santa?"

Trish nodded. "That's why I came back for you now. With a half hour to go till the mall closes, there's still a short line. I figure you guys will blend right in. There's no reason for anyone to link you to the big story of the day."

"What about Nick? Was he interviewed?"

"Nope," Trish said grimly. "I told her he'd refused. He had a lot going on as it was—the kid on his lap was screaming bloody murder." She grinned at the memory.

Amy smiled. "How did Nick take that?"

"Stayed right on script," Trish said proudly. "He never missed a beat with the ho-ho-ho's and asking what the kid wanted for Christmas."

"Mom!" Josh interrupted, clearly tired of waiting. "Can we go *now!*"

"Okay, okay," she said, regarding Trish ruefully. "Let's go."

As she put an exhausted and unprotesting Emma back into her stroller, Amy was filled with an unexpected sense of anticipation. It had been a lot of years since she'd been this eager to pay a visit to Santa.

The line was shorter now and they were at the end of it. No one came along to wait behind them. Exhausted shoppers were leaving the mall now in droves.

When Josh's turn came, he was still the last in line. The instant he climbed onto Santa's knee and Amy had placed Emma beside him, the photographer snapped their picture, then handed the instant photo to Amy. "No charge," he said as he packed up his things and left in a rush for whatever holiday festivities awaited him.

Emma leaned contentedly against Nick's chest and

closed her eyes. The sight of her daughter in Nick's arms brought an odd tightness to Amy's heart. She had a feeling this image would linger inside her long after the photo had faded.

"So, young man," Nick said to Josh in his booming Santa voice, "What do you want Santa to bring you for Christmas?"

She tuned out the sound of her son's words as he recited not only his own list, one with which she was thoroughly familiar, but Emma's. It was a modest enough list by most standards and she knew that everything on it would be under the tree. The only wish she couldn't grant was his longing to see his dad on Christmas morning.

When Josh's consultation with Santa was over, Nick left the village with Emma in his arms and joined her. "Are we still on for church tonight?" he asked. "I can give you directions and meet you there, and then introduce you to the rest of my family." He gave her a hard look. "Or was meeting my mother more than enough?"

"Your mother is incredible," she told him. "She's invited us for Christmas dinner tomorrow."

He didn't look all that surprised. "I had a hunch that would come up."

"You didn't put her up to it?"

"My existence as a bachelor is enough to put her up to it," he said dryly. "Keep in mind she's scheming."

"I gathered as much," Amy admitted.

"And?"

"And what?" she asked.

"How do you feel about her scheme?"

"I told her we'd be there tomorrow." Her gaze locked with his. "How do *you* feel about her agenda?"

A grin spread across his face. "Better than I did a few minutes ago," he revealed. "How about giving me a moment to get out of this costume and I'll walk out with you?"

Amy glanced pointedly at Josh. "Not a good idea," she said succinctly.

"Of course not," he said at once. "What was I thinking?"

He looked around till he spotted Trish. "Sis, any problem if I wear this home?"

Laughing, she merely waved him away. "Go."

Josh looked from Nick to Trish and back again. "Is she your sister?" he asked, his expression puzzled.

Nick winced. "She is."

"Then that lady, Mrs. DiCaprio, is your mom, too?" Josh pressed.

Nick nodded.

Amy held her breath as Josh absorbed that information.

Finally Josh looked Nick in the eye. "Awesome! I know Santa's real mom! The kids back in Michigan will freak when I tell 'em. Can I call tonight, Mom? Can I? They're not going to believe this."

"Sure, you can call as soon as we get home," Amy told him, relieved that the whole Santa illusion hadn't been ruined. If anything, it had been reinforced and improved on.

"Then let's go," Josh said, trying to hurry her along. "I'll push Emma's stroller."

"Just don't get too far head of us, okay?"

"Okay," he said, glancing repeatedly over his shoulder to make sure she and Santa were close on his heels.

"I guess your lecture got through to him," she told Nick. "I think it made more of an impact coming from you."

"He'll forget it soon enough," Nick said. "I'll have to stick around to keep reminding him."

"I imagine I could remind him," Amy said, though the thought of Nick being around to do it held a whole lot of appeal.

"You don't have the Santa factor on your side," he told her.

"And you'll look pretty strange wearing that costume in July," she countered.

"Think I'll be around you guys in July?" he asked.

"I guess we'll just have to wait and see."

"You know, there's something I forgot to ask you earlier," he said.

"Oh?"

"What do you want for Christmas, Amy?"

She met his gaze and her heart gave a little lurch. "I have everything I need," she told him. "My kids are safe and happy."

"And that's enough?"

"It is for now," she told him, unable to tear her gaze away from the intensity and heat in his eyes.

He leaned down and brushed a kiss across her lips, then came back and lingered a second longer.

"Then maybe that will give you a few other ideas for your list," he said when he finally pulled away.

Oh, yeah, she thought. It most certainly did. But having X-rated ideas on Christmas Eve would shove her out of nice and straight into naughty. She wondered what Santa would have to say about that.

One glance into Nick's mischievous eyes told her the answer to that. They were working from the very same list.

Before she could examine how she felt about that, a woman tapped Nick on the shoulder. When he turned around, his expression froze. It was exactly the look he'd had on his face earlier, when he'd dragged Amy inside that shoe store.

"Nick," the woman said softly. "Could I please speak to you for a second?"

"Sure," he said, but there was no mistaking his reluctance.

The woman cast an apologetic look in Amy's direction. "I'm sorry to interrupt, but this is the first chance I've had to speak to Nick since…" Her voice caught. She shook her head. "Sorry. I still can't talk about it."

"It's okay," Nick soothed. "Really, you don't have to say anything."

To Amy, he sounded almost desperate, as if he were willing the woman to remain silent.

The woman drew in a deep breath. "No, it's important. I tried to call you at the station, but they said you were on leave."

Nick nodded.

"Because of what happened," she guessed.

"Yes," he said tightly.

"I'm so sorry," she told him. "It's all my fault."

Nick regarded her incredulously. "Your fault? How can you say that?"

"If I'd told you right away about my ex-husband, if I'd warned you…" Her voice fell to a whisper. "Maybe things would have gone differently."

Nick put his hands on her shoulders and looked into her eyes. "No, Mitzi, nothing that happened was your fault. If anything, it was mine. I just stood by…"

"No," she said harshly. "That's just it, that's why I had to talk to you. I knew you were blaming yourself."

"Who else should I blame?" he asked heatedly.

The woman sighed heavily. "Maybe it was no one's fault, not even my ex-husband's. He had to be sick, right? To think that taking our boy and hurting him would somehow make me love him again." She shuddered. "Or even that it was a way to pay me back for leaving him. That's not right. He needs help."

"Hopefully he'll get it while he's locked up," Nick told her. "The important thing is that he'll never get another chance to hurt anyone else."

Amy listened to the exchange with mounting horror. She realized now why Nick had been so desperate to find Josh, so determined to stay right by her side until her son was safe. He was trying to make up for not being able to help another little boy, this woman's son. No wonder he was tormented. No wonder he'd asked so many questions about Ned. The search for Josh must have dredged up a thousand terrifying moments for him.

The woman spoke to Amy, "I'm sorry to intrude, but when I saw that Nick was here, I wanted to tell him that I don't blame him for anything that happened. I thought he might need to know that."

Nick did, indeed, look as if a huge weight had been lifted from his shoulders. "You have an amazingly generous heart," he told her.

"If I do, it's because I had an incredible boy in my

life for a few brief years. I'm so grateful for that. It was far too short, but he taught me so much. That's what I want to remember. Not the way he died, but the way he lived." She hugged Nick fiercely. "Merry Christmas, Detective."

"Merry Christmas," he whispered, his voice choked.

After she'd gone, Amy reached up and touched the tears on his cheeks. "I am so sorry that you had to relive all that today."

He met her gaze. "I'm not," he said eventually. "Not if it brought you, Josh and Emma into my life. How could I possibly regret that?"

He turned to Josh, who was rolling a laughing Emma in circles nearby. "Hey, guys, let's get going. It's Christmas Eve and Santa's got a very busy night ahead. I have toys to deliver."

His gaze shifted to Amy and he lowered his voice. "And maybe, if I'm lucky, I can even sneak a kiss or two under the mistletoe."

Amy laughed. "You can try. I've been wondering all day if that beard tickles. I couldn't tell earlier."

Grinning, Nick called out to Josh. "Don't look, okay?"

"Don't look at what?" Josh asked.

"Do as you're told," Amy instructed, laughing. "Mommy's gonna kiss Santa Claus."

Josh's expression immediately brightened. "Cool!"

Yeah, Amy thought, as Nick's mouth settled on hers. It was definitely cool. No, she concluded an instant later, actually, it was hot. Very, very hot.

Outside the mall, the air was icy and snow was falling, but Amy was still overheated from that kiss.

North Carolina might be in for some sort of rare blizzard, but for her this was quickly turning into the hottest Christmas on record.

# EPILOGUE

*Christmas, one year later*

"So, YOUNG MAN," Nick said to Josh in his booming Santa voice, "What do you want Santa to bring you for Christmas?"

Amy had no idea how Trish had persuaded Nick to play Santa for a day once again this year. He still claimed he'd hated every minute of it when she'd coerced him into it the year before. Maybe it had something to do with knowing that Amy would once again be bringing Josh and Emma to the mall for their Christmas Eve visit.

Josh studied Santa intently, then seemed to reach some sort of decision. He cast a quick glance toward Amy, then pulled Santa's head down so he could whisper in his ear.

Nick immediately glanced at Amy, a grin spreading across his face. "Well, now, I don't know about that, son. Maybe your mom should have a say about something that important."

Amy sighed. A puppy? He'd asked for a puppy. Josh knew they couldn't have one where they were living. What was she supposed to do now?

"Sweetie, I told you we can't have a puppy till we move to a house," she said, which oddly enough only seemed to make Nick's smile grow. She regarded him with confusion. "He didn't ask for a puppy?"

"Nope," Nick said, carrying Emma down to join her.

"What then?"

"A new dad," he told her. "And he seems to think having Santa for a dad would be pretty awesome."

Amy's cheeks flooded with heat. "Oh, no. I am so sorry."

"Don't be. I'm thinking it's something to consider."

She stared at him in shock. "Excuse me?"

"Not today, of course, but you know, down the road."

"Say sometime after you've actually had a chance to think about it?" she asked dryly.

He laughed, not the fake, booming laugh of Santa, but the amused chuckle of a man she'd discovered had a wonderful sense of humor.

"Oh, I've been thinking about it for some time now," he told her. "How about you? Has the thought crossed your mind?"

It was her turn to chuckle. "How could it not, with your folks and Trish pressuring me every chance they get?"

"So, what do you think?" Josh demanded impatiently. "Is he gonna be my new dad or not?"

"I think maybe we ought to give your mom a little more time to think about this," Nick told him. "She might even want a real, romantic proposal."

"What's that?" Josh asked.

"Candlelight and stuff," Nick told him. "Keep it in mind. You might need to know about things like that later. In the meantime, why don't I walk you all to your car. I've heard a rumor and I want to check it out."

"What kind of rumor?" Amy asked, confused by the hint of mystery in his voice.

"You'll see."

They walked to the same exit where Amy, Josh and Emma had entered the mall on that fateful day a year ago. When Nick pushed open the door, she immediately saw what he'd been talking about. Once again, snow was falling. It had already covered the ground and turned the rapidly emptying parking lot into a winter wonderland.

"Snow!" Josh screamed, running ahead and twirling around, his head thrown back and his mouth open so he could catch the fat snowflakes on his tongue. Suddenly he ran over and threw his arms around Nick's huge, padded waist. "Thank you, thank you, thank you."

Nick winked at Amy. "Sorry, kid, Santa can't take credit for this."

Maybe not, she thought, but he had a lot to do with the joyous expression on her son's face. He was also responsible for the amazingly lighthearted feeling inside her.

As far as she was concerned, Santa—*Nick*—had given them everything they needed and the promise of much more.

For last-minute shoppers everywhere,
may you find the perfect gift.
And for my Christmas-loving mother, Mary,
whose name should be spelled like
the Merry in the book.

# ASSIGNMENT HUMBUG

## Darlene Gardner

# CHAPTER ONE

MAYBE, AS HER FREE-SPENDING mother suggested, Merry Deluca really was shopaphobic.

She suffered through the quarterly trips to New York City showrooms that her wardrobe consultant insisted upon and hadn't stepped one high-heeled foot in a mall in more than a year.

Until today, the last frantic shopping day left before Christmas.

The shopping day hell had wrought.

From a bench positioned on the periphery of one of the wide thoroughfares, Merry watched the tide of shoppers grow and wished she could talk some sense into them.

Why rush through the mall on one of the most festive days of the year instead of spending quality time with family?

Merry certainly wouldn't be here on the outskirts of Charlotte at King's Mall if the assignment editor at WZLM-13 news hadn't sent her out to do this story.

Merry was an on-camera correspondent whose reports from the mall were scheduled to air live on the noon and six o'clock broadcasts. A taped version would appear at eleven.

She checked her watch. It was a quarter past nine in the morning, a little more than an hour since the mall had opened and fifteen minutes past the time she was supposed to have met her cameraman.

The technician operating the ENG truck wouldn't appear for another few hours to start setting up for the noon broadcast, but she'd arrived early to get a jump on the story. Her plan was to weave some taped interviews in with the live report.

So where was Danny Thompson?

She didn't suppose he was any happier about hanging out at the mall than she was, but a television reporter without a cameraman was like December without Christmas.

She crossed her arms over her chest and tapped her fingers against her upper arms, then turned her mental energy toward her approach to the story.

Betsy Anderson, the assignment editor, had told her to think light and upbeat. To try to capture that "air of excitement and anticipation that only comes around once a year."

As though that feature hadn't aired a thousand times by a thousand different television stations.

She gazed around at the cornucopia of stores with their attractive window displays, all competing to tempt dollars from passing shoppers. From the look of things, they were succeeding. Take the slim brunette in lambskin nearly toppling over from the weight of her purchases.

The labels on the smartly dressed shopper's bags—Harrington & Vine's, Crystal's, Saks—revealed that she'd managed to hit all of the mall's anchor stores in seventy-five amazing minutes.

It also marked her as the poster girl for Christmas excess.

A story very different from the one Betsy had suggested formed. Why not give the news reports a fresh feel by focusing on the buy, buy, buy mentality that had captured so many. Including her headliner, who was…disappearing into the madding crowd.

Merry scrambled to her feet and gave chase, thankful that her chosen method of keeping in shape was jogging around her neighborhood. The overburdened shopper didn't stand a chance of avoiding her.

Merry fell into step beside her. "Excuse me, can I have a minute of your time? I'm—"

"Merry Deluca of WZLM news," the woman finished for her. She stopped walking and beamed as brightly as a Christmas tree light. "I watch you all the time. I particularly loved your story about that new store in downtown Charlotte with the live models. What could be better than being treated to a fashion show while you shop?"

"Thank you," Merry said, while her nose for news went on high alert. The woman, who was middle-aged, darkly beautiful and sporting a ring the size of Gibraltar on her left hand, smelled as expensive as she looked.

"I'm going to report on the last shopping day before Christmas and wondered if I could interview you."

"Well, sure. What do you want to know?" The shopper's well-endowed chest, covered by an exquisite lambskin jacket in a tasteful shade of rust, heaved slightly from exertion. No wonder. She must have been hotfooting it to buy as much as she had in so short a time.

Why, the woman was as bad as Patrick, not that Merry would let herself think about him. But if she did, she'd make a parallel between Patrick's tendency toward extravagance and the shopper's.

Merry shoved Patrick to the back of her mind, where he wouldn't leave. She looked over her shoulder but still couldn't spot her cameraman.

*Where was he?*

"I couldn't help noticing how much you've bought," Merry said, plowing ahead. Her piece would be harder hitting with video of the woman, but she could still use the vignette. "Can you tell me why you waited until Christmas Eve to do your shopping?"

"Waited? I didn't wait. I started my Christmas shopping the day after Thanksgiving, and I'm still going strong." She laughed, a jolly, little tinkle. She seemed so willing to share that Merry felt guilty for reveling in her cluelessness.

But, really. Did the woman honestly believe that showering friends and family with a wealth of hastily chosen gifts would bring her love?

"Are you done for the day?" Merry asked.

"Probably not. Once I drop this stuff at the women's shelter, I may pick up one or two more things."

Merry's brows lifted. Her gut tightened. "The women's shelter?"

The shopper wrinkled her nose. "It probably sounds silly when the women at the shelter need so much, but I thought they'd appreciate getting some presents that aren't secondhand."

Merry pressed her lips together, wondering how she'd misread the situation. "No," she conceded, "it doesn't sound silly at all. It sounds thoughtful. And sweet. Really, really sweet."

Relief, as easy to read as the names of the neighboring stores, filled her face. "Bless you for saying that."

Trying to disguise her disappointment that she'd had the bad luck to stop a good Samaritan, Merry asked a few more questions and got the woman's name.

"Have a wonderful holiday," the woman called over her shoulder as she retreated, balancing the jam-packed bags as though she were the female version of Santa Claus.

"You, too," Merry responded, barely able to maintain her smile long enough for the woman to walk away.

She folded her arms over her chest and tried to look on the bright side. One bighearted shopper did not make a trend. It was early yet. As the day wore on, tempers would flare, shoppers would grow desperate to complete their Christmas lists and she'd rack up all the material she needed for her story.

But where was her cameraman?

"Top o' the morning to you, love."

She froze at the sound of the charming Irish brogue. There was nothing particularly suggestive about the saying—except that the sayer had a habit of snuggling up next to her in bed and whispering those words in her ear after he'd stayed the night.

The voice had come from behind her. Bracing herself, she turned, but her breath still caught.

Patrick MacFarland in the flesh stood a few paces away, pinning her with the vivid blue eyes that were such a striking contrast to his black hair.

He looked outrageously masculine in a beige cable-knit sweater and chocolate-colored chinos. Tall and wiry, he had chiseled cheekbones, a long nose and a sinfully beautiful mouth.

His looks, combined with the accent he'd brought over from Ireland at age twelve when his family immigrated, turned a lot of female heads. It had been his passion that turned Merry's. Not only his passion for life, but his passion for his family...and for her.

She drew air into her lungs, fueling her resolve not to let him know how much his mere presence affected her.

"What are you doing here, Patrick?" She tried to instill frost into her voice, a neat feat considering chipmunks chirped the Christmas song from the mall's sound system.

"The plan never was for me to stay in San Francisco over Christmas," he said in his lilting voice. "I had a devil of a time reaching you or I would have let you know when I was getting back."

"I'm screening my calls, Patrick," she said. "I don't pick up when I see one of your numbers."

"Did you get the long-stemmed red roses I sent?" he asked as though he hadn't heard her.

"Yes." She sighed. "And the chocolate. And the cheese-of-the-month club subscription."

"That one was inspired. You're a woman who likes her cheese," he said, seeming pleased with himself.

Considering what was between them, the inanity of the conversation struck her. "You still haven't told me what you're doing here."

"What better place is there but where you are?" He moved toward her with a panther's grace. Knowing how dangerous his nearness could be to her peace of mind, let alone body, she backed up only to come flush against a railing draped with holly. He didn't stop advancing until he was a hand's width from her. He brushed a strand of hair back from her face, touching her cheek in the process and sending her nerve endings skittering. "And is that any way for a woman to be greeting her fiancé?"

She fought an overpowering urge to breathe deeply of his clean, masculine scent and batted his hand away. "You're my ex-fiancé, Patrick. We broke up. Remember?"

"We?" He shook his head sadly, and her heart clutched. "I didn't break up with you, love."

"It only takes one to make it official."

"I hardly think telling me such a thing over the phone qualifies as official. One minute we're talking about the doves your mother wants released at the wedding, and the next you're breaking up with me."

"She wanted two dozen white doves to fly over us as we left the church. Two dozen, Patrick! And you said you didn't understand why I was against it," she accused.

"I also said I'd back you up no matter what. If you don't want doves, that's fine with me."

"That's beside the point. If we're not on the same page about these things, we shouldn't be getting married."

"But we are on the same page. I want you to have whatever you want."

She shook her head. How could she explain her doubts to him when she hardly understood them herself? She chewed on her bottom lip, thinking about how to proceed.

"You're right about one thing. I shouldn't have broken up with you over the phone." She didn't elaborate, because she could hardly admit that her will got so weak at the sight of him that she'd doubted she could end things in person. "But what's done is done."

"Have you canceled the wedding yet, love?" he asked in the same low voice he used when they were in bed together. Her resolve weakened, but she bolstered it back up.

"My name's Merry," she said. "I'd appreciate it if you'd call me that instead of *love*."

He trailed his forefinger along her jaw, then let it drop before she could protest. "Why should I be making it easier for you to ignore what's between us?"

Just like that, the endearment took on greater meaning. She remembered the day she'd accepted his proposal. They'd been at Charlotte's finest restaurant, and he'd asked her to marry him over champagne and caviar.

She'd have chosen a less ostentatious setting, but at the time it hadn't mattered. She'd been so in love with him, she'd been giddy with it.

She swallowed. "It's no small feat to cancel a wedding with three hundred guests, especially when my mother made all the arrangements. She's in Tahiti with my dad until after the holidays, you know."

Her parents, both attorneys who worked long hours, rewarded themselves with a holiday trip for two to a far-flung locale. When Merry was growing up, they'd left her at home with her grandparents and so many presents she never remembered what she'd gotten a few months later. Now that she was grown, they delivered the presents before the bon voyage, though they'd never once asked her to come along.

"If you talk it out with me, maybe we won't have to cancel at all," he said, still in that seductive voice that caused the hair on her arms to stand up.

Fearing that her body would take over from her brain, she stepped sideways to put some much-needed distance between them. "We have nothing more to talk about."

"We could talk about working things out rather than ending them. We could talk about how plenty of brides-to-be get cold feet before the wedding."

He touched her arm, and warmth spread underneath his hand. Nothing felt cold. Not her feet, not her body, not her heart. But it wasn't their physical relationship that was the problem. She took another step sideways so that his hand fell away.

"This is a bad time, Patrick," she hedged. "In case you haven't noticed, I'm working."

She detected the leather strap of the camera bag slung over his shoulder an instant before he replied, "So am I. I'm your cameraman."

The bottom fell out of Merry's stomach and her mind rebelled, even as the evidence that he was telling the truth stared her in the face. "Danny's my camera-man," she insisted.

"Danny's down with the flu. Seems like it's going around."

Merry couldn't dispute that. The mall's events co-ordinator had told her that King's Mall had been hit particularly hard this season. Employees were calling in sick in droves. And Danny had been at the mall just days ago getting footage of the mall's Santa. But that still didn't explain Patrick's announcement.

"But you can't be my cameraman. You quit your job at WZLM and gave up camera work. You're in corporate development now. Corporate developers do not take video at the mall."

He bent his dark head to hers. He smelled warm and wonderful, although she never had been able to identify the scent. Eau de Patrick, perhaps. He'd shaved recently and she knew his skin would feel soft and smooth if she reached up and stroked it. She leaned away.

"They do when the assignment editor knows how much the corporate developer wants to mend things with his fiancée."

"Ex-fiancée," Merry corrected firmly even as the reporter in her admired his resourcefulness and her traitorous body responded to the low timbre of his voice. "This isn't going to work. I'm going to call Betsy and request a replacement."

One of his dark eyebrows arched. "What's the matter? Afraid to work with me?"

"Of course not," she retorted even though he'd gotten it exactly right. She'd never had much willpower where Patrick MacFarland was concerned, which was why she'd agreed to a wedding before she'd thought things through. "It's just that I can't have you getting the idea that I want you back. You have to accept that it's over between us."

A challenge lit his eyes. "Then prove it to me."

"How can I do that?"

"Spend today working with me."

"That won't prove anything. I've worked with you plenty of times."

"Ah, but this time will be different." He lowered his head and leaned toward her. She felt the warmth of his breath on her lips. "This time, if you tell me the engagement's still off when the workday's over, I'll leave you alone."

PATRICK FOUGHT TO REMAIN confident as he waited for Merry's answer, deliberately downplaying the uncertainty in her eyes and the bare spot on her finger where he'd put a diamond engagement ring.

She loved him. He knew she did. The doubt she was experiencing had to be prewedding jitters.

He was partly to blame because he hadn't been around much in the past three months. After Merry accepted his proposal, he stopped indulging himself with camera work and took a job in mergers and acquisitions for an executive search and recruiting firm called The Goulden Group.

Because it had been five years since he'd gotten his business degree, he'd been lucky to secure the position. The firm was owned by a financial dynamo named Greg Goulden, who happened to be the father of one of his college roommates.

The hours were long and the work more than a little mundane, but Patrick couldn't complain about the money. The money was fantastic.

So, yes, he'd been busy establishing himself at work. But Merry was still the most important thing in his life. He wasn't so clueless that he didn't realize the wedding, an elaborate soiree for three hundred at a posh country club, was causing her stress.

That's why he repeatedly backed her up whenever she disagreed with her mother over an aspect of the planning. Like the doves. If Merry didn't want doves at their wedding, fine.

He couldn't accept that Merry didn't want him there.

"What do you say?" He stuck out a hand. "Do we have a deal?"

She ran her fingers through her long, glossy brown hair and stared back at him with the face that had helped her get a job in TV: sharp, angled cheekbones, a jaw more wide than narrow, a high forehead and eyes the color of evergreen. She wore a formfitting red sweater over a short green skirt that showed off her long legs.

If he hadn't known her better, he might have been intimidated by her appearance. But the woman inside the front she presented to the Charlotte viewing audience was even more beautiful than the package. Soft and sweet, like the center of a chocolate-dipped marshmallow.

For some reason, she kept that part guarded, as though it was a liability instead of the very essence of what made her who she was.

"Deal," she finally said without a trace of softness in her voice. But when she took his offered hand, the electricity they generated whenever they touched ran up his arm. She felt it, too. He could sense it in the slight quiver of her fingers.

"Aren't you Merry Deluca?"

A short blonde in a red jacket ringed with a white fur collar suddenly appeared in front of them. Merry pulled her hand from Patrick's and the brief moment when they'd connected was gone. She gave the woman her TV-reporter smile.

"Yes, I am," Merry said. "I'm reporting today from the mall."

"I've always wanted to be on TV." The woman gave her name as Kelly. She was on the plump side, with cherub cheeks and a rosebud of a mouth. "I could tell you about how I'm shopping for the perfect gift for my husband. We just got remarried last month."

"I really don't think—" Merry began at the same time Patrick said, "That sounds great, Kelly."

Kelly looked from Merry to Patrick and back again, obviously confused by the mixed message.

Merry, always the professional, kept her composure although Patrick picked up on the slight tightening around her mouth. For some unfathomable reason, she really hadn't wanted to interview Kelly.

"This is Patrick MacFarland," she told Kelly. "He's my cameraman."

Kelly's hand flew to her throat as she regarded him. "A cameraman? With your looks, I'm surprised you're not in front of the camera rather than behind it."

Wasn't she a charmer? Patrick smiled at her. "Thank you."

"I'm ready." Kelly clapped her hands, clasped them together and addressed Patrick. "So where's the truck and the big camera?"

Patrick chuckled. "The ENG truck—the initials stand for electronic news gathering—isn't coming until later. I have a camera but it's probably not what you're expecting." He picked up his leather bag and removed a lightweight digital camera. "This isn't the camera I use for live broadcasts, but it's plenty good enough to get you on tape."

"Then let's get the tape rolling," Kelly said.

She barely contained her excitement while Merry provided her with the questions she'd be asking. Patrick busied himself considering and rejecting back-drops for the interview, finally settling on a spot in front of a window display featuring snowflakes and candy canes.

A small crowd had gathered around them by the time he'd set up the shot. He'd missed this, he thought as he gazed through the lens and envisioned how the interview would look on TV.

Facts and figures didn't compare with the pleasure he got from bringing the world to television viewers. This simple assignment at the mall wasn't on par with some of the pulse-pounders he'd taped in the past— forest fires, riots, live concerts—but it was still more exciting than a day inside the glass and chrome building that housed The Goulden Group.

"I don't care if it takes me until the mall closes," Kelly said while looking into the camera exactly as he'd instructed her. "I'm going to find a gift that will let my husband know that this time I'm in the marriage for keeps."

Patrick zoomed out to include Merry in the shot, easily understanding why she'd been chosen over a few dozen applicants for the WZLM job. Not only did the camera love her, but she was good at her job.

Days after she began working at WZLM, they'd been sent out together on a live broadcast about the record cold temperatures. A naked man had streaked across camera. "As you can see," Merry had ad-libbed, "those of us caught unawares by the cold are in a hurry to head home and add more layers."

After Patrick had turned off the camera, she'd laughed until her eyes teared, then wiped off her ruined makeup. He'd expected her to reapply it, but how she looked hadn't mattered to her when she was off camera.

He'd fallen hard and fast. The next day was Valentine's Day. He'd sent Merry a three-foot-tall teddy bear holding a giant chocolate kiss and an invitation to dinner at a classy French restaurant.

She'd accepted, and he'd been charmed by her intelligence and kindness. Before the night was over, he'd vowed to himself that he'd marry her.

And he would. If he could convince her by mall closing that her doubts were simply prewedding jitters.

The interview concluded, Kelly thanked them profusely and then went off in search of that perfect gift. The crowd dispersed, and Patrick waited for Merry to acknowledge that he'd been right about putting Kelly on camera.

"That was a waste of time," Merry told him. "If she hadn't been so excited about the interview, I wouldn't have done it."

Patrick knew better than to smile when she was in this mood, but he loved the soft part of her that put other people's needs above her own.

"I'm sorry, love," he said. "But I don't know why you're saying that. I thought Kelly was great."

"That's probably because she fawned all over you."

Pleasure shot through him. "Don't tell me you're jealous of a married woman shopping for her husband."

"I am not jealous," she denied, not entirely believably. "I'm irritated that you didn't ask me what kind of story I was working on."

He thought back to what Betsy had said when she'd given him the assignment. "Aren't we supposed to capture the excitement and anticipation in the air?"

"That angle's been done to death. I'm going to show how the commercialization of Christmas is tarnishing the holiday."

He laughed. "You're joking, right?"

"It's no joke." She seemed offended by the very notion. "The mall is all about commercialism, with the Christmas shopping season starting earlier and earlier. Decorations went up in a couple of stores this year at the end of October! Not only that, a recent Gallup poll said that Americans spend an average of almost eight hundred dollars on Christmas."

"So?"

"So haven't you paid attention to the advertisements about the items we can't live without? The toys that our children absolutely must have? And it all comes to a head on Christmas Eve, when malls everywhere are teeming with people."

"What's wrong with that?" he said. "They're just folks who need to finish up their shopping."

"You're missing my point. The focus of Christmas shouldn't be on shopping. These people should be home with their loved ones instead of at the mall."

"They're at the mall buying things so their loved ones have presents to open on Christmas morning."

"They're here because these stores and their advertising dollars convinced them that this is where they should be."

"This is where they want to be."

She perched her hands on her hips. "Oh, really?"

He looked around them. Signs of the holiday were everywhere. Banisters bedecked with rich holly and giant red bows. Store windows decorated with Christmas scenes and carefully-crafted snowflakes. Pretty trees sparkling and winking from nearly every store. Shoppers wearing a disproportionate amount of red and green. He couldn't imagine a more ideal setting.

"Yes," he said. "It is."

"Well, I don't think so. And I'm going to prove it."

"Let me run this by you so I've got it straight," he said slowly. "You're wanting me to scour the mall with you looking for people who illustrate the negative side of Christmas?"

She nodded. "Exactly."

He angled his head. "Should I be shouting 'Bah, humbug' before I turn on my camera?"

"Not funny."

"It wasn't meant to be, but this idea of yours, I can't see how it'll work. It's Christmas. People are, well, merry on Christmas."

"Not people in the mall. They're so desperate to have their Christmas shopping over and done with, they'll buy anything."

"How about Kelly? She won't buy just anything. She's holding out for the perfect gift."

She snorted. "There is no such thing."

He disagreed. One of his coworkers at The Goulden

Group had purchased a day at the spa to show his wife she deserved to be pampered. Another had bought his girlfriend, who loved the winter, everything she needed for a trip to a ski resort. And his boss had gotten his wife a brand-new car with premium safety features so she'd be safer on the roads.

Patrick's thoughts raced. He'd already bought Merry a diamond tennis bracelet, expensive perfume, a black leather jacket and a digital camera but none of those things were personal enough to convince her of his love.

But such a present had to be out there. He gazed at the plethora of stores around him and thanked the Christmas star on top of the closest tree. For what better place than a mall could there be to find the perfect gift?

"Well?" she prodded, her voice cutting into his thoughts. "Are you ready to get started?"

Her arms were crossed over her chest, her expression conveying that she clearly expected him to argue some more.

"Absolutely," he said cheerfully.

Her eyes narrowed suspiciously. "You mean you're going along with me on this? Even though you think I won't be able to find material to back up my angle?"

"I don't believe you will."

"Then what kind of game are you playing?"

"It's no game, love," he said. "One of these days you'll understand that I'm on your side, no matter what. In the meantime, let's try to find somebody who isn't humming along with the Christmas carols."

## CHAPTER TWO

MERRY WANTED TO ARGUE with Patrick some more about disagreeing with the slant of her story, but she couldn't when he was being so agreeable.

"Now tell me more about what we're looking for," he said as they walked side by side on the highly polished floor through the mall. "Shoppers dropping a lot of cash? Shoppers whose nerves are frayed? Shoppers who don't care what they buy as long as they buy something?"

"All of the above," Merry said, while harboring serious doubts that he'd be any help at all. Patrick was one of the world's biggest optimists. Even if he were no longer openly questioning her plans, he couldn't truly be backing her up.

"Let's try the toy store," he suggested.

"Excuse me?"

"The toy store. You're looking for something useless that retailers are trying to get consumers to believe they need, right? What could be a better example than the Snickering Stone?"

"What's that?"

"According to a magazine article I read, only the hottest toy this Christmas. Did you ever hear of the Pet Rock?"

She nodded. It was hailed as the perfect pet—cheap, easy to take care of and exceedingly well behaved. Even though the fad had started before her childhood began, it had never totally died. Her parents had bought her one. But then, they'd bought her one of almost everything.

"The Snickering Stone is kind of like a Pet Rock with personality. It has a motion sensor. When you walk by, it laughs."

"And people are buying that?" she asked, even though it was a rhetorical question. People would buy anything at Christmas. Witness the Chia Pet and Singing Trout.

"Let's go to the toy store and find out."

They waited their turn at the mall directory. Once they'd located the nearest toy store, they walked quickly through the sea of shoppers to their destination.

The toy store was an affiliate of one of those chains that tried to get the most for their rented mall space, cramming an amazing amount of inventory into a relatively small space. It hadn't hurt business. The store was crowded and the lines long.

Merry hesitated at the entrance, surveying the crowd. "I don't see any salespeople who aren't busy either helping somebody or manning a cash register."

"Why do we need a salesperson?"

"To direct us to the Snickering Stone."

"Trust me, we'll find it all by ourselves," Patrick said and reached for her hand. "So we don't get separated," he explained.

He ventured into the store ahead of her, weaving through the cramped aisles. She was concentrating so hard on ignoring how good it felt to simply touch him that she jumped at the sound of a cackle that would put a wicked witch to shame.

"What was that?" she asked.

He grinned. "That's the stone's snicker. It didn't scare you, did it?"

"Of course not," she denied.

"Then why are you squeezing my hand so tight?"

She instantly let go of him, and he laughed. He gestured to the stone, which was on display alongside a stack of garish red boxes. A blurb promised that the stone would provide "the most fun you'll have this holiday season."

"It's great, isn't it?" Patrick asked.

She rolled her eyes. "How can you think there's anything great about a cackling stone?"

"It's funny."

He waved his hand. The stone cackled again, the sound so ridiculous that she couldn't help but smile. It was funny. It was also one of the most useless toys she'd ever come across.

"There's quite a few of them left," she said. "I wonder if the creators of the stone paid that magazine to say the toy was hot. You know, to create demand?"

"Now isn't that a cynical way to look at a Christmas toy?" He shook his head, but his expression was indulgent. "I'm thinking a kid would want the stone even if he didn't know it was popular."

"You're joking, right?"

"Look, Mom. There it is." A sandy-haired boy of about seven or eight years old dressed in an unzipped ski jacket was leading his mother their way. When the boy moved in front of the stone, it let loose with its maniacal cackle.

"I waaaant it," the boy said, his voice a plaintive whine. "I neeeeed it."

"Okay, Ronald. I told you we could get it."

Bingo. Merry smiled at Patrick. He was right. The Snickering Stone could provide exactly the ammunition she needed for her story.

"Excuse me." Merry raised her voice to be heard above the general commotion inside the store. "I'm Merry Deluca of WZLM-13 news. Could I talk to your son on camera about the Snickering Stone?"

The boy already had one of the boxes clutched to his chest in the spirit of true greed. Merry's heartbeat quickened.

"What do you say, Ronald?" The mother patted the little boy indulgently on the head. "Do you want to be on TV?"

"I like TV," the boy announced. No surprise there.

Before the mother and son could change their minds, Merry excused herself to find a store manager. She needed permission to get the stone out of the box and the boy out of the store. Five minutes later, Patrick had the shot set up.

"All I need you to do," she told the boy before Patrick turned on the camera, "is talk about why you wanted the Snickering Stone for Christmas."

"Oh, but Ronald's not the one who wants the stone," his mother interjected. "The stone's for Benjy."

Merry frowned. "Who's Benjy?"

"My little brother." Ronald held up the stone. "This is the only thing he put on his Christmas list."

"Ronald's going to pay for the stone with his own money," the mother said proudly.

Ronald reached in his back pocket and pulled out a wad of what appeared to be one-dollar bills. "I've been saving up my allowance."

"Are you going to buy a Snickering Stone for yourself, too, Ronald?" Merry asked, desperately trying to salvage her story.

"Heck, no," Ronald said. "I think they're dumb. All they do is laugh."

PATRICK LIGHTLY RUBBED Merry's upper arm as they exited the toy store. He preferred to believe she didn't protest because she was softening toward him, but she was probably still upset about what had happened in the store.

"I'm sorry those interviews didn't work out the way you wanted them to, love," he said.

After striking out with the boy, she'd convinced one of the store's cashiers to appear on camera. That hadn't gone her way, either.

"I can't believe I was so off track," Merry said. "Of all the employees in the toy store, that cashier looked the most unhappy. I was sure she'd tell stories about overindulgent parents and bratty kids and credit-card charges that would break a bank."

"Don't be so hard on yourself." He gently squeezed her shoulder in support. "You couldn't have known she was just tired because she'd worked a double shift yesterday."

"But why did she perk up the instant she was on camera?" Merry asked as they blended into the crowd and walked past one festive window display after another. "Why did she have to talk about that single mother she works with who needed to get her wrapping done?"

"You did ask why she'd volunteered to do a double shift," Patrick reminded, then quickly added. "Not that you're at fault. It was a question that had to be asked."

She gazed at him with narrowed eyes. "I don't get it. Why are you being so nice to me?"

"I'm trying to win you back. That's hardly going to happen if I'm nasty."

"So this is like the symphony orchestra thing?"

"I'm not following you."

"When my mother suggested hiring the twelve-piece orchestra to play at the wedding, you sided with me against it even though you didn't see anything wrong with it. Just like you did with the doves."

He couldn't prevent a sigh from escaping. "Do we have to talk about the doves again?"

She stopped walking so abruptly three people almost crashed into her. Two of them apologized.

"But don't you see?" she asked. "This is just like the doves and the symphony. You don't agree with the angle of my story but you're going along with it."

"I'm being supportive." He threw up his hands. "What's wrong with that?"

She stared at him mutely for a few seconds while he tried to figure out what was going on inside her head. He had no luck. "This, in a nutshell, is why it won't work out for us."

He released a frustrated breath. "Because I'm perfectly okay with letting you have your way?"

"Because you don't agree with what you're agreeing with!"

"Now wait just a minute," he said. "Plenty of couples don't agree, Merry. Not everybody thinks alike."

"We think less alike than most of them. That's why we shouldn't get married. We're incompatible."

"I disagree."

"Of course you do," she retorted. "See what I mean about us not agreeing?"

"That's not fair," he said. "The differences between couples are—"

The peal of her cell phone interrupted the reasoned argument he was about to make. She held up a finger and took the phone from the clip at the waistband of her skirt, which was concealed under her sweater.

"Merry Deluca," she said into the receiver while he mentally completed his thought.

A couple's differences helped keep a relationship fresh and interesting. So what if he didn't understand why Merry objected to the extravagant touches her mother kept trying to add to their wedding?

He personally thought Merry should have the best of everything, which was the major reason he'd gone to work for The Goulden Group. His salary was substantially higher than the television station paid, which would enable him to support Merry in style even if she chose one day to quit her job.

He liked the idea of a lavish wedding, the perfect backdrop for the beautiful bride she'd make. But he was willing to give on that. He had given, supporting her every step of the way. For whatever reason, Merry didn't want a fuss. Even though she deserved one.

She nodded a few times, then finished the phone call.

"That was Francine letting us know the truck is here," she said. Francine was not only the broadcast technician who'd been assigned to work with them but also a close friend of Merry's from her college days. "She's setting up in front of the mall. I'm going to meet her."

"Then we can finish our discussion later."

"I've said what I had to say. And it's already eleven o'clock. I need the time before we go live to work on my write-up."

She had quite a writing job in front of her to get the material they'd gathered to fit into a story about commercialism, but she probably already knew that.

"Are you coming?" she asked.

Making a snap decision, he popped the tape out of his camera. He preferred editing tape himself, but Betsy had told him he could delegate the task. It seemed prudent to take her up on it, because what he had to do was more important.

"Would you give this tape to Francine to edit?" he asked. "I'll be there in time to set up for the broadcast, but I have some errands to run."

"What kind of errands?"

His brain raced while he tried to think of something that would throw her off track, but she shook her head and said, "Never mind. I don't think I want to know."

She waited for a break in the crowd, then joined the throng of people rushing through the mall. Patrick watched her go, taking it as a positive sign that she glanced back at him.

If he could buy her the perfect gift, that might be all he needed to push him over the edge and back into her life.

His gaze ricocheted from a jewelry store to a candy store, but he dismissed them both. He'd been there, bought that.

He was about to enter Harrington & Vine's, one of the mall's popular anchor stores, when he noticed a bunch of shoppers gathered around a kiosk selling products that changed colors in the sun.

Intrigued, he moved closer and watched the salesman point an ultraviolet light at a canvas tote bag with a black-and-white ocean scene. The scene gradually came alive with vivid color: deep blue water, vibrant red beach umbrellas, rainbow-colored masts on the sailboats.

Merry enjoyed the unexpected and loved the beach. They'd spent a long weekend at Nags Head this past summer and took pleasure in every sunny second. Ten minutes later, he was finally at the front of the line.

"That bag's really cool," the salesman told Patrick while he rang it up. "I got my mom one. And my sister. And my aunt, too. Everybody loves them."

Some of Patrick's joy at finding what he'd thought was the ideal gift faded. If the color-changing tote had universal appeal, it wasn't personal enough.

While walking away from the kiosk, he overheard a teenage girl telling her friend about a store called Get Clocked. "They have this supercool alarm clock you can program with your favorite music. You can't go wrong with a present like that."

Patrick added one of the programmable alarm clocks

and a CD by Sheryl Crow, her favorite singer, to his growing stash of presents for Merry. While he was headed for the mall exit, he spied a bobblehead doll of Walter Cronkite, the former CBS *Evening News* anchorman who was an icon of television news. He bought that, too.

All of the choices were inspired, but he feared that none were perfect.

While he made his way out of the mall and toward the ENG truck, he vowed to find time later to continue the hunt. The woman he loved deserved nothing less than the very best.

"So did Patrick tell you exactly how he planned to change your mind about breaking off the engagement?"

Francine Collins pulled a chair up to where Merry sat at the computer in the ENG truck. Francine's curly brown hair was unruly, her color high, her Kewpie doll face animated. And her six-month pregnancy noticeably visible.

"Of course he didn't tell you," Francine said, answering her own question. "He wouldn't tip his hand and ruin his chances of sweeping you off your feet. But he must be planning something radical if he said you'd be back together by the time the mall closes. I bet it's something romantic."

Francine covered her heart with one hand. She was married, had two-year-old twins with a third child on the way and still managed to act as though life was a soap opera. Merry should have remembered that before confiding in her.

"Do you think you'll be able to resist him?" Francine

asked. "You never have before. Didn't you tell me you would have slept with him way before you did if he hadn't been such a gentleman?"

Merry rubbed her forehead, wishing she could erase the sudden memories of how right it felt to make love to Patrick. If she could, he would be easier to resist.

"Don't take this the wrong way, Francine, because you know I love you," Merry said. "But don't you have tape to edit?"

Francine shook her head so that her curls swung. "Not until you tell me what video you want to use in your report, I don't."

"I can't tell you that until I figure out the angle of my story." Merry checked her watch. "I only have fifteen minutes to do that before the noon news."

"Thirty-five. Your report won't air until twenty minutes past the hour. Besides, you're a whiz at this. It won't take you nearly that long." Francine barely took a breath before continuing, "Patrick thinks you have the prewedding jitters, doesn't he?"

Merry's fingers paused on the computer keyboard. "How did you know that?"

"It's the obvious conclusion. Things were going along fine until it sank in that the wedding's almost here. Then, bam, your nerves went haywire."

Merry stopped trying to work and leveled her friend with a penetrating stare. "It sounds like *you* think I have the jitters."

Francine shrugged. "That's not for me to say."

"You just said it."

"I was explaining the phenomenon. Most people experience the jitters to some degree before their wedding.

Take me, for example. Two days before I got married, Doug went off to a bar with his best man. I nearly called everything off because I didn't want to marry a drunk."

"But Doug doesn't drink," Merry said.

"Exactly. I'm just saying that second-guessing yourself is perfectly normal. In your case, it's even understandable. You said yourself you haven't seen very much of Patrick since he took that new job. You're alone too much."

"We haven't spent much time together lately," Merry acknowledged. "But that's only part of it."

"What's the other part?" Francine asked, all of her attention focused on Merry. When Merry hesitated, she prodded, "Talk to me, Mer. I'm here for you."

Touched by her friend's concern, Merry tried to put into words what she hadn't yet been able to work out in her mind.

"I don't know exactly. But since he took this job at The Goulden Group, he's different. Less playful. More serious. He works all the time. And for what? A Lexus and a big-screen TV he doesn't have time to watch?"

"How about a more solid future for his bride-to-be?"

"His bride-to-be didn't need a two-carat engagement ring." Merry sighed. "I'm not explaining it right. The more I think about it, the more convinced I am that we're incompatible."

"Because you don't want a Lexus or a big-screen TV?"

Merry tapped her chin. "I guess that has something to do with it. Did I tell you the latest about the wedding?"

Francine cringed. "You're not going to start in on the doves again, are you?"

"No, this isn't about the doves. It's about the six bridesmaids my mother suggested I add to the six I already have. Patrick didn't grasp why I wouldn't go along with it."

"Did he try to pressure you to agree to twelve bridesmaids?"

"No, but that's not the point. The point is that I don't understand him, and he surely doesn't understand me. After we broke up, he sent me flowers and candy and cheese. Cheese! Can you believe it?"

"You like cheese."

"Not enough to let myself get bribed. It was like he thought buying me those things would change my mind."

"You broke his heart, then you wouldn't accept his calls. He probably felt like he had to do something."

Merry bit the inside of her lip, dismayed at the notion of Patrick with a broken heart. She'd be loath to cause anyone pain, but especially Patrick. "You're only sticking up for Patrick because you like him," she accused.

"What's not to like?" Francine asked. "He's charming, he's smart, he's handsome, he plays with my twins and he had the good taste to fall in love with my best friend."

"Did he pay you to say that?"

"Certainly not. With that accent of his, all he had to do was ask."

Silence ensued, rare whenever Francine was anywhere in the vicinity. Merry's blood pressure rose, but then she noticed her friend clamping her upper teeth over her lower lip.

"You were kidding," Merry said.

A bubbly laugh escaped from Francine. "Yes, I was. I haven't talked to Patrick since you called off the wedding. Where is he, by the way?"

As if on cue, the door to the truck opened, revealing the man himself. His hair was windblown after the short walk from the mall, giving him a rakish air. Francine practically squealed. "Patrick! We were just talking about you."

He folded his long length into the truck, and cocked a dark eyebrow in piratical fashion. "Then I hope you were putting in a good word for me, Francy."

"Always," she said and grinned at him. "You know how much Doug and I want to keep double-dating. I'm way more partial to you than any of the guys Merry dated in the past."

"You'll have to tell me all about Merry's exes one of these days," Patrick said.

"Who do you want to hear about first?" Francine asked. "The rotten singer who serenaded her outside the dorm? Or the guy who crashed into the back of her car because he wanted to meet her?"

"One of her exes really did that?" Patrick asked.

"You are one of my exes," Merry reminded him without turning from her computer screen. Taking a hard line where he was concerned was easier when she wasn't looking at him. "And could you two be quiet so I can concentrate?"

She heard Patrick come up behind her and sensed him peering over her shoulder. *Eyes ahead,* she told herself. *Don't look at him.*

"Merry needs a few more minutes," Francine explained. "As you can see, she hasn't managed to write much yet."

Merry gave a long-suffering sigh. "Gee, I wonder why that is."

"Whatever you come up with, I know it'll be great. It always is." Patrick tenderly put a hand on her arm. "I'll just go set up."

Touched by his show of support and dismayed at her show of cowardice, Merry turned around to thank him—and noticed the shopping bags he held. Francine must have become aware of them at the same moment.

"Give me those bags, and I'll find a place to store them," she offered.

The "thank you" died on Merry's lips. On some level, she'd known what his errands entailed, but she hadn't wanted to acknowledge it. "You were *shopping?* That's why you didn't come with me to the truck?"

"It's the day before Christmas. I had a few things I still needed to pick up." To Francine, he said, "Thanks, Francy. It'll save me from walking to my car. I couldn't find a spot this morning so I'm about a half mile away."

After he collected his equipment and exited the door of the truck, Merry muttered, "He didn't hear a word I said."

"What was that, Merry?" Francine asked. "I didn't hear you."

"That was my jitters jittering louder."

# CHAPTER THREE

WITH HER SEGMENT quickly coming to a close, Patrick panned the camera in tight on Merry. A crowd of shoppers in high spirits had formed behind her.

Despite the earlier nonsense she'd spouted, Merry had given an upbeat report. She'd pieced together live material with taped snippets of Kelly discussing her search for the perfect gift, Ronald showing the allowance money he'd used to buy the Snickering Stone for his brother and the cashier talking about working a double shift to help out her coworker.

Merry flashed her even, white teeth at the camera. Because Patrick had watched her on the small screen many times, he knew viewers would think she was smiling specifically at them. He kept the camera trained on her as she finished her report.

"At King's Mall, where the shoppers have decided it's better to give than receive, this is Merry Deluca, WZLM-13 news."

Satisfied with a job well done, Patrick took off his headset and disconnected his camera from the cable drum that linked it to the truck.

From the corner of his eye, he watched Merry deal with the shoppers who approached her with the grace and good humor that were integral parts of her. Only someone who knew her well could tell that she was also frustrated.

"Thank you very much," she told a grandmotherly woman who complimented her on the message of her piece. "Yes, Christmas is a wonderful time of year."

He smiled to himself, thinking about how differently the sweet little old lady might have reacted to the story Merry had originally planned. When he was through returning the equipment to the truck, the elderly woman still had Merry cornered. He headed in their direction.

"It doesn't matter if I get a single present," he heard the woman tell Merry. "The looks of joy on the faces of my grandchildren when they open all the things I get them are all I need to have a happy holiday."

Merry suddenly perked up, her voice alive with interest. "Exactly how many presents have you bought your grandchildren?"

"Oh, I don't know." The woman's white head barely came higher than Merry's chin, making it necessary for her to tip her head way back. "I stopped counting a long time ago. But I can tell you this. The room in the basement where I hide those presents is filling up."

"If you've already bought that much, why are you still at the mall?"

The woman laughed heartily. "The sales, dear. There are such wonderful sales the day before Christmas. I save so much money that way."

"But isn't a sale a clever marketing scheme to make a shopper believe she's saving money when she's actually spending it?"

The poor woman looked flabbergasted by Merry's penetrating question. Her white eyebrows drew together. She scratched her head. She stammered. She needed help.

"Shoppers expect to spend a certain amount during the holidays," Patrick said, interjecting himself into their conversation. "Sales help them to spend a little less."

Ignoring the censure in Merry's gaze, he turned to the older woman. "I'm Patrick MacFarland, Merry's cameraman."

"And what a fine-looking young man you are. So smart, too." She was as sweet as she was small, the quintessential grandmother. "What you said about the sales, that's exactly what I was going to say."

Grandma, as Patrick had started to think of her, went on to tell them about the children's mittens she'd found for twenty percent off. When she got to the tins of popcorn she'd bought for a ten percent discount, Merry graciously extracted herself from the conversation. Giving Patrick a tight smile, she walked to the truck.

Grandma and the rest of the crowd were gone when Merry returned. The fire in her green eyes was still there.

"I'd appreciate in the future if you didn't sabotage my interviews," she said tightly.

"That's not what I did."

She lifted her chin to glare at him. "I finally find someone who fits into the story I'm planning and you give her an easy out. Sounds like sabotage to me."

Damn, she was mad. And making her angry was not what Patrick had intended. He resorted to reason. "Am I missing something here? Didn't you just do a piece on how it was better to give than receive?"

"Only because nobody I'd talked to before that grandmother illustrated how commercialism is tarnishing Christmas."

So they were back to that again. He shook his head in wonder. "Did it occur to you that not many people do illustrate your point?"

"That grandmother did. Before you wrecked things, I was about to ask her to go on camera and talk about how much money she's spent."

"Then you weren't paying attention to what she was telling you."

"She told me she's bought dozens of presents with no end in sight," Merry shot back.

"But she did it to see the looks of joy on her grandchildren's faces," he retorted. "That's hardly the stuff a hard-hitting report about the evils of commercialism is made of."

Merry didn't back down, but the tight line of her mouth relaxed. It was barely noticeable, but something he'd said must have gotten through to her. "Maybe she wasn't exactly what I was looking for, but she was close."

He softened his voice. Not deliberately, but to help her sort through whatever had led to her goal of becoming a television news Scrooge. "What exactly are you looking for, love?"

He gazed deep into her eyes, easily finding the generous, softhearted woman with whom he'd fallen in love. But then that woman turned away from him, breaking the gaze.

"I'll know it when I see it," she said. "As the day wears on, the mall won't be the happy place it seems to be now. Not everybody loves to shop."

Francine emerged from the truck, carrying her purse and walking as quickly as her pregnancy would allow. "I'll see you two later. Say, at five o'clock to get ready for the shoot."

"Wait," Merry said. "I thought we'd go to lunch together."

Francine scarcely paused, calling as she walked by them, "Sorry, sweetie, but I had a sandwich in the truck. I have shopping to do."

"I thought you finished your shopping."

"There are a few more things I need to get the twins," she said. "See you later."

"I can't believe she's going shopping." Merry sounded incredulous, as though a mall built expressly for that purpose wasn't standing a few feet from them.

"Why not?" Patrick asked. "I'm sure Betsy told Francine she wasn't needed until later. You know as well as I do that Christmas Eve is always slow. If any news breaks out, they can reach her by cell phone.

"Besides," he continued and quickly seized the opportunity that presented itself, "I'll take you to lunch."

A trapped look came into her eyes, before she said, "I'm not hungry."

Her growling stomach took that moment to disagree with her. She looked so guilty for having told him a fib that he laughed.

"Come on," he said, taking her lightly by the arm. "I'm hungry, too."

IF MERRY HADN'T SKIPPED breakfast that morning, she would have refused a lunch break.

Then she wouldn't be walking through King's Mall

with Patrick's large, warm hand cupping her arm, supposedly so they didn't get separated by the tide of shoppers.

She also wouldn't be afraid that the warmth of his hand would flow through her body and get near her heart.

The ironic part was that she couldn't wrench away from him. If he had an inkling as to how powerfully she still reacted to his touch, he wouldn't believe her when she told him at mall closing that the engagement was still off.

*Be casual,* she told herself. *Be cool.*

"Do you have to walk so close to me?" she grumbled.

He laughed, displaying the slightly crooked lower tooth that for some reason made him more handsome. When he spoke, his warm breath teased her neck. "The mall's crowded, love. I don't want to lose you."

She picked up on the double entendre but ignored it as he narrowly avoided missing a woman barreling toward the entrance of a kitchen store advertising a sale on snowflake flatware.

The crowd ahead of them thickened, the reason soon apparent. A line of children wound around an elaborate display resembling a winter wonderland. Fake snow, candy canes and an elf-staffed workshop contributed to the fantasy. Some of the children waited to talk to Santa while others lined up for a train ride.

The children's happy, excited chatter discounted them as story material, even though they were undoubtedly giving Santa an earful about all the things they wanted for Christmas.

Video-game systems, Barbie dolls, in-line skates, remote-controlled cars, electronic train sets...the requests would be endless.

Merry's gaze zeroed in on the bearded man on the throne. Even from a hundred feet away, she could tell his face was marred by a frown.

"That Santa doesn't look happy to be here," Merry said. "Maybe we should get some video of him."

"You're wanting video of a scowling Santa?"

"Who better than Santa to know how greedy people can get at Christmas?"

"Maybe later," Patrick said. Before she could protest, he added, "It'd be hell fighting through that crowd. Besides, I'm taking my fiancée to lunch."

"*Ex*-fiancée. And don't make it sound like a date. We're going to the food court."

"I'd rather go to the food court with you than a five-star restaurant with anyone else," he said in a low, intimate voice that sent shivers dancing up her arms.

She managed to ignore the shivers and rolled her eyes. "Do you have to say things like that?"

He gently squeezed her elbow. "How else will I convince you to come back to me?"

She swallowed. "Compliments won't do it."

"Then take pity on a poor Irishman," he said, thickening his brogue, "and give me some tips on what would do the convincing."

Despite herself, Merry smiled. When Patrick chose to be charming, which was nearly all the time, he was darn near irresistible. It made her conscious of how much she'd missed him these past months when he was spending so much time at his new job.

"My only need right now is food," she said. "I'm starving."

"Then let's feed you." Patrick still had hold of her arm as they rounded the corner leading to the food court. They both stopped short at the length of the lines.

"Can you believe how many people are here? Don't they know about online shopping? And whatever happened to staying home on Christmas Eve and baking cookies?" Merry mused. "Where are their priorities?"

"I'm sure a very many of them have already done their baking. How about you? Have you baked, Miss Crocker?"

"I'll have you know I baked snowball cookies and cranberry nut bars last night," she said. "And these wonderful Italian Christmas cookies my neighbor Angie Frencik made every year when I was growing up."

"Mmm. Sounds good. How about I come over later and have some?"

She was about to agree when she remembered why she shouldn't. The broken engagement. The breakup. How could those things have slipped her mind?

"No, you can't come over," she said, but didn't sound as convincing as she'd hoped. She quickly changed the subject. "Let's stick to the problem of the moment, okay? Which line do you think looks the shortest?"

They passed a place selling fast-food chicken, a burger joint and a Chinese eatery before stopping for pizza by the slice. A half-dozen pizzas were already out of the oven, kept warm under the lights on the counter. The line dwindled steadily until a man after Merry's heart, with a taste for extra cheese, was the only person in front of them.

"Two pieces of pizza and a lemonade," the teenage cashier said while he rang up the purchase. He was so fresh-faced Merry thought he looked like a singer in a boy band.

The man reached into his back pocket, withdrew his hand, then patted himself down with panicked motions. "My wallet's gone. How could my wallet be gone? I had it fifteen minutes ago."

Merry grimaced as her mind immediately conjured up mall pickpockets, searching the crowd for likely targets. This man, although not expensively dressed, had an air of absentmindedness about him that made him fit the bill.

"That's too bad, man," the good-looking young cashier said sympathetically. "Tell you what. Just take the pizza. My treat."

"Thanks, but I don't think I could eat it." The man did indeed look sick. "I cashed my paycheck this morning so I wouldn't be tempted to put anything on credit. I can't believe I lost all that money."

"You don't know that yet, sir." Patrick stepped up to the counter next to the man, his voice kind. "Why not check the mall office? It's Christmas. I'm betting someone turned in your wallet."

While the cashier provided directions to the mall office, Merry watched hope materialize on the face of the man with the missing wallet.

"I sure hope you're right about someone turning it in," the man told Patrick before rushing away, stopping to call back over his shoulder, "Thanks for the advice."

"I hope he gets his wallet back, too," Merry told Patrick while the cashier put their pizza on paper plates. "But if he does, I'm afraid his money will be gone."

"Why would you be saying that?"

"Even if somebody didn't deliberately pick his pocket, most people couldn't resist a wallet full of cash. Especially at the mall. There's too much emphasis here on what money can buy."

"Seems to me a cynical attitude like that is what got you in trouble earlier today," Patrick remarked. "Otherwise, you wouldn't have had to change the slant of your story."

Merry was still thinking about Patrick's remark when they sat down at a table for two with their soft drinks and pizza—pepperoni for him, extra cheese for her.

"I'll see plenty to back up my story before the mall closes," she told him. "We have a little more than six hours to go."

"Six hours until we're back together," he said and bit into his pizza. When he was through chewing, he asked, "When do you want to make the drive to my parents' house in Winston-Salem. Tonight or tomorrow?"

He took another bite of pizza, as though he hadn't said something outrageous.

"I'm not going to your parents' house for Christmas, Patrick," she said, even though she had a pang of regret when she made the declaration.

His parents lived in the middle of suburbia in a modest house that filled with relatives over the holidays. She knew that, not from anything Patrick had told her but because she'd witnessed it firsthand at Thanksgiving.

She'd frozen a step inside the MacFarlands' door when she'd gotten a look at the size of his crowd of relatives—two parents, three sisters, one brother, one brother-in-law, a sister-in-law and six nieces and nephews.

But then Patrick's hand had been on her back, propelling her forward, and soon she'd been enveloped in an atmosphere of love, laughter and acceptance.

The house would be like that at Christmas, too. Patrick hadn't talked much about it, but she envisioned a traditional Irish holiday with Celtic Christmas music, stuffed turkey, lots of spirits and plenty of love.

"Why wouldn't you come?" Patrick asked. "My family can be a bit overbearing, but I thought you liked them."

Overbearing? His family was wonderful.

"I do like them. But if I go to your parents' house, everybody will think we're back together," she said.

Patrick's eyes slid away from hers. She narrowed her own. "You haven't told your family the wedding's off, have you?"

He shrugged his broad shoulders. "You know mum and da love you, Merry. I didn't want to disappoint them."

Her irritation faded. How could she stay angry at a man who was more solicitous of his parents' feelings than his own?

"Besides," he continued, "I didn't see the point in telling them we're apart considering we'll be back together by the time we see them again."

Her shoulders squared. Good son or not, he could be awfully obstinate. "I am not spending Christmas with your family, Patrick."

"Would you be preferring that it just be me and you, then?"

"Not me and you. Me." She made a slashing movement with her hand. "Without you."

"Come on, love." His expressive eyes grew pleading. "If you're not spending Christmas with me, where will you be spending it? You're not joining your parents in Tahiti, are you?"

"No." She blocked out the momentary hurt that they hadn't asked her to accompany them, but then they never did. "But you know I don't count on them to be around at Christmas so I made other plans."

"Plans with who?"

"Francine and her family."

Patrick stroked his chin, drawing her attention to the cleft in the center. She was partial to a man with a cleft, but that could be because Patrick had one. "I suppose that's better than being alone, but you should be spending such an important day with the people who love you."

"Francine loves me."

He reached across the table and covered her hand with his. His eyes captured hers in a long, hot stare. "Not the way I love you."

She pulled her hand away. It was her turn to slide her eyes from his. "You're making this harder, Patrick."

"I'm trying to make it harder." All the lightness was gone from his voice and from his manner. "I don't want to break up, Merry. I want to work things out."

She stood. The food court was bustling with activity, but her eyes focused on nothing. "We have issues that can't be worked out."

"What kind of issues? And don't be starting in on the doves again. Or the symphony. Because those things don't matter to me. You matter."

She swung her gaze back to him as he rose and stepped toward her. He came into startling focus: the black of his hair, the blue of his eyes, the determination on his face. It almost hurt to look at him.

"You don't even know who I am."

"Then tell me."

"Let's just say that you and I are too different and leave it at that."

Reasoning with her was out. He'd tried that and it hadn't worked. Combing the mall for the perfect gift was an excellent idea, but that was taking time. Besides, that would prove that he loved her. But he needed something to show that she loved him back.

She'd raised her cute, little chin at a stubborn angle, her posture was unbending and her eyes stared straight ahead as she walked.

He recognized the signs of a woman who had set her mind on something. In this case, it was dumping him.

He looked heavenward, hoping for inspiration, and spied his answer dangling from the mall's high ceiling. He grabbed her hand and tugged, reminding himself that desperate situations called for desperate actions.

"Could you give me back my hand, Patrick?" she asked.

"No," he said and led her to the magic spot.

When he had her positioned where he wanted her, he shielded her with his body so that the shoppers behind them ran into him rather than her.

"Sorry, buddy," a man who plowed into him through no fault of his own said, patting Patrick amiably on the shoulder.

"What are you doing, Patrick?" Merry asked as he

held fast to her hand. "We can't stop in the middle of the mall. People will get angry."

But the shoppers behind the apologist parted, moving around Patrick and Merry without complaint.

"I'm doing something drastic," Patrick said.

"Something silly, you mean. I don't see—"

"If you looked up at the mistletoe, you would." Tugging on her hand to pull her even closer, he bent his head and kissed her.

Her lips were already parted, so he took full advantage, deepening the kiss before she had a chance to pull away. He'd kissed her a thousand times, thought about kissing her a thousand more, but every time the same thing happened.

He lost himself in her.

The world around them faded to black. Logically he knew they were standing in the middle of a shopping mall corridor, with last-minute shoppers crowding them on all sides, but it felt as though they were alone.

He laced his fingers with hers and brought his other hand up to brush the soft tendrils of her hair. His hand lingered on her cheek, stroking the utter smoothness of her skin as he kept kissing her.

But he wasn't only kissing Merry. She was kissing him back.

She flattened her palm over his wildly beating heart, left it there for a few seconds, then slowly and sensuously traced a pattern up his chest and over his shoulder. Her hand snaked around to cup the back of his neck, holding his head in place as though she actually believed *he* might pull away.

The passion that had always been between them flared, mixing with the heat and the love so that all he could think about was Merry…and why he heard applause instead of bells.

Merry must have heard it, too, because she looked confused when he lifted his head. Turned-on and dazed, but definitely confused.

"Do you hear clapping?" she asked him, sounding so breathless and looking so sexy with her lips red and swollen and her hair mussed he had to squash a desire to kiss her again.

He nodded. He heard not only clapping but a catcall or two. Slowly, without releasing her from the circle of his arms, he turned his head.

Only a few people had actually stopped to watch the kiss. The others applauded enthusiastically as they walked by. A redheaded, freckle-faced boy of about thirteen or fourteen provided the wolf whistles.

"Thank you," Patrick said, nodding in acknowledgement. "Thank you very much."

"I wish my man kissed me like that," a grinning woman remarked as she passed.

Merry found her voice. "He's my *ex*-man."

The woman, who hadn't broken stride, didn't hear her. Neither had anyone else besides Patrick. He grinned at the terminology she'd used. "I'm still very much a man, love. And if that kiss was anything to go by, we won't be ex-anythings for much longer."

Her kissable lips flat-lined and she wrenched out of his arms. The people who had stopped to watch the kiss didn't show any sign of moving.

"What are you staring at?" Merry asked them. "Get

shopping. There's not even six shopping hours left before Christmas."

"Hey, aren't you that TV newswoman?" someone asked.

"Maybe," she said.

She grabbed Patrick's hand, propelling him back into the stream of shoppers and anonymity. He stifled a smile. She probably didn't even realize that she had ordered their audience to do what she'd spent the day railing against.

"That was an underhanded thing to do," she hissed at him.

"I don't see anything underhanded about kissing under a mistletoe."

"You dragged me under that mistletoe."

"I'm not admitting to underhanded, but I will admit to desperate. I had to do something to prove you still love me."

He was so attuned to her that he knew she expelled air through her nostrils even if the mall was too crowded for him to hear.

"All that kiss proved is I'm still attracted to you," she said.

He didn't believe her. He'd kissed enough women in his lifetime that he could distinguish between kisses that spoke of love and kisses that screamed sex. Hers had been an exciting blend of both.

But there was no point in arguing about it. Not when she was weakening and he had hours yet to get her to face the truth.

"I think you're sexy, too," he whispered in her ear.

"Come home with me tonight and put us both out of our misery."

She seemed about to say something. Her chest heaved and her mouth opened, but no sound escaped. Then she shook her head, spun on her heel and stalked away.

But not before he winked at her. And followed. After all, he had a job to do. And his involved spending the day at the mall with her.

# CHAPTER FOUR

HER EX-FIANCÉ WAS absolutely infuriating. And so sexy that Merry's toes still curled inside her shoes. It was a wonder she could walk after that infernal, intoxicating kiss.

She should run. But that wouldn't do any good. It was still so crowded in the mall, she wouldn't get far. And, besides, a part of her didn't want to get away from him.

That was the part she worried about.

As she looked back on it, she realized her doubts about their relationship had mushroomed after he'd taken the job at The Goulden Group. He'd become caught up in making money, and she'd convinced herself she shouldn't marry him.

She imagined them growing further apart with each passing month as he devoted an increasing share of his time and energy to his job, again, not in a good way. Very little time would be left over for their relationship. She could only envision a long lonely future for each of them if they carried on as is. By ending things before they married, she'd prevented them from making a monumental mistake and saved them both from serious heartache.

Yet the reasons she'd accepted his marriage proposal still applied. He was good and kind, sexy and charming and enjoyable to be around. Especially when he kissed her. She closed her eyes briefly, frustrated that she couldn't shut out the memory of the kiss.

Determined to concentrate on work, she stopped the next shopper she saw and asked a few questions while Patrick stood patiently by.

"I purposely don't buy anything until Christmas Eve, because shopping helps get me filled with the Christmas spirit," the ponytailed young mother told her.

Merry's on-the-spot interviews didn't get much more productive after that. A trio of teenage girls without money had come to the mall to hang out because they liked the joyful atmosphere. A middle-aged father had brought his three sweet-faced little girls to see Santa. And just about everybody harbored the delusion that it would snow even though historically the Charlotte area had a less than five percent chance of having a white Christmas.

"Got any ideas about where we should head next?" Patrick asked, after a woman clutching a stuffed Santa talked about her white, frosty intuition.

"The mall's even more crowded now." She stated the obvious. "How about if we duck into Crystal's and find the longest line. After that, we can let human nature take its course."

"What do you mean by that, love?"

Love. There was that word again. She would have clamped her hands over her ears if it hadn't been so childish.

"Come with me, and you'll see." She took a ninety-degree turn into Crystal's Department Store and passed up lines that were four and five deep in favor of a long column of humanity in the housewares department.

"This one's good," she announced with satisfaction. "Let's hang back before we approach anyone. With the length of this line, things are bound to get ugly soon."

"You think people will become unpleasant when they get tired of waiting in line?"

She ignored the incredulity in his voice and answered. "Exactly. So could you get your camera ready? We can pretend to be looking at these wineglasses. I don't want people to see us and put on happy faces for the camera."

She indicated a selection of different types of glasses in which to drink wine: tulip-shaped for white wine, rounded with a larger bowl for red, and tall, thin flutes for sparkling wine.

After a moment's hesitation, in which she thought he might balk at her suggestion, Patrick went to the display of wineglasses and picked up a four pack. The glasses he chose were, of course, the priciest ones in the store.

"If I buy these flutes, we could drink to getting back together," Patrick suggested.

She cut her eyes to him. "Could you keep your mind on business?"

He grinned at her. "You are my business."

He behaved himself after that, although it was clear he didn't approve of her strategy. Maybe he was on to something, because five minutes passed, then ten, without a single temper flaring. Except, possibly, Merry's.

"I don't get it," she said. "I've been in lines way shorter than that and people always get impatient."

He smiled bemusedly at her. "Would you like me to incite the line for you?"

"Of course not. But the music alone should have them climbing the walls. Listen to it. I've never heard such bad instrumental versions of holiday songs in my life."

"I don't think the music is so bad," Patrick commented.

Merry smirked as an excessively homogenized version of the song about decking the halls began to play. "Come on, Patrick. Do you honestly think anybody could enjoy this?"

She'd no sooner finished her sentence when Patrick nudged her arm and nodded toward the line. "Look down."

She picked out a boot-clad foot tapping in time to the music. It belonged to a middle-aged man with a paunch and a smile.

"One toe tapper doesn't make a trend," Merry said.

"How about two tappers?" Patrick asked as a high-heeled woman behind the booted man joined in the rhythmic tapping. "Or three? Or four?"

A teenager in running shoes lifted the toe of his shoe up and down as did a young woman in clogs. And then nearly everybody in line joined in the tapping. Oxfords and boots and high heels, all following the rhythm.

Merry watched in disbelief as the last person in line, a heavyset man in his fifties who might have made a good Santa, belted out a surprisingly on-key, "Fa la la la la la la la la."

The toe tappers in front of the singer turned around and smiled. The singer smiled back. Merry felt her own mouth start to curve. But then Patrick positioned his camera, rousing her out of her Muzak-induced trance.

"That's not the tape I'm looking for," Merry told him.

"Ah, but it's too good to pass up," he said while he positioned the camera and went to work. The song's chorus rolled around again, and two others joined the singer in "fa la laing." One by one, the people in line chimed in until the "fa la la's" rang out louder than the music.

"There," Patrick said when the song ended and the "fa la la's" finally stopped. He couldn't hide his pleasure. "I think the video will stand alone, but you might want to interview the fellow who started the singing."

"I'm not interviewing him," she said, trying not to let the touching incident sway her. "I already told you. This doesn't fit with the story I'm planning."

"Then maybe you're planning the wrong story." He leaned toward her so she could feel the warmth of his breath on her face. "Where's your Christmas spirit?"

"It's not at the mall," she said but couldn't muster any real conviction behind the words. "So could you please help me keep looking for footage to back up my story?"

"Certainly," he said, but she could tell his heart wasn't in it. Truth be told, hers didn't seem to be, either.

Now how in the heck had that happened?

WHY DID MERRY KEEP resisting both him and the spirit of Christmas? Patrick couldn't make sense of it.

She couldn't completely hide the way she felt about him, especially not when he kissed her. Neither could she fail to notice that the mall was teeming with goodwill.

They'd spent another hour or so interviewing unfailingly cheerful shoppers, none of whom had provided fodder for her story. Then Francine called to invite them to take a break and meet for orange smoothies.

Merry had readily agreed, but Patrick told her he'd catch up with them later. Just in case she still didn't know how much he loved her, he needed to continue hunting for the perfect Christmas gift.

"You're sure this tennis racket is the best on the market?" he asked the salesclerk at the sporting goods store as he bounced the strings of pure natural gut against the palm of his left hand.

The clerk held up a finger to an approaching young man tall enough to play in the NBA and told Patrick, "That racket's top of the line. Made of titanium and graphite. At ball impact, the racket stiffens in the throat area, providing explosive power. They don't make 'em any better."

Sold by the sales pitch, Patrick purchased the pricey racket and slung it over his shoulder in the tennis bag he'd bought along with it.

He'd finally bought Merry the perfect present. He should have thought of it before. She played on a local adult tennis team and claimed there were very few activities that she enjoyed more.

A slender brunette with big eyes and a bigger smile fell into step alongside him while he was leaving the store. "I'm a tennis player, too."

"I'm not the tennis player. The racket's for my—" Patrick started to say fiancée, but reluctantly substituted another word "—girlfriend."

"Your girlfriend?" She put such a wealth of disappointment into the question that Patrick nearly apologized for not being available. "Did she tell you what kind of racket she wanted?"

"No, she didn't. It's a surprise."

The woman grimaced. "You're really not a tennis player, huh? Anybody even a little bit serious about the game likes to choose her own equipment. One woman's favorite racket is another woman's lemon."

He thanked her for the advice, which unfortunately made a lot of sense. Just as regrettably, that meant his quest for the perfect present wasn't yet over. He took a quick left and ducked into Harrington & Vine's. After a few minutes of wandering, he happened upon the electronics department.

Shoppers crammed the aisles. He noticed three teenage boys with gleams in their eyes clustered around the latest version of the Xbox. Patrick had a soft spot for video games himself, especially ones involving intergalactic battles, but shooting down aliens wasn't for Merry.

Neither was a very cool seven-inch television—when would she watch it? Or the mobile navigation system, which he'd tried and failed at another time to convince Merry to install in her car.

But an iPod…now Merry could go for that. He finally decided upon a deluxe model that stored up to five thousand songs and approached the sales counter feeling good about his choice.

"You're lucky we have any left," the salesclerk told him. "These babies are our number one seller this Christmas. Everybody's buying one."

Patrick frowned at the information that he'd chosen yet another gift with universal appeal but bought the iPod just in case.

After returning the tennis racket and deciding against perfume, he took video of the line of children waiting to see Santa Claus from a vantage point a floor above the Christmas village.

Then he wandered into a novelty shop, where his head spun while he looked at lava lamps, shrunken-down totem poles and feather boas.

"Can I help you with something?" a clerk asked during what Patrick assumed was a rare lull.

Patrick felt his spirits lift. The store was full of unique items. "I'm looking for the perfect gift for my lady."

"You and every other man at the mall," the clerk said. He went on to suggest a bra made out of candy, furry handcuffs and Chippendale stripper playing cards, none of which seemed right to Patrick.

He had better luck at Kitchen Accents, where he bought an indoor grill with removable plates. He added a soft stuffed pink pig from Toy Emporium. Of all the animals in the world, Merry had a weakness for pigs. This one squeaked when you squeezed it.

"This pig's really cute," the young, smiling cashier remarked while she rang it up. She gestured at a display of furry, stuffed animals behind her. "But the monkey's our biggest seller. He makes amazing screeching sounds."

"I'll take one of those, too," Patrick said.

It was only when he inadvertently bumped another shopper as he was leaving the store and the bag screeched that Patrick admitted to himself that he had absolutely no clue what he was looking for.

"I HAVE HAD THE BEST couple of hours." Francine regarded Merry over the lip of her orange smoothie, her eyes sparkling. "I only called you because my feet hurt."

"Gee, thanks," Merry said.

Francine laughed. "I didn't mean it that way. I only meant I was on such a roll, I would have kept shopping if pregnancy wasn't hard on the feet. After we finish our smoothies, I'm going to try one of those massage chairs so I can last another hour."

"You're that determined to keep on going?"

"Uh-huh. Sometimes it's hard for me to believe that you don't like to shop. I got the most darling stuffed reindeers with noses that glow when you squeeze their ears. And I found the most wonderful toddler-size University of North Carolina sweat suits."

"Excuse me for interrupting, but where did you find those?" a woman at the adjoining table asked. She wore felt reindeer antlers bedecked with holly with complete self-confidence. "My husband went to UNC, and I've been looking everywhere for just that thing for our eighteen-month-old."

While Francine breathlessly filled her in—the store sold UNC hats, T-shirts and bikinis, too—it occurred to Merry that her friend and coworker epitomized a Christmas shopper gone wild. Too bad, as an employee of WZLM, Francine couldn't appear on camera.

Her shopping tips finally exhausted, Francine turned from the woman wearing the reindeer antlers to Merry. "My aching feet weren't the only reason I suggested we meet. I want to hear if anything juicy happened between you and Patrick."

Unable to meet her friend's probing gaze, Merry's eyes dropped to the table. "No."

"Oh, come on. This is Francine you're talking to. You can't fool me. If nothing happened, you'd look me in the eye when you denied it. And you wouldn't be blushing."

Merry touched her cheek, which did indeed feel hot. She drank from her frothy smoothie in the hopes of cooling off, but there wasn't enough liquid left to accomplish the task. Across from her, Francine watched and waited. Merry rewarded her rare patience by finally answering, "Okay. Something did happen. He took me to lunch."

Francine raised both eyebrows. "And?"

Merry hesitated, trying to decide how much information to share.

Francine clapped her hands and grinned. "He kissed you, didn't he? Don't look so surprised. I'm your best friend. You called me the night Patrick kissed you the first time. You sounded just as dazed then as you look now."

"It was just a kiss," Merry mumbled. "It didn't mean anything."

"It means you're not as sure about breaking this engagement as you pretend to be," Francine shot back.

Merry massaged her temples. "I swear, Francine, you act like you want Patrick and me to get back together."

"I do. I like Patrick. And you love him."

When she was breaking the engagement, Merry had convinced herself that ten months hadn't been long enough to be sure that what she felt for Patrick was love. But if today at the mall had taught her anything, it was that she'd been fooling herself.

"I do love him," she admitted. "But that doesn't mean I should marry him."

The tinny refrains of "Jingle Bells" rang out, but the tunes came from a cell phone and not the mall's sound system.

"Excuse me." Francine held up a finger and dug into her voluminous purse until she found her phone. While she talked, Merry rubbed the back of her neck and tried not to think about how much she wanted Patrick to kiss her again.

Francine's face appeared pinched and drawn when she got off the phone, prompting Merry to reach across the table and cover her friend's hand. "What is it, Francy?" she asked, borrowing the nickname Patrick favored.

"It's bad news." Francine sighed heavily. "That was Doug. Seems like the twins have come down with a stomach bug."

"Oh, no."

"Oh, yes. Poor little guys. Doug says they're miserable but he can hold the fort until I get home. But this doesn't look good for tomor—" Francine stopped in midword and grimaced. "I know tomorrow is Christmas but maybe you shouldn't come over. I'd hate for you to get sick. Except that would mean you have nowhere to spend the holiday."

"Don't worry about me," Merry said and squeezed her friend's hand. "You need to think about your boys and yourself. Hopefully it is only a stomach bug. But if the twins have the strain of flu spreading through the mall, they're highly contagious. You'll have to be extra careful, with you being pregnant."

"Thanks for watching out for me, Merry," Francine said, withdrawing her hand from Merry's and running it through her hair. "But I've had a flu shot, which my doctor, bless her heart, encouraged exactly because of something like this. But what are you going to do? Where are you going to go?"

A mental image of the house where Patrick had grown up, decorated for the holidays and filled with people who genuinely cared about her, flashed in Merry's mind. She deliberately blotted it out. "I already told you not to worry about me, Francine. I'll be fine."

"How can you be fine if you're alone on Christmas? There must be someone else you can spend the holiday with." She stopped talking abruptly. "Patrick."

"No," Merry said. "Not Patrick. How many times do I have to tell you—"

Francine didn't let her finish. "I meant to say there's Patrick."

Merry followed the direction of Francine's gaze. Oh, no, Patrick. Tall, loose-limbed and darkly handsome, he strode with purpose toward the table where they'd been enjoying their orange smoothies. As always, her heart did a wild Irish jig when she saw him. Unlike always, sheer pleasure at seeing him wasn't the only reason. Francine had already risen from the table and was hurrying toward him.

Because she'd been struck dumb at the sight of him, Merry was too slow to react. She tried to make up for her lapse with wild hand gestures meant to snag Francine's attention, but her friend's back was turned.

Aside from a Christmas miracle, Merry had no chance of shutting Francine up before she informed Patrick that Merry no longer had anywhere to go on Christmas Day.

PATRICK WAS SO INTRIGUED by Merry's frantic hand movements that he didn't immediately notice Francine.

When he did catch sight of her, he couldn't help but smile. Her pregnancy was visible, her motherly appearance contrasting charmingly with her air of youthful exuberance.

"Have I told you lately that motherhood agrees with you, Francy?" he asked when she was within hearing range.

A flush of pleasure tinged her cheeks. "Almost every time you see me. And you get more charming every time I see you. I don't know how Merry could let you go."

"I'm working on rectifying that."

She leaned toward him and mock whispered, "You might try kissing her again. That made quite an impact."

Ah, that was interesting. He cast a glance at Merry, who had given up on the gesturing and was approaching them. "What's up?"

"Doug just called to say my boys have a stomach bug. I hope it's a twenty-four hour virus and not the flu. That way, Christmas might not be a total washout."

Patrick frowned, genuinely distressed that her boys

wouldn't be well on Christmas morning. He wasn't so old that he didn't remember the rush of excitement that woke him and his siblings in the wee hours. Or the mad dash down the stairs to see what had been left under the tree. "I'm sorry, Francy. Is there anything I can do?"

"Yes, there is," Francine said decisively while Merry closed the gap between them. My gosh, she was moving as quickly as a child on Christmas morning. "But I better not say or Merry will whack me with Santa's toy bag."

Merry appeared behind her friend and asked in a too-loud, too-bright voice, "Why would I want to do that, Francine? You haven't said anything you shouldn't have, right?"

The two women exchanged a look heavy with meaning while Patrick tried to figure out exactly what Francine wasn't supposed to say. "Francy was just telling me her twins are sick," he said.

"It's too bad, isn't it?" Merry looked sick to her own stomach. Doubtless she felt sorry for the boys, but there had to be more to her distress. It took him only a moment to figure it out.

"Not only is it too bad for them, it's too bad for you." Patrick strove to keep his expression innocent. "You won't be able to spend the holiday with Francy and her family now, will you?"

Instead of answering, Merry glowered at Francine. Her friend placed a hand over her stomach in the fashion of pregnant women everywhere. It could have been because she felt the baby move, but Patrick suspected Francine was using her pregnancy to win sympathy points.

"I've got to go get ready," Francine announced.

"The broadcast is two hours away," Merry protested.

"I meant get ready for Christmas. Since the boys are sick, a couple extra presents might help cheer them up."

She blew an air kiss at Merry and left them so quickly, Patrick felt a breeze. Merry stared after Francine, her mouth slightly open in what looked like dismay.

"I'm thinking this means your plans for Christmas Day have fallen through," Patrick pointed out.

"Then I'll make new plans," Merry said airily, as though she had a dozen options on where to spend the holiday.

"Exactly what I was about to suggest. Mum and da will be delighted to see you."

"Not when they find out we're not getting married, they won't." She sighed and rubbed the bridge of her nose. "I'd like to see them, Patrick. I really would. And I know Christmas at their house would be wonderful. But surely you understand why I can't go with you."

He stroked his chin while his brain worked overtime. "I have another idea then."

Her shoulders lifted, then dropped. Her dark hair fell long and loose around her face, which looked very pale except for the green of her eyes. "Why do you always have another idea?"

"You know I don't like the thought of you alone on Christmas, love."

She released a long breath, which told him she'd rather not think about being alone, either. She looked and sounded suspicious. Rightly so. "What's your idea?"

He leaned closer, taking in the subtle scent of Merry's shampoo and the peach moisturizer she smoothed on each morning. He breathed in those same scents when they made love. He lowered his voice to his most persuasive pitch. "Spend tonight with me."

She leaned toward him, as though longing to get closer to him the same way he craved to be near her. Just when he thought she might kiss him, she abruptly jerked back. He watched her throat constrict as she swallowed. "How would that solve anything?"

"It'll solve the problem of what you're going to do Christmas Day. You'll be at my place when you wake up. I'm thinking we can spend the whole day in bed while I convince you to put your engagement ring back on."

Her eyes were pleading, for what she probably didn't know. "Patrick—"

"Or you can put on your ring early in the day," he continued doggedly on. "Then we can drive to Winston-Salem. We'll be together so you won't disappoint my family by saying anything about a breakup."

Each shake of her head caused him pain so stark it was physical.

"What happened to your prediction that the engagement would be back on by the time the mall closes?" she asked.

"The prediction still stands." He sounded far more cocky than he felt. "The plan I just told you about, that's my insurance plan."

"I'm vetoing your insurance plan."

He lowered his voice so nobody but Merry could hear him. "Why? You did admit you're still attracted to me, didn't you?"

"Yes, but—"

Patrick had no desire to hear what came after the but, not when he'd finally gained an inch. "We can talk about this later, love. But for now, we better get back to work. We don't have much time until the mall closes."

Neither did he, and that's what worried him.

## CHAPTER FIVE

THE DAY WASN'T TURNING OUT the way Merry planned. She and Patrick had talked to plenty of free-spending shoppers, all so high-spirited that none fit into a story illustrating how commercial Christmas had become.

The most joyful shopper by far had been the man who'd lost his wallet. He'd nearly mowed down a half-dozen shoppers after spotting Patrick in one of the common areas. Somebody had turned in the wallet with the cash intact, and he'd wanted to thank Patrick for suggesting he check the office.

Another story that had a happy ending was that of a lost little boy that Trish DiCaprio, the mall events co-ordinator, had told her about. After the boy had been found, Trish had tracked Merry down to tell her the boy's family didn't want the story publicized.

Merry was happy for the man and the little boy's family, of course. And darn if she wasn't beginning to feel happy herself. It could be because she was having an increasingly difficult time remembering why a marriage between her and Patrick wouldn't work.

He'd ducked into one of those Christmas specialty stores a few minutes ago, insisting he needed to pick up something. She waited outside the store, wondering what could have been so important.

Her cell phone buzzed, and she actually wished that she'd programmed the tone to play a Christmas carol.

"Hello, dear," came Bridget MacFarland's lilting voice, a female version of Patrick's. The connection was surprisingly strong. "How are you this fine Christmas Eve?"

"I'm good, Bridget," Merry said slowly while she tried to figure out the reason for the call. She could count on one hand the number of times Bridget had phoned her. "But how are you? Is anything wrong?"

"Nothing's wrong, dear. But I was a far sight better before Patrick called and said you two aren't coming to Winston-Salem this Christmas."

Merry bit her lip so she wouldn't tell Bridget she'd changed her mind. When she had that impulse under control, she asked, "Did he tell you why we weren't coming?"

"Something about you having to work tomorrow. What a disappointment that was. But I'm a big girl. I know television news doesn't take a day off. And I can understand why Patrick won't leave town without you. But I did want to call and say you and Patrick are welcome any time at all, whether it be two days after Christmas or twenty-two."

A sense of loss swept over Merry. By breaking up with Patrick, she was also severing ties with his warm, loving family. He hadn't been able to tell his mother that the engagement was off, but she should. It was the right thing to do.

"Actually, Patrick and I aren't…" She trailed off,

unable to get the words out. "…sure of our plans. Everything's up in the air."

"Because of your work schedule," Bridget supplied. "I know. I'm not trying to make you feel guilty that you can't be here with us, dear. I called to wish you a merry Christmas and to say that both of you will be missed."

Her prospective mother-in-law's warmth carried over the phone line, and Merry's eyes misted. Her own parents loved her. Of that, she had no doubt. They'd made sure she attended the best schools and had everything she needed and more than she wanted.

But she'd been a late-in-life surprise, and the bond between husband and wife had been forged long before she'd been born. When they called her tomorrow from Tahiti, they'd tell her what a fabulous time they were having. They wouldn't say they missed her.

"Thank you, Bridget," she managed to reply.

"You're very welcome." Bridget paused. "Where are you, Merry? I can hear voices and Christmas music."

"I'm at the mall."

"That explains it. I love the mall, especially at Christmas. I love you, too, dear. Have a merry Christmas if I don't see you and Patrick."

"Merry Christmas," Merry said.

She disconnected the call, a certain tall Irishman uppermost in her mind. He emerged from the store with a floppy Santa hat perched over his thick dark hair.

"What do you think?" he asked, his eyes twinkling. He tugged the tassel. The hat stuck up, adding inches to his already considerable height.

"I think you look ridiculous."

"Well, now, that's not a very nice thing to say to a jolly Irishman."

It also wasn't entirely true. He should have looked ludicrous but didn't. The hat brought out the happy lights in his eyes, providing a glimpse of the fun-loving man she'd fallen in love with. The man who'd been largely absent these past months while he toiled at his new job.

"That Irish charm thing you do, does it always work?"

He grinned at her, seemingly unoffended. "You tell me."

"It seems to have worked on your mother. She just called me to wish me a merry Christmas. She was trying very hard to be understanding about me working tomorrow."

"So you know about the lie?" He grimaced. "I hated to do it, but it was only a white lie. I had to give her a reason we weren't going."

"But I don't understand why you're not going, Patrick."

"I expect you already know the answer to that one, love." He touched her cheek. "If you're not going to mum and da's, then neither am I. Even if you tell me tonight that it's over, I want to be around tomorrow. You know, in case you change your mind about being alone and want some company."

Her heart melted, right there in the middle of the mall. She already knew he didn't want her to be alone, but Bridget's phone call had made her realize how much Patrick was prepared to miss.

"Oh, Patrick," she said. "Why do you refuse to

accept that it's over between us. What have I done to encourage you?"

"Besides that X-rated kiss and confessing how attracted you are to me, you mean?" He pretended to contemplate her question. "Did you tell my mum you called off the wedding?"

"Well, no. But—"

"That's encouraging," he interrupted. He leaned down, positioned his mouth near her ear and asked, "Do you want to know what I think?"

She tried not to shiver. "Not particularly."

"I think you secretly want to spend Christmas with me," he finished.

She tried to deny it, but couldn't make her mouth work. She attempted to school her features into an impassive mask, but could tell she hadn't pulled it off. "You're not the only man in the world, Patrick."

"I know that." He smiled softly. "But we both know I'm the only man for you."

"That's terribly egotistical."

"It's the way it is." He gave her a warm smile. "Let's make another go of it, Merry," he said in a low, persuasive voice. "Just tell me what I did wrong, and I'll fix it."

"You're only making this harder."

"That's because you won't fight for us, love, and we have something worth fighting for."

"Not all relationships work out, Patrick." Her voice cracked. "Not all couples who love each other have happy endings."

"When you have something worthwhile, like we do, you fight to keep it."

She blinked away the moisture that had pooled in her eyes. "I don't want to fight with you."

"I don't want to fight with you, either." He cupped her cheek and looked at her with earnestness. "If you won't listen to anything else, listen to this. I love you. I always have. I always will."

"I've told you," she whispered. "Love isn't enough."

"That's where you're wrong, Merry. Love is always enough. Especially at Christmas."

PATRICK HADN'T REALIZED how much stress he'd been under these last few months at work until he felt it fading away.

Even though matters remained unresolved with Merry, spending another day as a TV news cameraman had plenty of side benefits. Not all of them involved operating a camera.

The latest perk had chubby cheeks, liquid brown eyes and curly, blond hair. He was a wee lad, not much over three feet tall. Patrick judged his age to be either four or five.

His mother, who was set to appear on camera, had left the boy at a food-court table with Patrick and Merry while she checked her hair and makeup in a restroom.

"You've got it wrong, lad," Patrick said. "I'm not one of Santa's helpers just because I'm wearing the red hat. The elves are the ones who help out Santa, and I'm way too tall to be one of those."

"They're tiny," the boy said, his eyes bright with pre-Christmas excitement. "And green. With pointy ears."

"They usually wear green, that's so. And it's true

their caps are red and their ears are pointy. But did you know that not all elves live at the North Pole?"

The boy's mouth dropped open, his attention thoroughly captured. Patrick wasn't Irish for nothing. He'd been taught how to spin a tale.

"Where else do elves live?" the boy asked.

"If you look real hard, you can sometimes spy the little people at the base of sacred trees in the thick woods. That'd be in Ireland, where my people are from. But you'd only see them at night for they're bashful of humans."

The boy's already big eyes widened. "Do they have a workshop where they make toys?"

"Not these elves. They mostly take care of wild animals. But they'll sometimes do a good deed for a person who's worthy." He ruffled the boy's hair. "Sort of the way Santa only rewards good boys and girls."

Merry had been listening to them with a slight smile on her face up to that point. He was so attuned to her that he realized he'd said something not to her liking. He didn't discover what it was until after the boy's mother explained on camera that she'd dyed her hair Christmas-bow red to show her Christmas spirit.

"Did you have to tell the little boy that nonsense about getting something for nothing from an elf?" she asked when they were alone. "Now he'll think Santa isn't the only one who'll bring him presents."

They were on the edge of the food court, between a bakery that featured oversize cookies and a candy store packed with sugary goodies he could smell from where he stood.

People all around them hummed along with the

canned music to the tune of "Frosty the Snowman," but he still heard the thick exasperation in her voice.

"You weren't listening closely enough, love. The Irish elves are picky about who they help. And they specialize in good deeds, which they do out of the joy of giving."

A dapper man dressed in a green suit interrupted to find out when the segment including the red-haired woman would air, then asked whether they thought Charlotte would have a white Christmas.

"Yes, I believe so," Patrick said. "I can feel snow in the air."

"How could you say that?" Merry asked when the green-suited man had gone. "There's no snow in the forecast. And have you looked at the sky? There aren't any clouds."

"There weren't any clouds earlier today, but there might be some by now. And I didn't say it would snow. I said I *believed* it would."

"What's the difference?"

"There's a world of difference, love. It's like the elves. I'd never say for sure that they exist."

She clearly wasn't following him. "But you believe they do?"

"I don't believe they don't. Belief is a funny thing. Take Santa Claus. You don't have to accept that a jolly fat man rides in a sleigh with flying reindeer to believe in the spirit of Christmas.

"The Irish stories are like that. Think of them as fanciful allegories for people who believe not necessarily in elves but in magic. Didn't your mum and da ever regale you with tales like those when you were a child?"

He saw her swallow before she answered and wouldn't have been surprised if she'd had a lump in her throat. "You know my parents, Patrick. They're attorneys. They're hardly the fanciful sort."

"A shame, I've always thought that was. Do you suppose that's why you can't see any magic at the mall?"

She didn't answer for a moment. "Maybe I can't see any magic at the mall because there isn't any magic here."

"Then why haven't you been able to find anything to back up the angle of your story?" He didn't wait for her answer. "I'll tell you why. The magic that's in the air, you have to open your heart to see it."

A short while later, as she and Patrick walked through the mall en route to the ENG truck, she was still trying to figure out what he meant.

Open her heart? Her heart was open. Hadn't he been creeping back inside it all day?

The commotion surrounding the Christmas village drew her attention as they passed. She turned in time to see a swirl of snowflakes descend over the children waiting in line for Santa.

She stopped and gaped at the scene. The children appeared to be caught in one of those crystal snow globes that transformed into a winter wonderland when shaken.

Hardly believing her eyes, she blinked. And the snow was gone. But she'd seen it. She knew she had.

Patrick was gazing at her curiously. "What's wrong?"

"Did you see that?" she asked. "Over at Santa's village?"

He groaned. "Please don't be telling me you're still wanting that video of the scowling Santa."

She shook her head mutely, trying to make sense of what had happened. But she couldn't, because a sudden snow squall inside the mall didn't make sense.

"Are you all right?" he asked.

"I'm fine," she said, and knew she spoke the truth. Because Patrick had been right. There was magic inside the mall, and she'd just seen some of it.

THE YOUNG WOMAN Merry had put on camera was more bubbly than a glass of champagne on New Year's Eve. Yet Merry found herself smiling at the woman's exuberance. Or maybe it was the man behind the camera who was the cause of her smile.

"I waited in one line for almost an hour for the display model of a DVD player, but the person ahead of me got it first," the woman told Merry and WZLM-13's live audience. "That was after the kid with the hot chocolate bumped me and scalded my leg but before I broke my heel."

Merry shifted the microphone in order to ask the obvious question. "Then will you tell everyone at home why you're in such good spirits?"

Although Merry had given the woman a preview of the questions she'd ask before they went live, the woman acted surprised. "Why wouldn't I be in good spirits? I'm at the mall, I'm on television and it's Christmas Eve."

Merry nodded, as though she agreed with the sentiment. By now, she supposed she did. She'd given up trying to find an angle that wasn't there and was going along with the flow.

She'd even had Francine edit the tape Patrick had shot of the fa-la-laing shoppers waiting in line and led her segment with it.

"And there you have it," Merry said when she was back on camera, being careful not to dislodge the Santa hat she'd borrowed from Patrick. "Despite the crowds, long lines and not much time left before the big day, the people here are filled with the indomitable spirit of Christmas.

"This is a very Merry Deluca, King's Mall, WZLM-13 news."

Patrick lowered the camera, grinned at her and gave her a thumbs-up. Pleasure shot through her. That charm of his was working overtime now.

They'd set up for the six o'clock broadcast just inside the main entrance of the mall. The people who had taken a break from Christmas shopping to watch the live report crowded around her, each one more upbeat than the last.

Merry listened to more stories of Christmas cheer, nodding and smiling. But not because it was expected of her. Sometime during the day, she'd actually started to feel cheerful.

Patrick had been right about more than just Christmas magic. How could she talk about how commercialism was ruining Christmas when everything she'd seen today confirmed that the spirit of Christmas was thriving?

Patrick, who hailed from a land of myth and leprechauns. A land where people believed in magic and love everlasting.

Patrick, whom she loved like crazy and couldn't wait to marry.

Giddy delight spread through her, and it took all her willpower not to shout her realization out loud.

*I want to be Patrick's wife.*

She wanted to spend tonight in his bed, tomorrow in his arms and the rest of her life in his heart. She cradled the bare spot on her finger where his ring had been, realizing how empty her life had been since she'd slipped it off.

Without Patrick, she wasn't whole.

She craned her neck and got a glimpse of him heading out of the mall to return equipment to the truck. Francine had already taken Merry's microphone and her earpiece, rendering it unnecessary for her to make the trip. She couldn't get away, anyway. The people around her were in no hurry to return to their shopping.

Keeping a smile on her face was no hardship. Merry doubted she could have prevented her happiness from shining through had she tried. She kept watching for Patrick to come back inside the mall, but instead caught sight of Francine. Her friend signaled that she was leaving and waved goodbye.

Merry blew her a kiss, amazed that only a few hours ago she'd been annoyed at Francine for trying to arrange for Merry to spend Christmas Day with Patrick.

Francine must have known what was in Merry's heart before Merry did herself.

"I cannot wait until Christmas," a woman about her age told her. She lowered her voice and whispered, "I bought myself a sexy red teddy today, but it's really a present for my boyfriend. It'll be our first Christmas together."

"Ours, too," Merry said.

"That's so great," the woman replied, but Merry

missed the rest of what she said. She caught a flash of dark hair on a tall man she knew instantly was Patrick. He moved toward her, as though in slow motion.

Their eyes met, and the fears that had shivered down her legs and settled in her feet disappeared.

So she'd gotten cold feet before the wedding. So what. It didn't mean that she and Patrick couldn't have a long, happy marriage. Sure, they had differences. But, as Patrick had claimed, those differences would spice up their relationship.

The love-struck shopper finally excused herself, leaving the path clear for Patrick to approach. His gaze was full of tenderness…and pride.

"That was good work," he said. "I liked the indomitable spirit of Christmas line. It's not always easy to report on what you see instead of what you want to see."

"You're the one who helped me see it like it is." She was amazed she could speak coherently. "Thank you."

He smiled into her eyes. "You're welcome."

Something rustled. Her eyes dropped. How had she failed to notice that his hands were full of shopping bags? Far more bags than he'd stored in the truck before the noon broadcast.

"I knew you were shopping," she said, "but I hadn't realized you'd bought out the stores."

He shrugged and looked oddly uncomfortable. "You know I like to splurge on my family at Christmas. There's quite a few of them, so it makes for a long list.

"By the way, Betsy called when I was putting away the equipment," Patrick told her. "She said she'd rerun the segment at eleven if we wanted to call it a day, but I told her we'll tape a new one."

"Why?" she asked, but she already knew.

"I need every one of the minutes we have left until the mall closes to convince you to take me back," he said. She was about to tell him she was already convinced when he added, "Besides, being a cameraman again has been a lot of fun."

The wistful note in his voice struck her. "More fun than being a corporate developer?"

His laugh sounded hollow. "Being a corporate developer is a lot of things, but fun isn't one of them."

Before she could ask him to expand, he nodded at his shopping bags. "I need to walk these bags to my car. Would you like to come?"

She nodded, and the giddiness traveled through her again. Because she doubted she could make it to his car and back without telling him all over again that she loved him and wanted nothing more than to marry him.

DAYLIGHT HAD FADED into night, marking the start of the true eve before Christmas. The temperature was still crisp, but some cloud cover had moved into the area.

Patrick couldn't suppress a burst of optimism that snow was on the way, but an unlikely weather event wasn't the only source of his optimism.

Merry's hard-line stance toward him seemed to have softened. She hadn't brought up those infernal doves in hours, and she met his eyes and smiled instead of avoiding his gaze.

After making the brash promise this morning that he'd leave her alone if the engagement wasn't back on by mall closing, he'd been terrified that she'd decide against him.

Now a burst of holiday hope rose inside him that

they'd be able to work things out and that he'd live the rest of his life with the woman he loved.

He'd left his winter jacket in his car, and a blast of cold wind cut through his knit pullover sweater. Merry shivered, too. He'd offered to retrieve her coat from the mall office, but she'd declined, pointing out they wouldn't be outside for long.

"I'd put my arms around you for warmth, love, but they're full at the moment." He held up his camera and a multitude of shopping bags.

"Then let me take a couple of those bags from you," she offered, and he handed her the two lightest. When the transfer was complete and he still didn't have a free arm, she added in a light, teasing voice, "Too bad the mall doesn't have shopping carts."

"We'll be at my car in a minute, love, and then I'll be able to put everything down."

"Promises, promises," she muttered.

If the parking lot had been emptier, he might have sprinted to his car. As it was, there were more empty spaces than ones containing cars. The farther they walked up the row where he'd parked, the fewer vehicles there were.

The cool air was filled with sounds of people opening and closing car doors, muted conversations and slow-moving traffic, but he could hear his own, shallow breaths. His palms grew damp despite the cold, and he recognized the signs of nervousness.

He'd planned to wait until the end of the night to ask whether she'd changed her mind about the engagement, but he couldn't get through another minute without knowing her decision.

The gold Lexus he'd bought as a present to himself after joining The Goulden Group came into view. It sat in virtual isolation, its golden color seeming to signify a new beginning.

Shifting the bags in his arms, he deliberately slowed his steps. The King's Mall parking lot wasn't the most romantic scenario, but it was the only one he had.

"My invitation's still open," he said.

For a moment, his words hung there in the cool, crisp air. His heart seemed to hang in the balance, too.

"Which invitation?" she asked just as casually. "The one to spend Christmas with your family? Or the one to spend it in your bed?"

He stopped in an empty parking space. All around them, people who'd spent the day at the mall were in their cars headed home to their families. Patrick found it difficult to breathe, but not because the parking lot smelled faintly of exhaust fumes.

"Either. Both." He cleared his throat. "Either or both."

She cocked her head. She was directly under a street-lamp, so he could see the smile in her eyes. "As you've pointed out repeatedly," she said softly, but not so softly that he couldn't hear, "I don't have anywhere else to go."

His heart drummed. Please let him have read the signals correctly. She'd seemed so gung ho against him this morning, but now...now, the signals she was sending out were as clear as the ones conveyed by candles shining in a window.

Was Merry welcoming him back into her life, the same way those candles welcomed visitors during the holiday season?

He pinned her with his gaze. The parking lot light shone down on her, bathing her in a warm glow. In front of him, he could see everything he'd ever wanted.

"I'm not inviting you to spend only this Christmas with me, Merry." He needed to make his position clear. "I'm asking for all the Christmases to come. Every one, for the rest of our lives."

She stared at him, this woman he'd loved almost from the moment he'd laid eyes on her, this woman he never wanted to live without.

"Why don't you just ask me if I've changed my mind about the wedding?" she whispered.

He couldn't contain the hope that soared in him now. It made him feel almost light-headed. She wouldn't prompt him like that if she meant to say no.

"Have you changed your mind, love?" He stepped toward her. "Will you marry me?"

"Y…"

The sound of a bag ripping followed by a thud interrupted her answer. He gazed down at his feet to see the box containing the indoor grill, which had crashed to the pavement a mere six inches from his foot. Talk about bad timing.

"What's that?" she asked.

He grimaced. "Nothing you need to see yet."

He reached down to pick up the box, and inadvertently dropped some of the other bags. Presents spilled from them. The stuffed pig, the iPod, the sun-sensitive tote. They all ended up next to the grill box.

Merry stared at the loot on the pavement.

"Those things you bought today," she said in a strange, strained voice, "they weren't for your family, were they?"

He'd meant the gifts to be a surprise but could hardly keep them a secret now.

"You're right," he admitted. "They're all for you."

She didn't say anything for a long moment, but stared at him as though she'd never seen him before. Her expression hardened.

"Then here's your answer." Her voice sounded strident, her words clipped. "No. I haven't changed my mind. The wedding's still off."

She dropped the bags she'd offered to carry, spun on her heel and left him amid the presents and his dashed hopes.

## CHAPTER SIX

THE COOL NIGHT AIR slapped Merry in the face as she hurried toward the entrance of the mall. Her eyes stung with the effort not to cry.

To think she'd been on the verge of telling Patrick that she loved him and wanted to go through with the wedding.

No matter how much her heart ached at the thought of never being his wife, now that was impossible.

"Merry, wait!"

Patrick was behind her, but she rushed blindly on, through the mall doors and down the main thoroughfare. She doubted she'd ever moved so fast in her life. The Christmas village was ahead, where she'd watched the improbable snow whirl around the happy children.

She saw the snow again, but this time she was approaching the scene from a different direction. This time she saw the oversize fan lifting the artificial flakes into the air. She stopped, her eyes blurring with unshed tears, as the magic she'd thought she glimpsed disappeared like snowflakes in the sun.

She hadn't seen a snow squall inside the mall. She'd seen a mirage.

"Merry, don't do this. Talk to me."

It was Patrick's voice, close enough behind her that she couldn't escape him now. She blinked a half-dozen times to dry her tears, then turned for the inevitable confrontation.

He looked both stunned and hurt, his hair tousled from his dash through the parking lot, his expression confused.

"What just happened back there?" he asked. "Why did you run off like that?"

The fact that he had to ask underscored their problem. She gestured broadly in the direction of the parking lot, where he must have abandoned all her unwanted gifts. But his brow furrowed, as if he still didn't understand.

"Because of the presents," she explained.

"The presents?" He sounded incredulous. "You won't marry me because I bought you presents?"

The knowledge that she'd been right to break the engagement caused her stomach to pitch and roll. How naive she'd been to get caught up in the excitement of the season and let herself believe they could work things out.

There wouldn't be any magical ending for her and Patrick, just as there hadn't been any magic in the Christmas village.

Her throat constricted but she didn't cry. "You don't know the first thing about me," she choked out.

"How can you say that?" He stepped closer so that she couldn't miss the sincerity in his expression. "I bought the grill because you like to cook. I got the stuffed pig because the pig is your favorite animal. The tote bag has a beach scene and changes colors in the sun, both of which you enjoy."

"Why can't you see that presents aren't enough?"

she said and realized she'd stumbled across the crux of the problem. She bit her bottom lip in a failed attempt to keep it from trembling. She steadied it with her top teeth, composed herself, then said, "They never have been. Not when they were from my parents and not when they're from you."

"Your parents? What do your parents have to do with this?"

"Nothing. Everything." She tried to compose her thoughts and then the words spilled out of her like water from a faucet. "There was never an occasion when I was growing up that they didn't shower me with presents. It took me longer than any kid I knew to open everything on Christmas morning."

"But that's what every kid wants."

"It's not what I wanted. I wanted parents like yours."

"Like mine? But there were five kids in our family. We hardly got anything for Christmas."

"Your parents watched you when you opened your presents. Mine were in Aruba or Cancun or Hawaii." She barely paused. "Would you be there for our kids, Patrick? Would you be there for me?"

"Of course I would."

"There's no *of course* about it. Don't you see the parallel? My parents bought all those gifts to make up for not being there. Since you changed jobs, you're not around, either."

"That's not fair. I just started at The Goulden Group, Merry. I need to establish myself so I can build a secure future for us. I want you to have the best of everything."

"But this is how it starts. Once you buy the big house

and the expensive car and everything else you think you need to be happy, you have to keep working those long, ridiculous hours. Because if you don't, you won't be able to afford to pay for it all."

He ran a hand through his hair. He appeared to be completely at a loss, the way her parents would be if she told them the same thing.

"I can return the presents," he said, his brow still furrowed. "This doesn't have to be a big deal."

"Not a big deal?" she repeated and shook her head. "You mean, like the doves?"

"Exactly. Like I keep telling you, I don't care about the doves."

But because he didn't have a handle on why *she* didn't care to have them at the wedding, similar items would crop up for the rest of their lives if she married him. It wouldn't always be something as ephemeral as doves, but it would always be something.

"You should return the presents. But it won't make any difference with me and you." She forced the next words past her trembling lips. "It's over, Patrick."

She watched sorrow descend over his face like a dark cloud and felt the same sadness envelop her.

"You really mean it this time, don't you?" he asked.

Again tears formed in her eyes, threatening to spill over. Again she held them back. "I really do," she said softly.

She could almost see the wheels in his head turning, but he didn't know her well enough to mount an argument that would convince her to change her mind.

"I'll give the engagement ring back, of course," she said through the thickness in her throat.

"No." His head shook. "You can sell the ring if you want, but I won't take it back. I gave it to you. It's yours."

He was so adamant that she nodded. She already knew she'd never sell the ring, and not because it was worth a small fortune. She'd keep it forever as a remembrance of a man she'd always love.

"Merry! Patrick!" A woman's voice rang out, reminding her they were in a public place. Merry turned to see a familiar blonde rushing toward them, dragging an oversize box. "I found it!"

She wasn't much more than five feet tall, her hair was a riot of curls and she had a spring to her step. After a moment, Merry placed her. Kelly, the woman looking for the perfect gift for her husband.

"Aren't those golf clubs?" Merry asked when Kelly reached them.

She nodded happily. "They most certainly are."

"What's perfect about golf clubs?"

"One of the reasons my marriage broke up is that I was always complaining about how much time my husband spent at the golf course," she said.

"Then you did it," Patrick said. "Congratulations. You really did find the perfect gift."

"Why?" Merry asked. "I still don't get it."

"By buying the golf clubs, I'm telling my husband I won't nag him about the time he spends away from me," Kelly said. "I'm telling him I accept him just the way he is."

Kelly strongly suggested they get her on tape so she could tell the WZLM-13 audience the ending to her story. Patrick's camera bag was still slung over his shoulder. He removed it, and Merry went through the motions until Kelly was through talking.

"Thanks," she said with a huge smile. Before she left, she looked from Merry to Patrick and said, "I just have to say this. You two would make the cutest couple."

Kelly bustled off, taking her high-spirited energy with her. Merry didn't want to think about her pronouncement, because she and Patrick would never be a couple again. He'd claimed love was enough. But it wasn't.

"You should go pick up those things you dropped," she told him. "I'll wait for you here."

He didn't speak, but nodded briefly. And then he turned away from her. She watched him go. Although he was only walking to his car, it felt as though he moved a little farther from her life with every step he traveled.

THE FALLEN PRESENTS lay where Patrick had left them, although anybody passing by could easily have run off with them.

The likelihood of that happening tonight, of all nights, was low. Bad things didn't happen on Christmas Eve. The night before Christmas was supposed to be full of wonder and magic.

So why on this enchanted night was he losing the only woman he'd ever loved?

Patrick couldn't make sense of how a day that had begun with such promise could be ending this way. He'd go to great lengths to fix whatever had gone wrong between him and Merry, but he wasn't exactly sure what it was.

He was forced to concede that she was right. He didn't understand her.

He picked up the presents he'd chosen so carefully, noting that the box holding the grill was crushed and the product probably broken. Like his heart. He took a deep breath, the cold like ice in his lungs, and loaded the bags in the trunk of his car.

His body on autopilot, he drove to a spot closer to the mall, parked and got out of his Lexus. His mind churned with the puzzle of why his quest to buy Merry the perfect present had backfired.

The women he'd dated in the past enjoyed receiving gifts, as did his mother.

When he began making money of his own, he'd showered his mother with the fruits of his success: jewelry for her birthday, electronics for Mother's Day, flowers for no reason at all and surprises galore at Christmas.

Bridget MacFarland had appreciated every last one of the gifts, probably because her husband had never been in a position to buy her much more than the necessities.

Patrick's father had ably supported his large family by laboring long hours on a construction crew after the MacFarlands had emigrated from Ireland. Any money left over after expenses had gone into savings.

Eventually Sean MacFarland had been able to invest in a roofing business, the profits of which were still paying for the college education of his two youngest daughters.

Patrick knew the value of hard work. He'd put himself through college on scholarships, grants and the money he made from summer jobs. But he'd never worked harder in his life than he had these past three months at The Goulden Group.

He'd taken the job primarily because he wanted to afford more than the necessities for Merry. So why couldn't Merry, like his mother, be pleased about receiving gifts that had come from his heart?

Among the people exiting the mall when he entered were an elderly man humming loudly to the tune of "Rudolph the Red-Nosed Reindeer" and a young couple with toddlers who'd probably spoken to Santa.

All was as it should be on Christmas Eve at King's Mall, except that he wasn't going to have Merry in his Christmas.

She was waiting for him at the directory near the front of the mall. So many people had crowded around the directory earlier today that it had been a struggle to get close to it.

But with less than an hour to go before the mall closed, the crowds were largely gone. Only a smattering of shoppers remained.

He squared his shoulders as he approached, aware that despite everything he hadn't stopped hoping for a Christmas miracle. He kept his voice light and asked, "What's the plan?"

She answered in her professional TV-reporter voice, the one that put distance between herself and the person she was talking to. "I thought we'd go back to housewares at Harrington and Vine's. That's where the longest line was earlier today."

The store where the jolly man had sung his fa la la's

was also where Patrick had fooled himself into believing in happy endings.

The mall was silent except for the soft sounds of the Christmas carols Patrick no longer felt like humming along with. He could hear the click of their heels on the floor—and angry voices. Patrick stopped walking.

"Do you hear what I hear?" He listened more carefully and heard two distinct voices, both of them male, both of them loud. "I think they're coming from the novelty shop."

"I think you're right," Merry said.

Together they moved toward the store, which Patrick recognized as the same one he'd patronized earlier today. Making sure Merry was safely behind him, he entered the novelty shop and followed the angry words.

Near the counter, two men who looked to be in their thirties shouted at each other. They were a good physical match, about six feet tall and two hundred pounds apiece.

One man had shoulder-length hair and a thick mustache, but his most prominent feature was a face turned red with anger. The other man, who wore his hair in a military-style crew cut, seemed more in control except for his clenched fists.

"I saw it first," Red Face shouted. "So it's mine."

"That's bull," Crew Cut retorted. Clutched in his hand was a familiar rectangular box. "Whoever grabs it first, gets it."

"You only got to it first because you shoved your way in front of me."

"It's not my fault you're slow."

Merry craned her neck to see around Patrick, whose body shielded hers from the confrontation. "What are they arguing over? What's in the box?"

Patrick took a closer look and realized why the box had seemed familiar. He had one inside his Lexus.

"It's the Walter Cronkite bobblehead. They're fighting over a doll," he said flatly and turned on his camera.

"What are you doing?" Merry asked.

"Getting some video." He gazed over his shoulder at her. "Isn't this the kind of thing you've been looking for all day?"

"Yes, but…"

Red Face's booming voice drowned out whatever she'd been about to say. "Slow? I'd watch what I said if I were you. I have a black belt."

"You're the one who should watch what you say to me," Crew Cut rejoined. "I played football in college."

The salesclerk, a small man with a build more suited to gymnastics than contact sports, ventured forward but stopped shy of the two men.

"Can't we settle this another way?" The clerk's voice sounded nervous. "I have other bobblehead dolls. Maybe one of you would rather have a Johnny Carson. Or a Jimmy Carter or a Ronald Reagan. We've still got all of those left."

"I want the Cronkite," Crew Cut bellowed. "My father will get a kick out of it. Cronkite was his favorite newsman."

"I want the Cronkite, too," Red Face shouted. "My son's planning to go into broadcast journalism."

"Cronkite retired more than twenty years ago. Your

son probably doesn't even know who he is. My father cried the night he went off the air."

"I'll teach my boy about Cronkite." Red Face's voice rose another notch. "I'll explain why he was the most trusted figure in America."

"Guys, please." The little salesman threw up his hands. "How can you act this way? It's Christmas Eve."

"I don't care what day it is. I want that doll!" Crew Cut shouted.

Red Face wouldn't let him have the last word. "So do I."

They looked daggers at each other, neither man giving an inch. Patrick usually kept his camera running and let situations run their course, but he couldn't in good conscience stand by while men came to blows on Christmas Eve. He shut off his camera and stepped into the fray. "I can settle this."

The combatants didn't break their stare-down, but the clerk acknowledged Patrick with a sad shake of his head. "I'm afraid the only way you can help, mister, is if you have another Cronkite bobblehead."

"I have one in my car that I bought earlier today," Patrick said, remembering the impulse that had led him into the store when he'd glimpsed the doll in the window. He'd thought Merry would get a kick out of it, but he'd obviously been wrong. "If you sell one of these men the bobblehead you have in the store, I'll sell mine to the other."

"Works for me." The clearly relieved clerk could hardly get the words out of his mouth fast enough. He addressed the men, who were still at a standoff. "Now which one of you is going to buy the doll from me?"

"I am," Red Face growled.

"No, I am," Crew Cut countered. "No way will I risk coming up empty-handed."

Patrick sighed. "I'll get my doll from the car and come back to the store. That way, both of you can be certain you'll leave the store with Walter."

He didn't wait to see if they agreed to his plan, but turned and left, walking past Merry without a word.

What could he say, after he'd finally shot the footage to back up her contention that Christmas Eve at the mall wasn't all that Patrick had naively claimed it was?

# CHAPTER SEVEN

MERRY EDGED OVER so Patrick could join her on the bench outside the novelty shop where she'd waited while he dealt with Walter Cronkite and the two obstinate men.

"Is everything under control?" she asked.

"I don't believe those two will come to blows anymore, if that's what you mean. But neither do I think they'll be tossing down a few cold ones together anytime soon."

He seemed disheartened, a condition Merry didn't associate with him. She squashed an urge to reach over and take his hand. Clearing her throat, she said, "It was nice of you to give up your bobblehead doll like that."

He shrugged. "Since it was for you, I probably would have returned it anyway. You made it clear that you didn't want it."

But she did. The realization hit her like a bolt of lightning. It would have been a nifty conversation piece to keep on her desk at work. Cronkite had been an icon of television journalism, and the doll uttered his signature line: *And that's the way it is.*

But those weren't the only reasons she would have enjoyed the present. Patrick had obviously put a lot of thought into what she would like.

The silver-colored bars that signaled the novelty shop was shutting down for the night lowered into place. Merry checked her watch. Fifteen minutes remained before the mall officially closed, but she couldn't blame the clerk considering what had just happened.

Patrick gestured to the store. "The scene of the crime is a good place to tape the top to your story for the eleven o'clock news. If that anecdote doesn't put Christmas shopping in a bad light, nothing will."

Everything inside Merry rebelled at airing anything about the two abrasive men. The canned Christmas music that had grated on her nerves earlier still filled the mall corridors, but she found that she liked the sound. Christmas should be filled with music, joy and, yes, magic.

Nothing about two men battling over a bobblehead doll was magical.

"I think it would be better if Betsy reran the footage we got earlier," she said. "Or we could tape a new top and use that material of Kelly explaining how she'd found the perfect gift."

"You said there was no such thing as the perfect gift."

"And all day you've said that I was on the wrong track with my commercial Christmas idea. Why would you change your mind now?"

"Maybe I've come to believe you were right about the public thinking they need things they could do without. Neither of those guys needed that bobblehead, now did they?"

She couldn't fault his logic, which sounded like

something she might have said this morning. But since then she'd begun to view the situation differently.

"Those men acted horribly," Merry agreed. "But as misguided as they were, they still weren't entirely on the wrong track."

Patrick lifted one of his dark eyebrows. "Would you mind telling me how you arrived at that conclusion?"

"One of those men wanted the bobblehead for his father. The other was going to use it to inspire his son. If you think about it, both those men could have fit into the first report I did today. About how it's better to give than receive."

Now that she'd begun putting her thoughts into words, they coalesced and led to a startling revelation.

"I get it now," she said in wonder. "All those people dashing through the mall weren't doing it out of greed. They were looking for gifts to show a special someone how much they were loved."

"That's what I've been trying to tell you all day, love. And that's why I bought you all those presents." He smiled a strange, sad smile. "I don't entirely understand why you got so angry when my bag broke, but I thought about it and I do understand what you meant about wanting what my parents have.

"I've always taken my family for granted, but I realize how lucky I was to grow up in a house with so much warmth and love. I want that for us, Merry. But I want you to have nice things, too. I happen to believe that you deserve the best of everything."

"My parents think so, too."

He sighed. "Are you going to compare me with your mum and da again?"

"I can't help it, Patrick. Not one of you understand the only present I ever wanted was the gift of your presence."

His eyes widened. "You have that, love. Why do you think I took the assignment today if not to spend time with you? Why do you think I've been pressuring you to spend Christmas with me? And why do you think I'm going to quit my job the first chance I get?"

Her mouth dropped open. "You're going to quit your job? When did you make that decision?"

He scratched his head, looking as bemused as she felt. "Just now. Quitting seems the thing to do now that I've faced the fact that I rather hate working there."

HE HATED BEING a corporate developer. Once he'd made the admission, Patrick realized how true it was. The stress he'd been under at work these past months had disappeared when he'd gotten behind the camera lens, where he belonged.

"But then why haven't you quit before now?" Merry asked.

The idea had been brewing inside him since his first week—no, his first day—at The Goulden Group. But he'd been afraid to acknowledge it. Until now.

"Because I convinced myself you wanted to be married to a successful businessman who could give you anything you wanted."

"What if all I ever wanted," she said in a soft voice, "was you?"

"Then all you have to do," he said just as softly, "is forgive me for being such an idiot."

She smiled. "You think *you* were an idiot? I let you sell my Walter Cronkite bobblehead."

He laughed and reached for her. She came willingly into his arms, and for a moment he just held her.

"Aren't you going to kiss me?" she asked, her voice faintly muffled.

"In a minute," he said, still holding her tight against his heart, which had started a wild beat of joy.

"Because if you kiss me right now, I'll marry you."

He put his hands gently on her shoulders and held her back from him, so he could see her face. "Are you serious?"

She nodded and started to say something else, but he didn't wait to hear what it was. He leaned in and kissed her. He savored the feel of her lips against his, the sweet smell of her hair, the taste of her mouth, the sensations all the stronger because he'd thought he'd never experience them again.

He wasn't sure how long the kiss lasted, but when it ended he already wanted to kiss her again.

"You didn't give me a chance to finish what I was going to say." She sounded breathless. He smiled and smoothed her hair back from her hot cheek.

"What was it, love?"

"Even if you hadn't kissed me right then, I still would have married you."

He knew she'd meant for him to laugh, but her message was too important. "You don't have to marry me if you're not ready."

"Oh, believe me, I'm ready," she said. "I'd be ready if the wedding was tomorrow. I love you, Patrick. I always have."

"Then let's find a justice of the peace and do it."

MERRY FELT SURE HER MOUTH hung open, because Patrick looked completely and utterly serious about marrying her in a civil ceremony.

"But tomorrow's Christmas," she said. "We'd never find a justice of the peace who worked on Christmas."

"Then let's fly to Vegas. I bet you can get married any day of the week in Vegas." His eyes sparkled, as though he'd always dreamed about walking into a chapel on the strip with his bride-to-be.

"But what about the big, splashy wedding? You're the one who thought the doves and the symphony and the dozen attendants were good ideas."

"If that's the kind of wedding you want, they are good ideas. But if you don't, I'm with you. Don't you see, love? I'm on your side no matter what. It doesn't matter to me if we get married by a justice of the peace or an Elvis impersonator. All that's ever mattered is that you marry me."

"Then let's get married in Charlotte on Valentine's Day, just like we planned," she decided.

"Why should we do that after all those things you said about not wanting a big wedding?"

"Because now that I know you'd marry me in front of a justice of the peace, I'm satisfied." She paused. "I'd like for your family to see us get married, Patrick. I really love your family."

"And they love you back, which they'll probably tell you repeatedly when we show up in Winston-Salem tomorrow," he said. "But my family would understand if we got married in Vegas. They'd probably insist on seeing us married in a church when we got back, but they'd understand."

"My parents wouldn't," she said. "They won't be satisfied unless they can give me this wedding. That's the way they show their love, Patrick. By giving me things. I can accept that now."

He looked doubtful. "Does that mean you won't make me return all those things I got you for Christmas?"

"Not all of them," she conceded and stroked his face. "As long as you realize that the perfect present for me is you."

A short time later, after they taped a new introduction to her news report and retrieved her coat at the mall office, they walked out of King's Mall hand in hand.

Merry stopped short, hardly believing her eyes. In front of them, against the backdrop of night, snowflakes floated gracefully to the earth and stuck. Already the parking lot resembled a winter wonderland.

"I can't believe it," Merry exclaimed. "It's snowing."

"Just one more Christmas miracle to add to the collection," Patrick said. "We're engaged again, aren't we?"

She raised her lips and met his mouth in front of a mall where magic wasn't supposed to happen but had. She felt that magic shimmer through her, right down to the bottom of her toasty warm feet.

For George and Marilyn. Even though we're not under the same roof during the holidays, you're always in my heart.

And thanks to Dr. Makarowski and Eda Burhenn, CRNP, for all the rheumatology information.

# DECK THE HALLS

## Holly Jacobs

# *CHAPTER ONE*

JOY O'CONNELL WASN'T very…wasn't very joyful that is.

As a matter of fact, if she heard one more version of "White Christmas" she just might scream. So far this morning she'd been treated to a reggae version in the car on the way to work and then a classic Bing Crosby version as she entered the store.

She could manage those.

Barely.

But this new rap one that was blaring in the elevator?

She shuddered. It wasn't that she had anything against rap, but whatever happened to good, old-fashioned elevator Muzak?

She hurried through the doors as soon as they slid open, past the vacant customer service desk, then down the hall to her office without anyone seeing her. She shut the door to escape the noise.

She glanced at the clock. It was nine on the nose. Just nine more hours until they closed their doors and Christmas season officially ended for the store and she could turn off the Christmas music. And it wasn't going to be a moment too soon.

Harrington and Vine's company policy demanded

that Christmas music start being piped into the upscale department store about the same time the Christmas decorations went up.

Joy had been working in retail for almost twenty years now, and it seemed that each year the Christmas season was just a bit earlier than the last.

This year, the powers-that-be had mandated the season start in October, before the Halloween decorations were even down.

Maybe that explained why Joy O'Connell was less than joyful.

Or maybe it was simply that here it was Christmas Eve and she was in Charlotte, North Carolina while all her family and friends were across the country in San Diego, California. It was her first holiday alone. Even back in college, she'd gone home for the holidays.

Just thinking of the annual parties and gatherings she'd attended her whole life, but would miss this year, made her feel glum. For instance, last night she'd had a bowl of popcorn and watched the antithesis of a holiday movie…a classic slasher film while across the country her whole family had been at Aunt Lois and Uncle Jack's party.

As she watched yet another stupid heroine go into the dark basement, she imagined Aunt Theresa and Aunt Colleen, her cousins, her parents all gathered in Aunt Lois's small dining room, laughing and visiting, then exchanging gag gifts. Every year previously she'd been right there in the thick of things.

Except this year.

She'd eaten her rather metallic-tasting popcorn, watching a movie heroine who was TSTL, too stupid to live.

Oh, she wasn't totally alone on the East Coast. She had one friend, Morgan, who had recently moved to Pittsburgh. But even though they had both transplanted east, the northwestern Pennsylvanian city was still too far to visit just to have a sense of connection, of home for the holidays.

Christmas carols, no family—those were both enough in and of themselves to put Joy in a holiday funk. But the topper on her Scroogeish mood was the fact that a third of the store's employees were out with the flu.

Joy glanced at the clock. She had to shake off this morose feeling and get to work. She hung up her coat, wishing she'd had something a bit warmer in the face of the day's nasty weather. It was overcast, ominous and downright cold for North Carolina. Then she went and poured a cup of coffee, thankful Susan, her assistant manager, had come in early and started it.

She took a sip as she sat down to enjoy a carol-less, peace-filled moment when her phone rang.

Joy wanted to ignore it.

If there'd been anyone else in the office besides her, she would have. But as the new manager of Harrington and Vine's, the buck stopped on her lap. Most days she didn't mind, but it seemed this holiday season she had a whole flock of bucks stopping and she couldn't face one more.

Not one.

Unfortunately there was no way out, and she had to pick up the continual-bearer-of-bad-news telephone. Wondering what could go wrong now, she answered, "Hello?"

"Ms. O'Connell," croaked a voice she couldn't place.

"Yes? Can I help you?"

"It's me…." The sound of someone hacking up a lung went on for a seemingly unending amount of time, before the croaker finished, took a deep inhale and said, "Jamie. It's Jamie."

"Jamie?" Joy set down the mug, knowing that coffee wasn't going to restore her flagging spirits. Nothing but the end of the Christmas season—of the flu season—would. On the long shot that she was wrong, she continued, "That was just some food that went down the wrong tube. You're not sick. Not you. You're made of sterner stuff. Right?"

Jamie didn't respond.

"Say you don't have it, too."

But Joy knew Jamie's denial wouldn't be coming. Jamie Anthony, Harrington and Vine's Personal Shopper, did indeed have the flu.

H&V was an anchor store for King's Mall. It brought designer-brand products to the Charlotte area and catered to the type of clientele who demanded just a little more service than most.

Jamie was a big part of the store's answer to caring for those customers. She shopped for those who didn't have time to shop for themselves, and assisted those who had the money, but not necessarily the inclination, and frequently not the taste.

"Sorry," Jamie rasped. "But I do. I'd be there if I could. You know I love shopping most days, but this time of the year—"

Another coughing jag brought the sentence to an

abrupt halt, but Joy didn't need Jamie to finish. Jamie had been rhapsodizing about the holiday season since the day in mid-October when the store had put up the first artificial tree.

Yesterday, Jamie's abundance of holiday spirit had been driving Joy nuts, but today she'd give anything to have the Personal Shopper waltz into her office and sing the praises of the season.

"Fine." Joy knew there was no option but to face the inevitable. Jamie was obviously not shopping today. "Then tell me your calendar was basically empty because everyone finished their shopping bright and early this year."

She crossed her fingers and vowed to be the picture of good cheer if Jamie assured her that her calendar was empty—barren even.

"I don't have any clients…" Another long bout of coughing. "But I do have the contest winners. And Joy, that was pretty much going to be an all-day affair. Publicity photos, lunch, shopping…"

"Oh, no."

Harrington and Vine's had partnered with King's Mall to offer a Christmas Eve shopping spree for one lucky family. And it looked as if one unlucky store manager was going to fill in for a flu-ridden Personal Shopper and assist them.

Accepting that her fate was signed and sealed, Joy asked, "What is the family's name, and when are they arriving?"

"Hall. The Halls will be there at eleven. You'll find the file on my desk. They sent in a shopping list, and the three boys have an allowance of seventy-five dollars per person in their immediate family—their mother, father, stepfather, half siblings, grandparents and themselves. It's all in the file. Their names, the day's itinerary and all the other information you'll need."

Joy glanced at the clock counting down the minutes she had available before they arrived. Her dark Christmas mood seemed so much bleaker.

"I'm sorr…" More coughing.

"Jamie, don't you dare apologize. Go to bed, get better. We'll need you for the after-Christmas rush. Do what you can to enjoy tomorrow."

"Thanks."

"Merry Christmas, Jamie."

"You, too," Jamie croaked, then hung up.

Joy got up and walked down the hall to Jamie's office to retrieve the file and desperately tried to think of a way out of this.

There had to be someone—anyone—she could palm the family off on.

She didn't have to think long.

As she walked back toward her own office, file in hand, she spotted Susan Thomas, her coffee-making assistant manager. Joy decided Susan's arrival was a sign from above. Why, she didn't even have to call out and ask Susan to wait because her assistant manager walked into Joy's office.

It was a spider-and-fly moment for sure.

Susan could handle anything, even a family shopping spree on Christmas Eve.

Yes, Susan could fill in for Jamie and get Joy off the hook.

Feeling better than she had all morning, Joy followed

Susan into her own office. She'd hand the Halls off to the Assistant Manager and then savor her cup of coffee before heading into the holiday trenches.

Susan was sitting in the chair in front of Joy's desk, her head down.

"Hey, Susan," Joy said as she walked around and took her seat. She put the file down and reached for her coffee when Susan looked up.

Her face was a lovely shade of green that had nothing to do with the holiday outfit she wore, and everything to do with her complexion.

Joy's momentary optimism collapsed.

"No," she said firmly, as if forbidding it would cure Susan. "You are not sick, Susan."

Mind over matter. That's all Susan needed—a little mental coaching.

"Sorry, Joy, but—" Susan sprang out of the chair and made a mad dash toward the restroom.

Joy headed after her to see if she was okay, all the while knowing that Susan wouldn't be dealing with the Halls.

Joy would be.

Merry freakin' Christmas.


"TEN MINUTES. If you're not in the car, I leave without you."

Dr. Edward Hall stood waiting by the kitchen door as he listened to what sounded like a herd of cattle stampeding on the house's second floor. He smiled, despite the fact he hated running late, and since the boys moved in full-time, running late had become status quo.

As an afterthought he called out, "Rule Number Eleven."

Despite the fact his three sons didn't own even one punctuality gene between them, he loved being a father.

Always had.

But maybe he'd fallen out of practice with the day-to-day sort of things in the five years since his amicable divorce.

Well, it hadn't been amicable at first, but he'd worked hard with his ex to do what was best for their boys. And the best meant learning to get along. They had. They'd shared custody and parenting right up until three months ago.

Then the boys had spent most weekday nights with their mom, simply because the continuity made going to school easier. But Ed had kept them weekends, holidays, whenever the opportunity presented itself.

He'd been, and still was, a hands-on father. Being a rheumatologist, meant he had very little in the way of emergency calls, and was able to keep a fairly normal work schedule. Nine to five on weekdays, and Saturday mornings. It was an ideal schedule for a father and he rarely missed the boys' activities.

He'd coached teams, cheered from sidelines, driven for field trips…just generally been there for the kids.

But everything had changed when Lena's new husband had been offered a dream job two and half hours away in Raleigh. The boys had been adamant about not leaving Charlotte. They were of an age where their friendships were established and they'd found their niches in their respective schools.

Lena had been stuck between a rock and a hard place.

The boys' two half siblings were young enough not to care about the move, but for two teens and one almost teen, leaving friends and schools mattered a lot. In the end, Ed and Lena agreed the boys would stay with him full-time during the school year, and spend all the time they could in Raleigh with her. Weekends and holidays, summers whenever possible.

Ed had hired a nurse-practitioner in order to further minimize his workload, and had settled into full-time parenting.

He'd have Christmas Eve, then Christmas morning with them, after which they'd leave to spend a week in Raleigh. But before any of that there was a matter of living through today.

Shopping.

Ed hated it most of the time, but especially hated it on Christmas Eve. The mall would be total chaos, filled with procrastinators. For someone who thrived on being punctual and getting things done ahead of the curve, all those last-minute, crazed shoppers were annoying at best. He'd rather deal with Mrs. Majors, his toughest patient ever, than shop on Christmas Eve.

But there was no help for it. And if he had to go, he was going on time.

"Ten, nine, eight..." He started to count down loudly. It had the desired effect. The trio barreled down the stairs and stood breathless in front of him.

"Where's the fire, Dad?" Jake, his sixteen-year-old, asked as he pushed his wild brown hair out of his eyes. "I won the contest. They'll wait if we're a little late."

"Son, it's Christmas Eve, and I'm betting the woman

who's graciously agreed to shop with us today has better things to do than wait around for three boys."

He looked at his younger two sons, replicas of their older brother. Hair too long, dark eyes filled with mischief. Fifteen and twelve, almost thirteen. In another month he'd be the father of three teens. The thought boggled. He remembered them all as diaper-bottomed babies and felt a swift wave of nostalgia.

"Plus there's Rule Number Eleven, right Dad?" T.J. asked.

He laughed. "Yes. Life Lesson Number Eleven." He eyed his two younger sons. "Tim, T.J. You both ready?"

"Yes," the pair answered in unison.

"Do you think you might need coats? It's freezing out there. They're saying it might even snow."

The boys laughed at his concern.

Ed remembered the days when looking cool mattered more than comfort. Maybe that was the beauty of reaching the ripe old age of forty…comfort won out. He grabbed his leather jacket and just gave the boys his version of *the dad-eye*.

They seemed particularly unmoved.

"Our sweatshirts are fine," Jake assured him in a tone that said poor-Dad-he's-so-out-of-touch. "You're a doctor, which means you worry too much about us getting sick, 'cause that's what you work with all day. Sick people."

"It has nothing to do with being a doctor. It's just that I'm a dad. Worrying is part of the job," he corrected. And he knew there was no such thing as worrying too much for a parent, whether he or she was a doctor or not. It came as naturally as breathing. "And I'm a dad who likes being prompt. So everyone in the van."

"Want me to drive?" Jake asked.

Ed knew the real question was, can-I-drive?

Jake had only had his permit a couple months, and Ed had tried to avoid having him drive when his younger brothers were in the car, but Jake had been doing very well, and it was Christmas.

He didn't answer, merely dangled the keys.

Jake snatched them up. "Great. Everyone in the van. And make sure you use your seat belts."

Ed laughed, despite being late; despite the fact the weather was rotten; despite the fact the boys would go to their mother's tomorrow afternoon and he'd be left to rattle around the house on his own for the rest of the holiday.

He laughed because, despite the funk he'd been in this week, it was Christmas. He didn't go back to work until next Wednesday, his boys were healthy, and they were about to shop on the Harrington and Vine's dime.

The laughter didn't quite lift his bah-humbuggy mood, but it moved it up a notch closer to a real Christmas spirit.

Even given the uncharacteristic weather and the fact that he had to go shopping Christmas Eve, it wasn't going to be such a bad day.

As Jake settled into the driver's seat, Ed began, "Okay, when the weather's bad, it's important to turn on—"

"The lights, even though it is ten in the morning. I know, Dad."

"Let's go," T.J. hollered. "I can't wait to get to the electronics department."

"Now, remember the rules…" Ed droned rules for

polite behavior as they drove to King's Mall. It was rather like a chorus. His lecture was the lead vocal, while the boys' groaning provided the harmonies and backup. One part wouldn't sound nearly as good without the other.

Jake got them to the mall in one piece, and parked the SUV way at the end of a row. Way, way at the end. Ed figured they were lucky to have found a space even if it was in the outer parking limits. He couldn't believe so many people left their holiday shopping until the last minute, but looking at the crowded parking lot, it was obvious that they had.

Ed led his trio through King's Mall and into Harrington and Vine's. The upper-end store was decorated with taste, despite the vast amount of reds and greens that were liberally distributed throughout. Christmas music flooded the sound system, but did little to drown out the general hum of activity from the myriad of last-minute shoppers.

Ed wished the contest would have scheduled this particular shopping trip a bit earlier in the week so as to avoid this tidal wave of late gift buyers.

He hated crowds and…

He tried to beat back his negative thoughts.

This was about the boys, and they certainly had enough excitement buzzing between them to make up for whatever Ed lacked.

"Onward and upward," he said and was chorused by a trio of groans.

"Come on, Dad. Let's all try to pretend to be normal for one day," Jake pleaded as they all headed up the escalator to the second floor, as per the contest instructions.

"I can't promise anything. But if you three try and behave, so will I." Ed had found the threat of embarrassing the boys was frequently the key to keeping them from embarrassing him.

"Hello," he said to the gray-haired woman at the Customer Service desk. "We're the Halls. We won a contest and were instructed to meet a Jamie Anthony here today at eleven o'clock."

"Oh, Mr. Hall, we've been expecting you. Let me just get Ms. O'Connell for you."

Ed glanced at the paper which clearly said, Ms. Anthony. "There's been a change?"

He wondered if the thought of shopping with three boys Christmas Eve had intimidated Ms. Anthony so much she'd palmed them off on a colleague.

But the woman shook her head. "The flu. About a third of the staff is out with it, including Jamie. But don't you worry. You'll enjoy Ms. O'Connell."

He realized the boys were behind him and way too quiet. "Jake, Tim and T.J., if I turn around and see what you're doing, you're going to find yourselves grounded on Christmas Eve, so I suggest you stop." He smiled at the woman. "Sorry."

"Don't you worry. I have two of my own, and have started in with grandkids now. I know what it's like." She started through a side door. "I'll be right back. I'm sure you're anxious to start shopping."

Anxious?

Ed turned around and the three boys gave him their best angelic looks—looks that didn't fool him for a second.

If anyone should be anxious, it was the poor Ms.

O'Connell who was going to have to shop with them today.

"We didn't do anything, Dad," Jake protested.

"Yes he did, but I didn't," T.J. assured him. "Him and Tim were…"

Ed's phone rang midway through the excuses and accusations. He flipped it open and thought about the woman who would be spending the day with them. He hoped she knew what she was in for.

## CHAPTER TWO

JOY WAS TRYING, really trying, to work up some holiday enthusiasm for the family she'd be spending the day with as she hurriedly tried to clear paperwork off her desk.

About a half hour ago, she'd even turned on the intercom and listened to the piped-in carols on purpose, trying to remember a time when Christmas music didn't give her hives. She worked at remembering when carols had signified the holidays—the joy, the surprises, the time with family.

She tried to recall the butterflyish feeling that used to settle in her stomach Christmas Eve morning and last until Christmas Day night.

She tried very hard to remember a time when she would sing the carols every chance she got. She'd jingle bells and hark angels. A time when glowing noses made her day.

All that trying must have worked, because as Betty opened Joy's door and walked into her office, Joy was humming an ode to Christmas trees with more than a touch of enthusiasm.

"They're here." Betty's voice had a delighted sort of inflection in it.

Joy's humming stopped abruptly. Betty's obvious delight filled her with trepidation.

That kind of glee from Betty was rather ominous.

The Customer Service manager had spent the last week praying for the holiday season to end. People coming to the desk during the holiday rush weren't known for Christmas jolliness. That made Betty's newly discovered good humor worrisome, and try as she might, the trepidation overrode the almost holiday spirit Joy had just hummed her way into.

"What do you think of them?" Joy asked.

Again, Betty smiled.

It was unnerving.

Really, it was.

"I think you're going to have your hands full. As the father was introducing himself, the boys were behind him, the two oldest, hanging the youngest upside down."

"Great," Joy muttered. "Shopping with a group of boys."

"And a man," Betty piped in helpfully.

"And a man," Joy repeated. "Yeah, that's just what I need the day before Christmas."

Yes, her newly acquired almost-holiday-spirit vaporized instantly.

"Actually, maybe it is just what you need," Betty said. "I think you've lost the spirit of the season."

"Now, isn't that the pot calling the kettle black? The wreath calling the tree green, maybe. Weren't you the one just yesterday claiming that Christmas was nothing but a marketing gimmick and you were going to boycott next year? And I'll have you know, I was actually humming along with the Christmas music when you came in."

"You're not humming now."

"No, because you just told me I'm not taking a nice, well-behaved family around, I'm shepherding a group of *boys* through the store. I babysat a group of brothers for exactly one summer when I was in high school."

She'd spent the years since trying her best to block out the memory, but hadn't succeeded. Water fights, muddy playdates, bee stings and a broken arm when the youngest in the family, Ronny, wearing his favorite superhero cape, decided he was giving up saving the world in favor of being a rugby player and dived on the ball—from the top of the swing set.

That was the day Ronald discovered old baby blanket capes didn't help rugby players defy the laws of gravity. It was also the day Joy decided she was never babysitting again, no matter how bad her financial straits got. "It was the longest summer of my life."

When the family asked her to babysit again the next year, she'd turned them down flat and taken her first job at a local department store.

But there was no turning down this brotherly trio.

*"Boys,"* she said again, knowing the word sounded rather like a swearword.

Betty chuckled her Mrs. Santa sort of laugh, deep and from the belly. "Did you grow up with brothers?"

"No. An only child. But I had cousins. Between them, and babysitting it was enough to convince me boys aren't really human. Sure, sometimes they grow up to be men, but sometimes they just stay *boys* their whole lives."

The last guy she'd dated seriously, was a Peter Pan sort of grown-up boy. His inability to function as an adult was why they'd eventually broken up. Missed dates, never arriving on time, frequently changing jobs—mainly because of the never-on-time part.

What had started out as cute and carefree, eventually became annoying and aggravating. Joy had enough stress in her life and finally decided he wasn't worth the trouble.

She didn't really miss him.

That's not to say she didn't miss having a man in her life.

She just wasn't attracted to boys.

And now, today, she had to shop with… "Three, right? Three boys?" she asked, praying Betty would disagree. Maybe she'd misheard Betty and Jamie's file was wrong. Maybe there was only one boy. And if the three part was right, maybe three girls.

Even two girls and a boy.

But Betty just laughed even harder and nodded. "Yes, three boys. And their father. Since there's no mom in tow, I'm guessing he's an eligible man. Just what you need to discover some real Christmas cheer."

Joy made a snorting sound. "You're sounding cheerful enough for both of us. What happened to the Ebenezer Betty that's been working the desk the last few weeks?"

"It's Christmas Eve and I'm spending the evening with my grandbabies. My cheer's been quite restored, thank you very much. And here's hoping yours is, as well, before the day is done."

"Ha."

"Hurry up. They're waiting."

Joy took the file and checked Jamie's itinerary. First step? A photo op with the mall's Santa.

How hard could that be?

Feeling in control, Joy took the file and went out to meet her shoppers.

She found the family waiting in the small grouping of chairs by Customer Service. They didn't seem to notice her, which gave her a few minutes to assess what she was going to have to deal with. Two older boys were fighting over which was superior, Marvel Comics or D.C., and the younger one was ripping apart a magazine, folding the pages into paper airplanes.

The father was talking on his cell phone, seemingly oblivious to the chaos erupting around him. If Joy had met him anywhere but here under these circumstances, she might be inclined to notice that he was hot.

Dark brown hair that bordered on black, with just the merest hint of silver at the temples. His sons probably put each of those gray hairs there, she thought, and refused to give any consideration to the man's well-proportioned body.

She looked for something negative to concentrate on. There. His nose was too prominent and sharp. But then she noticed it had a slight bump in the middle that softened the line and he wore a small smile that crinkled at the edge of his lips. It was a warm expression that seemed at home on his face.

Okay, so he was nice to look at, but she was going to ignore the fact he was attractive and remember that this was business. The sooner she started, the sooner this shopping trip would be over.

The two older boys were still arguing, and the youngest ripped another page out of a magazine, while hunky dad continued his conversation.

To add insult to injury, "Hark the Herald Angels" was blaring over the intercom and, as if on cue, the phrase, "Peace on Earth" rang out. Peace might be on earth, but it certainly wasn't going to be in Harrington and Vine's…at least not until Joy could get this shopping trip over and the boys out the door.

She cleared her throat.

The comic debate continued, Mr. Hall kept talking on the phone, laughing at something that was said. But the youngest boy looked up and lobbed one of his dozen airplanes at her. Joy deftly caught it.

The boy smiled.

And despite the fact Joy was allergic to boys, she didn't find it overly difficult to offer a little smile back. "Are you ready to do some shopping?"

The comic boys stopped, the youngest picked up his arsenal of planes and stuffed them in a back pocket, and the father said, "Goodbye," and snapped his phone shut.

"Hi." Joy forced a smile. "I'm Joy O'Connell. I'll be assisting you today as you shop."

"Hello, Joy. I'm Edward Hall." The man took a step toward her, hand extended.

Joy took it and it would have been all aboveboard and professional, if his fingers hadn't grazed the inside of her palm. The touch sent a spurt of adrenaline racing through her bloodstream, causing her heart rate to pick up its tempo.

Joy quashed the breathless feeling the sensation left her with. "Uh, Mr. Hall, it's a pleasure—"

"Dr. Hall," the youngest boy interrupted. "My dad's a doctor. Not a real doctor. I mean, he doesn't cut people open and look at their guts or anything. A real doctor would do that. He just goes to his office, then comes home. I'm T.J. You caught that plane like a boy, not some girl."

The boy offered the last part up as if it were the biggest compliment he could give.

Despite the fact boys made her itch, Joy grinned. "I'll have you know that girls can catch, and even make paper planes, every bit as well as a boy can, T.J."

He scoffed, as if at the ripe old age of—what, thirteen?—he knew that boys could outplane girls.

Maybe if they survived the day, Joy might just show him a thing or two.

Dr. Hall nodded at the two older boys. "And these are my sons—"

"Mr. Marvel Comics, and Mr. D.C.," Joy supplied.

"Jake and Tim," Dr. Hall supplied.

"Jake, Tim," she acknowledged with a nod. "Now that the introductions are made, let's start our day. Jamie is superefficient and left me her schedule for you all. It's going to be busy. Our first stop is a quick visit to see Santa Claus."

She tried to sound enthusiastic about the schedule, but she obviously didn't quite pull it off because the boys groaned.

"Oh, come on," Joy said, trying even harder to sound excited at the prospect, though she felt anything but. She forced another broad smile. "It's just a few snapshots for publicity. How bad could it be? You have a couple pictures taken, then you get to shop."

Dr. Hall shot her a look that said he was sure it could be pretty bad.

Joy was inclined to agree, but continued to hold her brittle smile in place as she shepherded the family down the escalator and toward the mall's Santa display.

She realized the intercom was playing "Here Comes Santa Claus." It should be playing, "Here Come the Halls."

She hoped Santa was ready for them.

## CHAPTER THREE

TURNED OUT SANTA WASN'T ready for the Halls.

And neither was Joy.

How hard was it for three boys and one man to stand next to a mall Santa and smile long enough for a picture to be snapped?

The answer was, it had been very hard.

Very, very hard.

"I'm sorry," Dr. Hall said…again.

It was just after noon and they were standing in line at the coffee shop that was located directly across from H&V's side entrance. The boys had run ahead to the electronics department, while the two adults tried to recuperate over the restorative properties of coffee.

"No problem," Joy repeated.

She tried to issue her assurances with conviction and forced yet another upturn of her lips. But of course, all her reassurances were big fat lies. This shopping trip was a problem, and the pictures with Santa? That had moved beyond problem to pure torture.

She kept forcing that smile as they waited for their coffees.

She'd read somewhere that it took fewer muscles to smile than frown.

She had her doubts about the veracity of that particular study because her facial muscles were feeling very strained at the effort of maintaining her happy facade. She turned away from Dr. Hall a minute and scowled at no one in particular.

It felt wonderful.

She almost groaned as she forced a smile back in place and turned back to him.

"Santa didn't appear to be any more thrilled with the whole picture-taking process than the boys were," Ed said morosely.

"Or you were." She tried to pass the comment off as a joke, even though joking was totally beyond her capacity right now.

"Forty-four," the counter girl called out.

"That's us," Ed said, claiming their coffee cups. "Shall we find a table? We can take a moment and muster our collective strength for the actual shopping."

"Maybe the boys will manage a few items on their own while they're in the electronic department?"

She was hopeful. It would be wonderful if, rather than a better part of the day, they were able to finish their shopping in short order. Then she could feed them a quick lunch and be done with the Halls.

Ed shook his head as he steered them toward the only empty table in the small coffeehouse. "Not going to happen. We've already let them loose. I guarantee shopping for their half siblings is the last thing on their minds. New video games, stereo equipment and the like is all they're thinking about right now. I love my boys, but I have no illusions. They'll be shopping for themselves."

"Great." Joy caught herself. That was a mutter. A disgruntled, non-holiday-spirited sort of mutter.

"Great," she tried again, infusing a good measure of enthusiasm into her voice. "Today's about them having a good time. And they each get to buy something for their brothers, so even if they just get some shopping done for themselves, we'll have moved forward. So, while we drink our coffee, why don't you fill me in on who they need to shop for."

"They have two younger half siblings. Their mom, their stepfather and two sets of grandparents."

"And you, of course, Dr. Hall."

"Ed," he corrected. "Once two people have survived something like Santa pictures, they can't stand on formalities. I'm just Ed."

"And I'm Joy." She took a long sip of coffee and felt a bit better for it. "Any suggestions on what sort of gift for you I should steer them toward?"

He was a doctor. What sort of things did doctors do for enjoyment? "Golf equipment maybe?" she tried.

"I don't golf."

"Oh." Okay, she was stereotyping. That didn't sit well. She tried to be open-minded about people. Not all doctors golf.

She took a sip of her very hot coffee.

"So, Dr. H—" His frown stopped her midword. "Ed," she corrected. "So, Ed, what do you do for fun?"

"I'm so busy with the kids' schedules that if I ever had a hobby just for me, for fun, I've forgotten it. I work, I do dad stuff and…" He paused, as if trying to think of something else he did, then shrugged. "I guess I'm a bit of a bore. But for me the dad stuff is my fun."

"You're no bore," she contradicted. "You're a good father. Putting the kids first. So, what could they give you that would make your Christmas merrier?"

"Merrier." He gave a little snort.

What was that?

That was definitely a disgruntled snort.

Did she detect something a little less than holiday spiritedness in the man who kept cheerily assuring her that the pictures were no problem?

He'd just smiled bigger and broader each time he told her that this take—the twentieth take for instance— was going to be the one where none of his sons made devil horns behind a sibling, or stuck out his tongue, or punched a brother.

Could Dr. Edward Hall be a Christmas-bah-humbug kindred spirit?

"You're not feeling all warm and mistletoey today?" she asked slowly, testing his Ebenezer level.

"If by *mistletoey* you mean dry and prickly, then yes. I'm feeling that way today…pretty much all season."

"But you seemed so holiday gung ho. Even through the worst of the Santa pictures." She deepened her voice and did her best impression, *"Come on, boys. This is the picture, I can tell."* She laughed. "You outcheered Santa, who actually wasn't hard to outcheer. I'm pretty sure he was ready to be done with the whole picture thing after the first shot. He's not the jovialest mall-Santa I've ever worked with. Actually, he's probably the most cantankerous one."

"It was all an act—mine, not Santa's—a horrible fraud," Ed told her in a conspiratorial stage whisper. "I thought I could pretend some Christmas spirit, but Santa convinced me I can't. I mean, the man was chanting the word *coal* like it was some kind of mantra. And after that small problem with the boys snapping the string that held his beard in place, he got a bit more explicit in what he'd like to give them for Christmas. When you said, 'Everyone say Ho Ho,' he said 'Bah Humbug.'"

Ed took a long sip of his coffee. "Even at that, Santa has more Christmas spirit than I've been feeling. I'm to take the boys to my ex-wife's in Raleigh tomorrow afternoon. They'll be there for a week. And though they're a bit of a handful, I'll miss them. I know, it sounds pretty lame, but there it is. They drive me crazy, but not having them home will sort of take something out of the holiday."

"Your first holiday since the divorce?" Joy asked with sympathy. She knew that the absence of family could put a real damper on the holiday spirit.

"No. It's been years since the divorce. But my ex has lived here in Charlotte up until this year, so we've been able to yo-yo the boys back and forth. A few hours, or even a day without them is a respite, but a whole week, especially during the holidays?"

"I understand." Joy felt the same way about her family. All those Christmas gatherings could get to be a bit much, and over the years, from time to time she'd fantasized about skipping out and hitting some Mexican beach for the holiday.

But now that she was actually not going to be home for the merry-go-round of parties? There was a hole. The holiday had lost some of its luster for her. "Really, I understand."

Ed sighed. "I know I shouldn't complain. The boys are with me most of the time. They wanted to stay in their schools, and I give Lena a lot of credit for allowing them to stay here, so I shouldn't complain that they'll be with her over the break…"

Joy heard the unspoken but. "But you'll miss them."

"I know, after the entire picture-with-Santa debacle, you probably can't imagine why, but there it is. Yes, I'll miss them."

He took another sip of his coffee and looked up. Their eyes met and held for a moment, maybe longer. Then he said, "Sorry. I don't mean to bring your holiday spirit down."

"Down?" Joy was pretty sure the word came out as a scoff. "I don't think my holiday spirit could go any lower, even if we had to spend the entire day taking pictures with Santa. And to be honest, that's saying something."

"But you seem so jolly." This time it was his turn to look puzzled. "You're a fraud, too?"

"I'm a very good actress. It's going to be my first holiday here in Charlotte. My family's all back in San Diego. The only friend I have on the East Coast, is up in Pittsburgh, and though I'm sure Morgan wouldn't mind my visiting, it's still too far. So, I'm here on my own. There's been a flu bug going around and about a third of my staff is out and—" she lowered her voice to a notch above a whisper "—try as I might, I'm so sick of Christmas carols that I swear if I hear one more song using the words *holly, jolly* or *merry* I might scream. And if it's a rapped carol?" She just shook her head, not willing to describe her upcoming reaction.

"Oh, yeah? My receptionist is pregnant and due to give birth any day. I'll spend the next three months having to cope with a temp."

He grinned, almost daring her to beat that.

Joy realized they were playing a game of one-up-manship. Whose holiday was the suckiest. "Oh yeah, Dr. Hall—"

He interrupted. "Ed."

"Ed," she agreed. "Well, Ed, truth be told, I'm the store manager and simply filling in for Jamie, Harrington and Vine's Personal Shopper. She's out sick. Shopping with four males, three of them teens or thereabouts, wasn't in my job description." As soon as the words were out, she worried that he might take offense, but he just laughed.

"She's out with the flu that's making the rounds?"

She nodded.

"Fine. But I can top that."

"Oh, I don't think so. We've both been pretty even. Both going to miss family. Both with missing, or soon-to-be missing employees. But shopping on Christmas Eve with four males? I win the suckiest-Christmas-award hands down."

"Seriously, I can beat it. You see, I have to help the boys shop for my ex-wife, her husband and their two children. Even your aversion to Christmas carols—"

"I've been listening to them since before Halloween and company policy won't allow me to turn them off until the day after Christmas," Joy argued, even though she knew the truth of it. She'd lost this battle.

Ed shook his head, even as he grinned. "Sorry.

Shopping for an ex and her new family trumps even three months of Christmas carols and Christmas Eve shopping with boys. I win."

Joy raised her frappacino for a toast. "I bow to your win and commend you for officially having the suckiest Christmas season."

As his coffee cup knocked against hers, Joy realized that the day suddenly didn't feel nearly as sucky.

As a matter of fact, she was sitting having coffee with a handsome man, laughing and carrying on as if she didn't have a desk filled with problems to attend to and the last few hours of the holiday season to wrap up before starting the postholiday season, which was as crazy or even crazier.

But at this particular moment, all that was easy to forget. For the first time in a long time Joy didn't feel lonely and realized she could easily stay right here for a lot longer.

Knowing she had to get back, she took a final long, appreciative swallow of her coffee. "I suppose the sooner we get the shopping done, the sooner you'll be out of your misery. Well, at least part of your misery."

As if he'd read her mind, he said, "And the sooner we're done the sooner you can get back to your normal job and forget about the horrors of shopping with four men on Christmas Eve."

She realized that horror wasn't quite the word she'd use to describe the experience, despite the whole Santa thing. "To be honest, I don't mind this as much as I thought I would."

He laughed. "Just wait. The pictures and the coffee break were cakewalks compared with making my three shop for anything other than computer games and DVDs."

"That bad?" she asked, her uplifted mood sinking a bit.

He grimaced. "Worse."

## CHAPTER FOUR

As THEY WALKED BACK into the store across the still-bustling hall, Joy's cell phone rang.

Ed walked a couple steps ahead, trying to give her some privacy for the call, but he couldn't help glancing back. She was a decidedly average-looking woman, if you took in each of her features one by one. Blondish-brown hair…his mother used to call it dishwater blond. He'd guess she was about five-five which wasn't tall or short. She had pleasant, albeit average features—a small, perky nose and light brown eyes.

But, there was nothing average about Joy O'Connell. When she'd laughed over coffee as they vied for first place in the suckiest Christmas contest, there was a spark there…a spark Ed hadn't felt in years.

He pulled his thoughts away from his decidedly less-than-average shopping hostess and tried to take in the mall.

With only a few hours left to shop, the activity level in the main concourse was frantic. People scurrying from one store to the next, racing the clock to finish crossing names off their lists.

Ed had finished his shopping weeks ago. He'd even

wrapped all his gifts. No frantic last-minute sprees for him.

He just about had his hormones under control when Joy rejoined him and sent them spiraling out of control again.

"Sorry, about that. Do you mind if we stop at my office before picking up the boys? There are a couple papers that I need to look at and sign."

"No problem," he assured her.

"Will the boys be okay?" she asked, looking a bit unsure.

After their behavior with Santa, he didn't blame her for asking the question.

"Jake's sixteen. I think he can handle his brothers for another few minutes. Especially in your gaming section. They're probably all lost in the demos, trying out new games."

Even as he said the words, he prayed he was right. Maybe he should go back and wait with them, but for reasons he couldn't explain, he didn't want to leave Joy.

"Great," she said, a smile, a real smile, on her face.

Okay, maybe he could explain his reluctance to leave her. Maybe it had to do with her smile, which made her averageness all but disappear. It sort of lit her whole face up and overshadowed everything else.

They walked in silence back toward the Customer Service area. He had to admit, if only to himself, that he wasn't just attracted to her…he was very attracted.

It had been a long time since that had happened.

Oh, he'd dated, and certainly noticed good-looking women when he encountered them. He wasn't dead, after all. But he was busy, too busy to follow up on the casual dates he'd gone on or attractive women he encountered.

They reached the second floor and he watched Joy as she chatted with the receptionist.

He drew closer.

"Okay, I guess I'll have to do it, Betty," she said. "It's not like I really have a choice. But I'm starting to feel like the Little Red Hen, doing everything by herself. Only I know at the end of this particular story, there will be no cake for me, just more work."

"Sorry, Joy. I'd do it myself after work if it weren't for my grandchildren…." Betty let the sentence trail off.

Joy nodded. "I know. Could you ask someone to load it all in my car? My keys are in my purse."

She signed her name to something.

Betty nodded. "Sure thing."

Joy turned back to Ed. "Okay, are we ready?"

Without waiting for his answer, she started walking back toward the elevator.

"What happened now? Another sick employee?" he asked.

She shook her head, sending her hair swishing to and fro. "Actually, a sick volunteer. Volunteers, rather."

Her hair was slightly askew. Ed almost physically had to stop himself from reaching out to push it back into place. It looked soft and inviting. Too inviting for his peace of mind.

She looked so forlorn that he had more than just an urge to stroke her hair. He wanted to wrap her in his arms and comfort her, just as he'd done when the boys were small. He wanted to hold her tight and assure her that things would get better.

"So what other job are you going to have to do today?"

"It's not a job, actually. To be honest, it might be fun. Harrington and Vine's partnered with a local holiday organization, Secret Santas. It's a volunteer group that works with various businesses in the Charlotte area, partnering them with a needy family. The families in question don't have a clue they've been chosen.

"On Christmas Eve, their volunteers pick up presents from the business and drop them off at the family's house. Our volunteers are down with the flu, and the organization doesn't have anyone else to send. So either someone from H&V takes the gifts, or it doesn't get done. And that would be a shame. We adopted a single mother with two kids of her own, raising three others she's taken in from her extended family. There won't be much under the tree if we don't help put it there."

"And you're elected to play Santa's elf and deliver the gifts?"

She shrugged. "Hey, I'm in charge. It's one of those the-buck-stops-here things. I can't imagine this woman. Five kids…" She let the sentence trail off.

"I can barely handle three," Ed said.

"That's what I mean. I'm just worried that there's so much that I won't be able to drop it all off without getting caught."

"When were you supposed to deliver the gifts?"

"The neighbor has a key and the family will be out until around three. I'll just have to go later in the day and try to sneak the stuff onto the porch."

"Or…"

"Or?"

"Maybe we could help? Why don't we have your staff load the gifts in my van. With five of us, we can make short work of dropping off the gifts. It would do my boys some good to volunteer and give us a chance to help you out. Then we'll come back, try to get our shopping done so we can let you get back to your real job."

"Dr. Ha—"

He gave her his dad-look and was surprised to find it worked just as well on adults.

"Ed. You don't have to do that. I'm sure you have other plans."

"Nothing that can't wait another hour or so. I mean, if you can put your plans on hold to help out, so can we." He paused, and then asked for a second time, "Speaking of plans, what are you doing tonight? We're just staying in and having a quiet family meal."

Rather than answer, she said, "You cook?"

"I have three boys, so of course I do. I mean, have you ever seen three teenage boys eat?"

She shook her head.

"Well, feeding them is scary. I had to learn to provide food often and in massive quantities or risk them turning on me. But I'll confess, I'm having tonight's meal catered at eight. A patient has a start-up catering business, and it was a great way to throw a job her way and guarantee we eat a bit better than our standard daily fare."

"Which consists of?" she couldn't help but ask.

"Let's just say there's a certain company that manufactures macaroni and cheese that we're personally responsible for keeping in the black."

Joy laughed. "Hey, that's better than my usual bagged salad dinner. I mean, at least yours is hot. Maybe I should get that patient's catering business's number?"

He reached into his pocket and handed her a set of keys. "Let us help. The van's in row K, way at the very end. It's a maroon Chevy Lumina. I'll go get the boys and meet you...?"

She handed the keys back. "Better yet, why don't you go get the van and take it to our service door, around the side of the mall? You know where your van's parked, after all. I'll go get the boys and meet you there."

"You're sure?" he asked.

"You don't think I can get three boys to the van un-aided?"

"It's not so much the getting them to the van, it's the getting them away from the video games."

"I manage a department store, surely I can manage three boys."

Ed tried not to worry about the famous-last-words feeling that came over him as Joy assured him she could handle it.

Getting the boys out of an electronics department... Well, he'd had years of practice, but even he wasn't looking forward to the job.

He loved his boys, but understood their weaknesses. Video gaming certainly fell into that category. He kept strictly enforced time limits on the gaming at home.

He walked at least half a mile back to the van.

Okay, maybe not that far, but the uncharacteristic cold and gloomy weather certainly made it feel that way. The clouds were dark and ominous, just as his mood had been before his coffee with Joy.

He realized he was whistling a very off-key rendition of "Deck the Halls" and couldn't help a small internal chuckle. He hoped his earlier sentiment wasn't Joy's before the day was through.

She still hadn't said what she planned to do for the holidays. Knowing she was new to the area, that her family was on the West Coast, that she admitted her only friend was up in Pittsburgh, he suspected she didn't have any plans. And that didn't feel right to him.

He found the van and climbed in, kicking on the heat to warm it up before the kids and Joy got in.

He drove to the service entrance, as she'd instructed, and was surprised to find she was already waiting there, boys in tow.

"What on earth did you do?" he asked, as the boys obligingly offered to help put the presents in the back of the van. "I'm their father and doubt I could have gotten them away from the games that fast. And they're all too old to use Santa and lumps of coal as a threat."

"I don't know," Joy said with a wicked smile. "I did suggest that rumor had it the pictures we took with Santa weren't all that wonderful and maybe we'd have to do retakes, but if I got these presents delivered on time, I could probably be counted on to simply Photoshop what we had on hand."

"You're a devious woman, Joy O'Connell." He paused a moment and added, "And it looks good on you."

"Ah, that's not it. If that didn't work I was totally prepared to threaten some cheek pinching aren't-you-cutes in a loud, draw-attention-to-them manner."

"My appreciation for your deviousness only increases."

"But worse than that, much worse, was my final threat. It's so bad, I was hesitant to even say the words out loud, much less act on it."

"Dare I ask?"

"Christmas carols. I was going to serenade them. My first choice was 'Deck the Halls'…the rap version."

"I was just thinking there was a possibility that might become your favorite song before the day's over." He laughed.

Her laughter harmonized nicely with his. "To be honest, today is going much better than I anticipated."

"Really?" he asked.

She nodded and shot him a smile that heated areas of his body Ed had almost written off as hopelessly atrophied and unusable.

"Much, much better," she told him, her voice all throaty.

"Me, too," he admitted.

JOY REALIZED she'd been flirting with Ed.

She couldn't remember the last time she'd flirted with anyone, not even her most recent ex. He'd been the flirter in their relationship. He'd spent so much effort at it, she'd felt almost obligated to date him. Then she'd felt obligated to go out again since he'd spent so much effort on setting up their first date.

After that, she'd sort of fallen into the habit of him. Then one day she'd realized, that there was no way their relationship could progress further. Habit and a sense of familiarity wasn't enough of a reason to date anyone. So she broke up with him and concentrated on work.

Things had gone well, she'd been busy, happy, then she'd moved. And now?

She was still busy, still happy, but…

She realized she wanted more.

She glanced at Ed, who was driving his van, then turned around to see what the rather quiet trio in the back was up to.

"So who are these presents for?" Jake asked when he saw that Joy was looking at him.

"A family who doesn't have a lot. A single mom with two kids of her own, who's opened her home to three more children. Their neighbor suggested that they might need a few things, so…" Joy nodded at the back of the van. "The store donated the gifts and we're going to deliver them, covertly. The neighbor's going to let us in and we'll put everything under the tree, then leave."

"But she won't know that it's you," T.J. said.

"It's not me, but Harrington and Vine's. And the family not knowing, well, that's the point. Sometimes knowing you've done something that needs to be done is enough. That's the point. It's not having anyone else know you did it. It's just knowing that you did it—that you made a difference."

"I think this is it," Ed said as he pulled up in front of a modest, two-story brick home.

Joy nodded. "And that one should be the neighbor's. Let me just go get her and then we'll see how fast you guys can move."

She hurried to the small ranch-style house and knocked on the door. The door opened and a gray-haired lady with a smile that seemed to bubble up straight to her eyes said, "Merry Christmas," by way of a greeting.

"Mrs. Jeffreys?" The woman nodded. "I'm Joy O'Connell from Harrington and Vine's."

"Oh my, you did make it. The woman on the phone said the volunteer was out sick." If it was possible, her smile seemed to grow even broader.

"That's true, so we're filling in."

"Wonderful, wonderful. They're going to be so surprised. Just let me get Anne's key and my jacket."

"I'll tell the guys to start unloading." Joy hurried back out to the van. "This is it, fellas. Let's start emptying the car. Mrs. Jeffreys is coming over to unlock the door."

Ed and the boys opened the back of the van and started carrying the myriad of packages to the front porch.

"Hey, it's snowing," T.J. hollered.

"Snowing is a bit of a generous term," Ed noted.

He was right. The sky had opened and a scattering of big, lazy flakes drifted down, hit the cement and immediately melted. Then abruptly stopped.

"Ah, it's done already," Tim said, looking forlornly at the sky, as if waiting for more.

"Hey, we're in North Carolina. This counts as snow," Joy told him as she juggled a stack of gifts.

"Unless there's enough for a snowball, I'm not counting it," Jake grumbled, but despite his words he was grinning.

Mrs. Jeffreys hurried over onto her neighbor's porch. "Here we go," she called as she unlocked the front door.

"We're just going to put them all under the tree," Joy instructed her crew.

The tree looked as if a lot of care and attention had been spent on it. The decorations were predominantly the made-them-in-school-as-an-art-project variety. Construction paper stars with school photos in the middle, cotton ball snowmen. And some frozen orange juice lids with designs that had been very cleverly punched through.

"These are cute," Joy said, more to herself than anyone else. She knelt on the floor and began piling her stack of gifts under the tree, arranging them as neatly as she could.

"Oh, they're always bringing home things like that from school," Mrs. Jeffreys said. "I don't think Anne's seen the front of her refrigerator in years. It's completely covered in artwork. Come to think of it, neither have I. The children keep me well supplied in addition to their mom."

"It looks like my tree at home." Ed set his load down in front of the tree. "I've got the angel T.J. made in kindergarten at the top of mine."

"Dad," T.J. hollered.

Joy looked up and Ed grinned. "I don't think it's cool to talk about a teenager's kindergarten angels in public."

"Talking about it is almost as bad as putting it up on the tree," Jake teased. "Dad gets all sentimental, pulling out those old bits and pieces. Why, when he looked at the little construction paper circle Tim made that read World's Best Dad I swear he got tears in his eyes."

"I might have gotten a bit sentimental, but there were

no tears." Ed looked as affronted as T.J. had a moment ago. "And there's nothing wrong with having a father who thinks you hung the moon…or made the Christmas star as it were."

The three boys just rolled their collective eyes.

Joy started to stand and Ed offered her a hand up.

"Lame jokes aside, some day you'll all understand," Joy assured the boys.

Their expressions said they doubted it and that made the adults laugh again.

She realized she was holding something and looked down. It was Ed's hand. How on earth had that happened?

She dropped it as if it were a hot potato.

When he'd helped her up they'd somehow forgotten to let go.

She didn't even make eye contact to see if he noticed they'd been holding hands and weren't now.

"Come on, guys," she encouraged, "let's finish this before the family comes home."

It took a few more trips to bring in everything. They spent a few more minutes making sure it all looked perfect.

"You all do good work," Joy assured them. "And speaking of work, what do you say we head back to the store and see if we can get to work on your shopping lists?"

The boys hollered their approval and hurried out past the adults to the van.

"I just want to thank you again," Mrs. Jeffreys said as she locked the door. "They're a very special family and I just know this is going to mean so much to them."

"We were delighted to help," offered Joy.

She and Ed started back to the van.

"Joy?" Ed said.

She ignored the quiet nature of his voice, suggesting whatever he was going to say was for her ears alone. She felt nervous and uncomfortable as she suddenly remembered her initial assessment of Ed's attractiveness. This was business, not a date.

She pretended she hadn't heard him say her name and instead called out, "Let's go, boys."

"Hang on a minute," T.J. said. He hurried back to the porch and left the mass of paper airplanes he'd had in his back pocket on a chair.

"Maybe the kids'll like them," he said with a quick shrug.

For a moment, just one brief second of insanity, Joy wanted to take Ed's hand again and give it a squeeze. Instead, she made eye contact and smiled.

"Nice kid," she mouthed.

He nodded back, agreeing.

"Okay, guys. Time to shop."

## CHAPTER FIVE

"Now, YOUR DAD SAID you'd put together a shopping list? Why don't we start in the toy department and get your half siblings done."

"Can't we just buy them each a Game Boy?" Tim asked.

Jake shook his head. "Nintendo DS."

Not one to be left out of a fray, T.J. cried, "PSP."

Joy could see another comic-book-type argument starting. Hoping to circumvent it, she said, "When you're shopping for other people you're supposed to look for something that will make them happy. Do you really think your little sister wants a handheld game?"

"She might," Tim said, not looking very sure.

"Nah, probably not. She can hardly walk. I bet she couldn't use the controller very well. But she does like all those kids' shows on TV. Maybe we could get her a stuffed animal of one of those characters?" Jake suggested.

The boys started squabbling about which sibling might like what. More bantering than fighting, they reminded her so much of her cousins, of her family. It made her miss the whole O'Connell clan—even Uncle Fred—all the more.

And missing Uncle Fred was saying something, since his idea of holiday cheer came from a bottle—a bottle he seemed determined to empty on his own each year. About halfway into it, he'd start singing risqué bar songs. You could always tell a party was winding down when he finally reached "Honky Tonk Woman."

Most years she cringed when Uncle Fred was around, but at this moment, she sort of wanted to hear his rendition of "Grandma Got Run Over by a Reindeer." It had to be better than most of the Christmas carols.

"Come on, guys," Ed said, pulling Joy from her memories of Christmases past.

The words were mild enough, but she heard the current of warning in his tone and saw a dad-look in his eyes. "Ms. O'Connell is being generous filling in for Ms. Anthony, who's sick. She's got a lot of things to attend to, things that don't include herding us through the store all day."

And though she'd thought that very thing not too long ago, Joy realized that at this moment she couldn't think of anything she'd rather be doing. So she smiled reassuringly at the boys. "Okay, so the toy department for the younger kids. Any other thoughts?"

"Yes," said Jake. "The three of us thought we'd pool our gift allowances for each other and give ourselves a joint present. The new gaming system and its accessories. We did the math, took our spending allowance for each other, added them all together and it was enough. We can do that, can't we? It's within our budget."

"Yes," Joy assured them. "You can do that. It's nice that you're all willing to share. And I'm glad you figured out what to get each other, but you have a long list. So what about the others? Do you have any ideas?"

Three dark-haired heads shook, the youngest's so vigorously that Joy worried he'd rattle something loose.

"Well, then," she said, trying for that holiday cheer again, "Let's go start at the toy department and see what other ideas crop up."

On the way there, they passed by the electronics section. She stopped a clerk and asked him to put one of the new gaming systems behind the counter for the boys.

"No use hauling that huge box around the rest of the day," she told Ed.

Ed held back a bit as the boys raced ahead. "Sorry this is going to take a while. I can shop with them, if you like, then call you when we've finished so you can approve the presents."

"You know, if you'd asked me first thing this morning, I'd have probably taken you up on your offer. But now? Well, let's just say, this shopping trip isn't as bad as I thought it would be."

He cast a meaningful glance at the boys. "Really?"

Joy nodded. "Really."

She felt a warm glow that lasted until the boys started fighting about which game to get with their new system. "The space one, not the race car."

"The noisier the better, right?" Joy asked Ed.

Ed nodded, even as he cast the boys his evil-dad-eye and said the single word, "Boys," in a tone that would have guaranteed Joy's cooperation.

It didn't seem to have the desired effect on the boys, though. Oh, they got a bit quieter, but she noticed they were still whispering their argument, and caught the sly pushes and slugs whenever their father's attention shifted.

"Let's try and finish here, then we'll come back to electronics if you like. How about this for your four-year-old sister?" Joy tried, holding up a princess doll. She didn't watch much children's television, but she did work retail and knew it was a good seller.

"She doesn't like girlie toys, she's a tomboy," T.J. maintained. "I know you thought she might want a toy, but Dad, she's going to want—"

"Let me guess," Ed said. "Some sort of electronic game?"

Three heads nodded in unison, like a trio of bobble-head dolls.

"Is there anyone on your shopping list who won't want electronics?" Joy asked softly.

All her warm glowing personal family memories faded, as well as the leftover warm glow from their present-delivering time. Joy suddenly recalled that after those first few aren't-they-precious moments, visits with her family's youngest members routinely sounded like this moment right now.

And truth be told, Uncle Fred sang off-key.

Very off-key.

"I guess the baby might want something that wasn't electronic," Tim admitted. "I mean, she still puts all her toys in her mouth. And you always say water and electricity don't mix."

"Rule Number One, as a matter of fact," Jake offered.

Ed looked slightly embarrassed. "I started preaching that after Tim thought his fish might enjoy listening to the radio and dropped it in the tank." Ed paused. "An electric radio, not a battery operated one."

Joy wished she'd brought another cup of coffee along with her. She could use a jolt of caffeine to bolster her sagging spirits, though she doubted it would do much to erase the picture of the electrocuted goldfish from her mind.

"Come on," Tim protested. "I was only six at the time and didn't know better."

"Yeah," Jake said. "But those fried fish and the shorted-out socket are why the electricity and water don't mix rule went on the board."

"Board?" Joy asked.

"Dad got this great idea. He made a list of life lessons for us. Rules that would keep us out of trouble." Tim didn't look as if he felt the life lesson list was all that great an idea.

"He posted a whiteboard in the basement and adds to it," T.J. explained. "The Hall Family's Life Lessons."

Ed was looking very uncomfortable. "That's enough boys. I'm sure Ms. O'Connell would like to finish off this shopping trip so she can get back to work."

"No, actually, I'm fascinated by your life lessons. What else made the board?"

All three tried to answer at once, but T.J. was the loudest. "Change your underwear every day. That was mine after Dad did a week's laundry and didn't find any of my underwear in it." He paused and added, "I've outgrown that one now."

"I added the rule about showering every day at the same time," Ed told her.

"Don't light arrows then shoot them. I think that's Number Twenty-three," Jake hollered.

"Let me guess, that was yours?" she asked him.

"Actually, my friends Katie, Joey and Ryan prompted that rule."

"You were there, though, and didn't have the sense to leave," Ed said. "Which is why we added Rule Number Twenty-four—if friends are doing something dangerous, either make them stop or leave and tell."

"The telling part is tough, but sometimes you have to," Jake said. He looked very adult at that moment, and Joy wondered what had happened with a friend.

The mood didn't stay somber long.

Tim grinned, casting a look at his dad that said he knew Ed was going to yell. "And then there's the excuse-me rule, Number Eighteen. If you make a rude bodily noise, just say excuse me. That one's all mine. I'd learned this saying, *Excuse me please, that wasn't smart, but if it would have come out the other end it would have been a—*"

"All right, I think Ms. O'Connell has the idea and I'm pretty sure she's had enough highlights of the Halls' Life Lessons." Ed eyed all his sons looking stern.

Joy laughed. "To be honest, I liked them."

Just then the rap version of "We Wish You a Merry Christmas" came over the PA system. "You can go home and add, *no Christmas carols should be played until after Thanksgiving,* if you like."

"*And no carol should be rapped...ever,*" Ed added, shooting her a secret, just-between-grown-ups smile.

Despite the fact they'd been wandering through the toy section for what felt like an eternity and hadn't managed to buy even one present, Joy couldn't help but smile back.

# CHAPTER SIX

IT WAS AFTER TWO-THIRTY and the boys had managed to pick out two presents for Hannah, the still-chews-her-toys half sister. The beautiful princess doll, and a football. The boys agreed that their sisters shouldn't be allowed or encouraged to get too girlie.

"Guys like girls who play sports," Jake said, all sage wisdom and grown-up-like.

The doll, the football and two silver frames, which they'd picked up in the nearby homeware department, one frame for each set of grandparents was all that they'd managed in the hour they'd been shopping.

When Ed said he thought he had a picture of the three of them, Joy had laughed and said leave that part of it to her.

He'd studied her suspiciously as she'd gone and whispered to one of the employees who'd looked at Ed and laughed, then hurried away.

Joy looked like a Christmas angel. Yes, it was a totally mushy and nonHe-Mannish thought, but there it was. Joy O'Connell was a picture of wide-eyed sweetness. But her expression? It belied the image. She was way too devilishly pleased with herself.

"What are you planning?" he asked suspiciously when she came back.

"Nothing," Joy replied, batting her eyes in what he was sure was an attempt to appear innocent.

It wasn't the type of technique the boys would use, nonetheless he recognized that it was just a ploy, designed to throw him off his suspicions.

"I have a nurse-practitioner working at the office who gets that precise look on her face right before she does something diabolical. Em's got a wicked sense of humor that finds frequent expression in horrible practical jokes."

"Oh? Like what?" She leaned toward him, all attentive.

"Uh-uh. Do you think I'm going to give you any ideas?" He shook his head. "No way. I may have just recently met you, but I already know you're far too dangerous as is. You don't need any tips on how to cause trouble. And don't deny you're up to something. I'm the father of three boys. I recognize trouble when I see it."

"I'm not trouble," she maintained with another way-too-innocent grin.

A smile that made him want to kiss her.

The mere thought was beyond a surprise.

Ed hadn't wanted to kiss anyone in a long time. Between the boys and work he'd been busy. Oh, he dated occasionally, and had kissed more than one of the women, but he hadn't felt this type of pull. This type of desire.

Trying to hide the feeling, he called, "Boys."

They were currently embroiled in a new fight over the merits of sea monkeys for their other half sister.

For once he was glad to have their arguing to deal

with. It was just the distraction he needed to chase the thoughts of kissing Joy O'Connell out of his head.

"She still eats everything." Jake thrust the package back at his father. "You're a doctor. Do you think eating these would kill her?"

Ed put the package back on the shelf. "If you know she's probably going to eat them, you probably shouldn't buy them for her."

"Then that's it. There's nothing else here to buy," T.J. said. "That means—"

"Back to electronics?" Jake asked, hope in his voice.

Joy glanced at her watch. "Listen, before you all head over there, what about a lunch break? We're running late because of delivering the presents, but lunch was part of the prize. You all must be starving."

Ed wanted to protest that if she fed the boys this really was going to be an all-day excursion, but he stopped himself. Truth be told, spending a day with Joy, even if it meant shopping, wasn't such a bad prospect.

And even if he had protested, the boys' enthusiastic chorus of yeses would have certainly drowned him out.

Joy was smiling as she simply said, "Let's go." Surprisingly, the boys fell right into line and followed her.

"You're sure?" he asked. "I know we're keeping you from work."

She nodded. "The work will be here the day after Christmas. Plus, they can page me if something earthshattering crops up. We'll feed them, then do some power shopping in the—"

"Electronics department," he finished for her.

They both laughed and the urge to kiss her swept

over him again. They'd stopped dead in their tracks and fallen behind the boys now. He looked at her, and she at him for a second, a minute…longer?

Ed couldn't tell for sure.

They'd drawn closer and for a moment, he thought they were indeed going to kiss inside the bustling store, but Joy suddenly pulled back. And Ed knew a keen sense of disappointment.

"Yes, the electronics department. We can finish there and get you all home in time for your Christmas Eve dinner."

He remembered what she'd said about all her family being in San Diego. "Do you have somewhere to go for Christmas Eve?"

"So, let's go…lunch," she said merrily, but Ed noticed that she hadn't answered his question.

New to town, her family on the West Coast. What was Joy going to do for the holidays? Spend them alone?

But she obviously didn't want to share her plans with a near stranger. He didn't blame her, but he was still bothered by the thought of Joy on her own.

"There's a Patty's across the hall," she offered.

"They have good pizza," Tim replied, as if that was all the affirmation she required.

Jake and T.J. agreed.

"Looks like Patty's it is," Joy said.

Ed walked next to her as they made their way across the hall. "I think the crowd is getting thicker."

"I think you're right. A lot of people enjoy waiting until the last minute. They seem to enjoy the rush. I don't get it myself."

Their group walked into the restaurant and Joy told the hostess, "Five."

"Okay, a quick lunch, boys, then we'll finish this shopping off in short order," Ed said.

The boys mumbled their agreement as they all followed the hostess.

The woman settled them in an oversize booth, passed out menus and set a basket of rolls down. "Your waitress will be with you in just a moment."

Ed and Joy sat opposite each other. He had the two younger boys on his bench, she had Jake on hers.

In no time the boys started comparing orders. Ed tried to concentrate on the menu, tried to decide what sounded good but kept finding his gaze drawn back to Joy.

"Rudolph the Red-Nosed Reindeer" came on the PA system and he noticed her grimace. "So, if you weren't wincing at Christmas carols, what would you be listening to?" Without taking his eyes off Joy, he barked, "Number Fifteen!"

"Fifteen?" she mock-whispered.

"No food fights."

"I shudder to think what prompted that one?" she half asked, half stated.

"Let's just say, there's a certain chain restaurant here in town that we're banned from. A lifelong ban. And it's not just this one in Charlotte, it's from the entire chain, all of them. Nationwide."

"I think the manager said worldwide, Dad," Jake added helpfully.

"Do you think he sent our mug shots to all those other stores?" Tim asked hopefully. "Maybe they have a book they keep of people who are banned. If you walk in and they recognize you, do you suppose they'd call the police?"

"That would be cool," T.J. said. "Maybe we can get Mom to take us when we get to Raleigh."

"Yeah, we'd be in a crowd, so maybe the manager won't recognize us," Tim chimed in.

Jake snorted at his brothers. "They don't really have a book with our pictures. But it was a cool food fight."

Ed shot him a look as Jake continued, "Not that we're proud of that fact or anything. Rule Number Fifteen shall be especially obeyed in all public places," he quoted very neatly.

Joy tried valiantly, but she couldn't help it, she laughed. The sound felt a bit rusty and she knew it had been a long time since she'd done more than a social chuckle.

The stress of the move across the country, starting a new job, then the holidays. She'd let it all get to her.

"I've got a new rule for you, that is if friends of the family can suggest them."

"Sure," the boys chorused. Ed smiled and nodded.

"Laugh at least once every day, no matter how stressful life seems."

*Good one,* Ed mouthed.

She bowed her head acknowledging his comment, even as the boys began to talk one over the other, vying for her attention and comments.

They paused long enough to place their orders when the waitress came around.

As Joy sipped her water, the boys talked about a neighborhood boy who made everyone laugh with his antics. "He makes us look good, doesn't he, Dad?" T.J. quipped.

Ed was very vehement in his agreement.

"They have a future in stand-up," Joy told Ed during a lull.

"I figure they'll all go on to do amazing things…or end up in jail. I just don't see any hopes at middle ground for them," he joked.

As they finished their meal, the boys talked about school, about the holidays, then the conversation turned to their upcoming trip to their mother's.

"She misses us," T.J. said. "It was better when they lived in town."

"She did her best." Jake eyed everyone at the table, as though he was daring someone to accuse his mother of doing less than that.

"Yes, she did," Ed agreed. "Leaving you boys with me was one of the hardest decisions the two of us ever made."

Joy noticed he included just himself and his ex-wife in the decision-making process, making sure the boys knew that both their parents had stood united, and that the decision ultimately belonged to the adults, not to the boys.

Her respect for the man shot even higher, if that was possible.

"We should get her something special," Tim murmured.

"Something that will let her know we miss her, but don't blame her," Jake added.

"Hey, Joy, what do girls like?" T.J. asked.

"Women," Ed corrected.

"Hey, I've reached an age that being thought of as a girl is rather flattering," Joy said. "And as for what we like, that's hard to say. You want something that will let your mother know you're thinking about her, that you miss her, that you know that this move is as hard for her as it is for you."

"Jewelry," Jake said. "She's got that ring she wears all the time, the one that her grandmother gave her. She says she wears it because it reminds her of Grandma and reminds her she was loved. We could get her something to remind her we..." He let the sentence trail off.

Ed had said Jake was sixteen. That was probably too old to go around spouting off in public how much he loved his mother and how much he missed her, but he did both—Joy could see it. Just as she could see echoes of those two emotions in Jake's brothers' eyes, as well.

"I think that's a lovely idea. We'll head over to the jewelry counter when we go back, but first things first. Our lunch isn't complete without dessert."

"Are you sure you have time?" Ed asked.

"Yeah, we don't need it," Jake assured her, though the two younger boys were already arguing over sundaes or pies.

Joy smiled at Ed. "I have time." To Jake she added, "This is Christmas Eve lunch. And everyone knows you can't have any holiday meal and not have dessert."

Jake didn't need a second invitation. He was already discussing the dessert possibilities with his brothers.

"After lunch, we'll go to the jewelry counter," she told Ed. "It won't take us long to finish."

That should have been a welcome thought. Instead, it left Joy feeling... She searched for the right word.

Lonely.

As odd as it felt, she knew she was going to miss the Halls when they left.

## CHAPTER SEVEN

ED'S CELL PHONE RANG as they were wending their way through the crowds.

He fell behind and Joy was left with the boys.

She'd started the day with a definite bias against boys, believing all males should be ignored until well into their twenties. But as the three young men talked about holidays past, she had to admit they had a certain amount of charm, albeit a deeply buried, you-really-had-to-dig-for-it sort of charm.

"...and remember that year T.J. didn't want that oozy stuff that was all over his favorite TV show. He asked Mom what to do if he got it, and she said, just say thank you and set it aside," Jake said.

The other two boys laughed, and Joy felt as if she'd missed something important. "So did he get some?"

"Yeah," Tim said. "And we didn't even buy it for him. My grandmother thought she was being so smart when she got it for all of us. When he opened his—"

"I said thank you," T.J. protested.

"But he didn't just set it aside and open his next present," Jake told Joy. "He threw it. It hit the wall with a splat, and blew open, sending green ooze flying all over the room, a big old glob of it in Grandma's hair."

"She screamed," Tim added.

"Turns out she thought she was being cool buying it, but she wasn't cool enough to want to play with it," T.J. said. "And definitely not cool enough to want to wear it."

Jake laughed. "She wanted to do something different from her usual grandma box."

"Grandma box?" Joy asked.

Jake nodded. "She always gets us pajamas—"

"Even though we tell her we sleep in shorts," Tim added.

"And a toothbrush, even—" T.J. said.

Jake cut him off. "Even though we tell her the dentist always gives us one."

"But she hasn't brought us any cool toys since that Christmas," T.J. continued. "We're back to plain old grandma boxes."

"Joy, you could pick out old lady pajamas, right?" Jake asked.

"That's Ms. O'Connell, Jake," Ed said, rejoining the group. "And who is she buying old lady pajamas for?"

"Grandma. We thought we'd give her back a Christmas box. Pajamas, a toothbrush and some of that green ooze stuff. They had it in the toy section. She'd think that was funny, wouldn't she?"

Ed smiled. "Yes, your grandma would think it was funny. Remember that Christmas she bought you all the ooze?"

"We just told Joy," T.J. said, then quickly corrected himself. "Ms. O'Connell."

"Joy's fine. It's a lot less of a mouthful."

The three boys looked at their dad. "If Joy prefers being Joy, then let's compromise on Ms. Joy."

"Why don't you three see if there's anything that you think your mom would like," Joy prompted.

As they raced around the jewelry counter, she noticed that Ed was practically radiating pleasure.

"A good call?"

"Good news for one of my patients. That's what took so long. I'd brought their number from the office, just in case I got the results, so I called. There's nothing like delivering good news on Christmas Eve. We thought it might be cancer, but it wasn't."

Without thinking, Joy reached out and took his hand and gave it a squeeze. "That's wonderful."

He squeezed hers in return. "Yes, it is."

She realized what she'd done and pulled her hand back. What was with her? She didn't seem able to keep her hands off Ed Hall, and that wasn't like her at all. She'd just met the man.

Enough was enough. She was just going to help them finish, then forget all about this weird attraction to Dr. Hall.

"Uh, let's check on the boys' progress."

"Ms. Joy," Tim called excitedly from the far end of the case. "Come see."

He pointed through the glass to a group of necklaces. "That one."

It was a beautiful locket. Three small flowers were etched on the front, anchored with three small diamond chips.

"She could put our pictures in it and wear it, so that even if we're not there, we'll sort of be there." Jake looked embarrassed, as if that were too mushy a sentiment for a sixteen-year-old boy to have.

Joy's throat felt clogged with emotion but she swallowed hard and nodded to a clerk. "That one," she told the girl, pointing at the locket.

The girl laid it on a piece of felted board and the boys oohed and aahed over it.

"How much?" Jake asked the clerk.

Joy had known it was expensive and well out of the shopping-spree price range the boys had been given, but even she had to gasp at how much out of that range. Seventy-five dollars didn't buy much in the jewelry department. The store had some moderately priced jewelry, but the locket wasn't one of those pieces.

"How about with an employee discount?" she asked.

The girl did some calculations and gave them another slightly lower quote, but not nearly low enough.

"Okay, how about at the after-Christmas sale price, plus the employee discount?" Joy tried.

It was better yet, but still too much.

"Sorry, boys." She turned to the clerk, trying to remember the girl's name. "Aubrey," she said, finally managing it. "Could you find us something more in keeping with the boys' budget? Something under one hundred dollars?"

"Sure, Ms. O'Connell." The girl started studying items on the shelf and began to set out a selection.

The boys drew back, whispering among themselves.

"Ms. O'Connell?" Jake asked. "Could we take our present allowance for each other? We each got seventy-five dollars, and if we add that to our allowance for Mom's gift? I did the math, and we're close. We could take the rest from our account, if Dad would loan it to us for today."

"No problem, and not a loan. I'll pitch in the rest."
Ed's voice sounded thick with emotion.

Joy could only nod. To talk, to try and say anything
would allow the tears that had formed to escape.

She struggled a minute and finally said, "Aubrey,
would you wrap that up for the gentlemen?"

"And," Jake said to his brothers, "you can't tell her
that we gave up our game, guys. Because sometimes
just knowing you did something nice has to be enough,
right Joy?" He corrected himself, "Ms. Joy?"

"Right," she said, amazed that she got the word out.

She took back every horrible boy-thought she'd ever
had. Boys were wonderful. Sweet. At least these ones
were. They were—

"Thirteen," Ed barked.

As if they'd used up all their good behavior on that
one very nice act, the three of them had started a noogie
war that had escalated. T.J. was upside down again,
held between his two older brothers.

"We'll be back, Aubrey," Joy said, deciding it would
be safer to keep the boys moving. "Come on, guys.
Let's see about finishing off your shopping."

ED LOVED HIS BOYS, and knew he was probably biased
in thinking they were just a bit above the ordinary. But
today, they'd shown just a bit wasn't quite enough.
They were extraordinary.

He looked at the woman walking next to him.
"Thanks for all the discounts and for letting them do
this."

"How could I not?"

Ed loved his kids with a father's sort of prejudice.

But at this moment, in addition to that love and general father-pride, there was so much more.

"They're some kids," he said.

Joy nodded. "I know I told you that when I learned I had to take the Hall family around today, I was less than enthusiastic. But truth be told, for the first time this holiday season, I'm feeling my old sense of…"

She seemed to be struggling to find the right word.

"Joy?" Ed supplied.

She laughed. "Yes. Joy. It's just been missing. But today, your kids gave me back some. They really are great. And, Dr. Hall, I don't want this to go to your head, or anything, but so are you. Pitching in for your ex-wife's present…that takes a very big man."

"I might not have been so inclined the year or so after the divorce. It wasn't as nasty and bitter as some, but at the time all I could see was the negative. Distance has made me see Lena for who she is…a great woman who just wasn't a great fit for me. Which is fair because I wasn't such a great fit for her, either."

At that moment, he looked up and shouted, "Boys!"

Joy looked over. The boys had been sidetracked at the makeup counter. The store had had a manicurist painting nails a festive holiday red. The girl must be on a break because she was nowhere to be seen and Jake and Tim were holding T.J.'s hand down on the counter and painting his nails while he protested both verbally, and with his feet. Kicking his brothers in the shin in turn.

"Boys!" Ed said again. Two guilty faces looked up and one furious T.J. yelled, "Dad, did you see what they were doing?"

"I saw."

Just then Rachel, the holiday manicurist, approached them. She took in the scene and said, "Oh, Ms. O'Connell, I'm so sorry. I should have cleaned up my station better before I went on break. I—"

"No harm, no foul," Joy assured her. "If you could just remove the polish for T.J.?"

"Sure thing."

Joy moved in to comfort the youngest Hall, while Ed practically dragged the other two away.

"You know, one minute I'm so proud I could burst with it, and the next—"

Before he could finish both boys said in unison, "Sorry, Dad."

"I'm very disappointed in you both."

"We were just kidding with him."

"If the two of you are laughing, but he isn't, that's not kidding. Rule Nine."

"Be smart, behave and be kind," Jake quoted.

"Were you?"

They didn't need to answer. Ed could see that they knew they'd acted inappropriately. "So what are you going to do about it?"

"Apologize to T.J." Tim shot his younger brother a less than apologetic look.

"And?"

Jake heaved a sigh of the mightily put-upon. "To Ms. Joy."

"Right. She's been truly helpful to us, so I don't think it's too much to ask that you make things as easy on her as possible."

The boys looked contrite enough for Ed to feel

they'd been sufficiently lectured. "Fine. Let's go get those apologies out of the way, and finish shopping so that Ms. O'Connell can get back to work and get out of here on time."

The boys ran over to Joy and T.J. Ed stayed back and just watched them. Joy had helped T.J. remove the polish and was listening intently to what the two older boys said.

She smiled, nodded, then reached out to casually mess their hair. T.J. seemed to accept the apology, as well.

Then the four huddled together talking rapidly about something. The closer Ed got, the more hushed the discussion became.

"What's up?"

"We were wondering if maybe you had some private shopping you needed to attend to," Joy said.

She had the look that Ed recognized because he saw it so often on his sons. A look that spelled d-a-n-g-e-r. "What are you up to?"

"Don't you know you never should ask that question at Christmas?" Joy scolded. "We need a half hour, so basically, get lost, Dr. Hall."

"Yeah, Dad. Get lost," T.J. parroted.

"You're sure you want to try to handle these three on your own?" Ed asked, the enforced nail painting had to still be fresh in her mind.

"They'll behave."

Ed looked at the boys, and all three nodded.

"We made up, Dad," T.J. assured him. "Jake and Tim said I could go first on the Xbox for the next week 'cause they were sorry."

"Well, then okay, if you're sure?" It was more a question than his agreement.

He watched her bristle at his doubt and had to admit, if only to himself, she was cute when she was annoyed.

She drew herself up, spine straight, shoulders squared. All that was missing was her shaking a finger in his direction. "Dr. Hall—"

"Ed."

Her eyes narrowed and she folded her arms. "Ed, I can manage an entire store, have survived moving across the country and leaving behind everything I grew up with. I think I can manage three boys." She pointed toward the escalator. "See you in about twenty minutes in the electronics department."

Looking at her, all ruffled and annoyed he felt another overwhelming urge to kiss her. Since his boys and a large contingent of holiday shoppers surrounded them, he opted not to try. Instead, he shot the boys a warning dad-eye and smiled at Joy. "Well then, have fun."

# CHAPTER EIGHT

WHAT HAD SHE BEEN THINKING?

*I can manage an entire store, have survived moving across the country and leaving behind everything I grew up with. I think I can manage three boys.*

Joy knew she had said the words with such certainty. She'd believed them.

She was a capable, competent woman. Surely she could handle taking three boys to buy their dad a Christmas present on her own.

At least anyone looking at her curriculum vitae would think she could.

And to be honest, the boys hadn't been bad. There was no poking, punching or nail painting.

What there had been was incessant, loud arguments about what constituted the perfect present for their father.

And taking boys upstairs by the fine china, crystal department? Oh, she'd tried to steer them away from that section. The problem was, the homeware department was the first one, straight ahead, as you got off the escalator.

"That's going to change," Joy muttered more to herself than to the boys.

And after the harrowing trek, they'd found nothing. Nada. Zilch.

"Dad's hard to shop for," Jake said in the biggest understatement of the day.

"You guys can't think of anything? Does he go to a gym?" The boys' amused looks answered that question.

"Tools? I mean is he into cars or building things?"

This brought about a bunch of snorting and laughter.

"Pajamas?" she tried, feeling desperate. "In keeping with Grandma's tradition?"

Jamie would have figured out something unique and wonderful within seconds and here she was reduced to pajamas. "I mean, everyone can use a new pair of pajamas."

"Dad sleeps naked," T.J. said.

An image of a naked Dr. Hall flitted through her mind's eye…more than flitted. It just sort of hung there, front and center, until Jake thwacked his younger brother on the head. "You don't talk about that in public. Rule Number Twenty."

"Sorry, Joy." T.J. did look contrite.

Jake gave his younger brother a nice clone dad-eye.

"Ms. Joy," T.J. hastily corrected.

"That leaves us nothing."

"Hey, I have an idea," Tim cried. "We could get him—"

Joy knew what was coming. "Let me guess, it involves electronics?"

"One of those personal organizers things," Tim continued, excitedly. "You can put in appointments and birthdays, so you don't forget."

"What he's saying is he doesn't want Dad to forget

*his* birthday. It's in January," Jake told Joy. "And that's a dumb idea. Dad still hasn't figured out how to run his iPod. We have to help him with the updates. What makes you think he could figure out something even harder."

"iPods are easy," T.J. said. "He just doesn't like messing with the computer, and he has a whole bunch of CDs to put on the computer and says it would take too long."

"You know," Joy said. "Sometimes it's not how much you spend on a gift, but how much thought went into it. What if you all re-gave him his iPod. Give him a certificate under the tree saying you'll get his CDs onto the computer, then program his iPod for him? It might not cost you a lot, but it's something he might really enjoy."

"He probably would," Jake agreed. "He always complains about our music. If we fix up his with all his old stuff he could listen to it instead."

"What do you consider old?" When Joy thought old, she thought Lawrence Welk, but she couldn't quite picture Ed liking Mr. Bubbly.

"Meat Loaf," Tim said helpfully.

"Hey, I like Meat Loaf, and I'm not old," Joy protested. The collective expressions of the boys said differently. "Gee, thanks."

"We could spend his Christmas money and get him an adaptor, so he can play his iPod in the car," Jake continued.

The three boys talked amongst themselves for a few minutes, then turned to Joy. She could see that they wanted her opinion.

"I think that's a great plan."

She was off the hook. Yes, Jamie would probably have come up with something unique and wonderful. Programming an iPod for Christmas wasn't exactly unique, but Joy figured it could count as wonderful if you wanted your music loaded.

"Listen, Ms. Joy," T.J. said. "Dad's waiting down in electronics. Do you think you could get rid of him? We'll get that adaptor."

"I'll take him up to my office with me. I really should check in. When you've picked out the adaptor, just give it to the clerk behind the counter. He'll get it bagged for you, so your dad doesn't see it."

The boys shouted their approval of the plan.

"Okay, but then you're going to have to finish your shopping. It's after four and I'd hate to have to close the store without everyone having something."

"We'll be fast," Jake promised, and his brothers echoed his promise.

"Okay. And you know your family rules?"

The boys nodded.

"You have to obey every one of them while we're gone." They looked far too thoughtful for Joy's peace of mind. "Every single one of them."

Grimaces and sighs abounded, but finally all three said, "Promise."

They headed back and found Ed readily enough. "Dr. Hall, I wonder if you'd come with me for a few minutes. I'm sure the boys will be fine here, won't you?"

A chorus of *yeahs* and *sures* rang out louder than the Christmas carols on the intercom.

"See, they'll be okay. I have to go up to my office and need you, as their guardian, to sign some waivers."

"What kind of waivers?" Ed asked.

"Oh, you know, one that will allow us to use that picture of your family in promotion, one that says if any of the gifts you bought on our shopping spree blow up, Harrington and Vine's isn't responsible for damages." She shrugged. "That kind of thing."

He still looked hesitant about the boys, so she tried something risky. She'd seen her mom do it, seen her cousin do it, as well…she tried parent-speak.

Okay, she wasn't a parent, but she knew the phenomena existed. She'd witnessed it. But since she hadn't ever used it, she wasn't sure she could get it to work for her. *Come with me,* she tried, willing the message to move from her to him without any words being spoken.

It was all in the eyes. She knew that. So she opened wide and tried again. *Come with me.*

Ed stood there, looking totally unaware of her silent message.

Maybe he needed something less cryptic. She tried again.

*Come on, you doofus. Can't you see your boys are practically itching for you to leave so they can get your Christmas present?*

This time his eyes widened, and she could see a question in them. A very articulate, parent-speak, *huh?*

*Come with me,* she tried again, then vocally said, "Dr. Hall—"

"Ed," he corrected.

"Ed. This really will only take a few minutes. The

boys are going to wait down here and think about gifts so that when we get done, we can finish up fast. Jake will be in charge. Right, Jake?"

"Yes, Ms. Joy. We'll follow all the rules, Dad. And we'll be ready to finish up as soon as you get back."

"There, you see," she said to Ed, while parent-speaking *come on*.

"Uh, fine."

Afraid he'd change his mind, she said, "Go on, boys," then took Ed's hand and pulled him out of the electronics department.

"I didn't think you were going to get my message."

Ed looked confused. "What message?"

"I was using parent-speak to tell you to get out. The boys figured out your gift and needed a bit of privacy in order to get it."

"Parent-speak?"

Joy felt her cheeks warm. "I know it's not scientific, but I've seen my own parents use it. And you obviously got my message because you agreed to come."

"I thought maybe my kids had finally caused you to burst a vessel. You looked like you were having some sort of stroke and I decided you needed a break." He chuckled and she heard him murmur, "Parent-speak."

She couldn't take offense. It did sound sort of funny, but no matter what he said, she knew it had worked because here he was, walking next to her, holding her hand.

She dropped his hand quickly. "Sorry."

"You don't have to be sorry," he said.

"I…"

As if he sensed her discomfort, he said, "So are there really things I need to sign?"

Joy took a deep breath and nodded. "Just a waiver for the pictures, if that's all right. And, if you don't mind, as long as we're up there, I should probably spend a couple minutes checking on things."

"I don't mind."

They walked, side by side up to the reception area. Joy nodded at him to follow her, and they cut behind the counter where Betty was looking a bit frazzled. "How are things up here?"

"You've only had a couple calls, I forwarded them through to your voice mail. Oh, and that rush job you asked to have taken care of? It's done and everything's on your desk."

"Great," she said. "How did it turn out."

Betty chuckled. "I think you'll be pleased."

Joy couldn't wait to take a look. She turned back to Ed. "Let's go back and I'll get those messages, then you can sign the paper, then we'll check on the boys."

"Fine."

When Joy opened her door, and turned to let Ed in, Betty followed right behind him.

"Yes?"

Betty cleared her throat and looked up. Ed was standing under mistletoe.

"How did that get there?"

"No idea," Betty said innocently. Much too innocently.

"Don't you have a line a mile long out there?"

"Yes, I just wanted to be sure you both got to your office all right. Merry Christmas, Joy." Betty glanced at the mistletoe again. "Some presents aren't wrapped and under the tree, but they're enjoyable nonetheless."

Joy shook her head as Betty left her office. Ed was still standing under the mistletoe looking confused. "Was that more parent-speak, because I might be a parent, but I was lost."

"No. That was woman-speak. Or more accurately, Betty-speak. That's enough to make anyone lost."

"So are you going to tell me what it was all about?"

"Betty came in here while we were gone and put up some mistletoe."

Ed looked up and then back down at Joy. He looked amused, but there was something else there in his eyes. Something that didn't have anything to do with humor.

"So?" he sort of drawled.

Joy's mouth felt dry, which made speaking hard, but she managed to croak out, "So?"

"So are you going to leave me standing here all alone under the mistletoe?" He paused half a beat then before she could respond, he added, "And before you answer, let me assure you that if you do leave me here, I'll probably need therapy because your rejection will produce a crippling sense of self-doubt."

She took a hesitant step toward him. "Well, I wouldn't want to be responsible for crippling you."

"I should think not."

She took another step. She was close enough now to smell his cologne. Warm and woodsy. "You smell good."

"A Father's Day gift from the boys. Come a little closer so you can really get a good whiff of it," he said softly.

Joy took the last step and closed the gap without saying another word.

"So?" he asked.

She drew in a deep breath. "Very nice."

He leaned forward and she could feel his breath whisper against her neck. "You do, too." He looked up. "So what do you think? I'm pretty sure I've read that if you're under the mistletoe and don't kiss, it's bad luck."

"We can't have that." And before she could remind herself that she'd just met this man, Joy stood on tiptoe and gave him a quick kiss.

She pulled away and instantly took two steps backward. She was surprised that something so small and chaste could leave her heart skipping a fast, erratic beat.

"Now you have to move," she said, wanting him out from under the mistletoe so she wasn't tempted to go back and try a second, longer kiss.

"You don't want to tempt yourself?"

"I don't want to tempt fate. Your boys are running loose in my electronics department. We've obeyed all traditions, and you've got papers to sign while I pick up my messages so we can get back to them."

"Right."

JOY SEEMED FLUSTERED after their kiss, and despite the fact it only amounted to a small peck, Ed had to admit, so was he.

He hadn't reacted so strongly to a woman in a very, very long time. And to be honest, he wasn't sure what to do about it. Joy had admitted that she was less than comfortable with his crew when they'd first arrived. But as the day unwound she seemed to feel more at ease.

At ease enough to date a single dad?

Ed knew that dating long-term would be tough. It's why he'd always kept things so casual. It wasn't that he was against getting serious about a woman, it was just that he hadn't found one he thought was worth the effort of juggling the kids, work and dating.

Until today.

Until Joy.

Suddenly he was thinking that maybe the effort of dating would be worth it.

He watched her bustle around her desk, thumb through a file, all the while casting glances his way.

He didn't need parent-speak to see she was nervous. That led him to believe that maybe their kiss had affected her as much as it had him.

"Here you go," she said, pasting a way-too-bright smile on her face. "If you could just read the release, then sign and date it, that will be done. While you're doing that, I'm going to check my voice mail."

She sank into her chair and pressed a button on her phone base. She made notes, pressed more buttons, all business until suddenly she broke out into a small smile, that progressed to an out-and-out grin.

"Good news?" he asked as she hung up.

"The best. My cousin's had her baby. It's a girl. Six pounds, nine ounces, twenty-two inches. She's tall and skinny. My cousin's husband says she looks like Yoda, but she yelled in the background that she's beautiful and threatened to name her Leia. He told me they're naming her Noelle Joy."

"After you."

She nodded. "I hate that I'm not there."

"Can you get back for a visit sometime soon?"

"Not soon enough. The after-Christmas rush is crazy. But hopefully, in the new year I can get home for a few days."

"It's hard, isn't it? I know when the boys spend the rest of the break with their mom, I'll be wandering around the house and nothing will feel quite right, which is odd because most days I'd give my eyeteeth for a bit of peace and quiet."

"I know what you mean, it's weird. When I was in San Diego, I used to chafe with all the family stuff we did together. I mean, I'm an only child, but we have a big extended family and everyone lived in each other's back pocket, so sometimes it was hard to remember that I was an only child, if you know what I mean."

He nodded.

"I used to wonder what it would be like not to spend my holidays jumping from one relative's to another's, a string of holiday meals and parties. It got exhausting. Now I know what it's like not to have to do that and it's not as great as I imagined."

Ed couldn't think of anything to say to that, so he simply said, "Sorry."

She gave herself a little shake, and shot him a forced smile. "It's okay."

"Oh, before we head back, I have those picture frames the boys bought for their grandparents. And I have something for you."

Ed noticed the three identically wrapped gifts on

the corner of her desk. She took the top one and handed it to him. "Open it now."

She was grinning in a way that reminded him of the type of expression the boys wore when they'd done something particularly diabolical. "Do I have to be careful of things jumping out at me, exploding or something else horrible?"

"No, you're safe."

He ripped off the paper and opened the long, shallow box. There was a frame, identical to the two the boys had chosen. In it was a picture. A picture of a very disgruntled Santa, the three boys and Ed. Jake was in the back, making devil horns over T.J.'s and Tim's heads. T.J., for his part, had crossed his eyes and Tim was reaching for Santa's beard. Ed noted his own expression was one that someone on their way to the gallows might wear.

When the picture was snapped, he'd been frustrated, now he was simply amused. "It's perfect."

"The wonders of digital photography. I saw it as the photographer discarded it. He was right, it wouldn't work for Harrington and Vine's purposes, but I thought you might like it."

"Joy, I—" He wanted to tell her that today hadn't turned out the way he thought it would. That although shopping on Christmas Eve wasn't exactly his idea of fun, meeting her was an unexpected treat.

He didn't get to say any of that because she suddenly went all business on him. "Let's head back and see what your boys are up to."

He noticed she gave the mistletoe, hanging just inside the doorway, a wide berth. But he didn't. He walked right under it and cleared his throat.

She turned and immediately registered where he was standing. "You did that on purpose."

"What can I say? I'm a guy. Sue me."

She sighed a very put-upon sigh, but he thought he saw a hint of a smile as she leaned forward and gave him an even more peckish kiss than the first time. Rather than let her ease away, he pulled her in closer and gave her a longer one, an introduction to the kind of kiss he'd really like to give her. "There."

She looked torn between confusion and annoyance. "Why did you do that?"

"You looked like someone who needed to be kissed."

"I… You…" she sputtered. "Oh, come on."

Ed followed her out of the office and down the hallway, as the piped-in music started a rousing rock version of, "I Saw Mommy Kissing Santa Claus." It struck him as very appropriate and he enthusiastically hummed along.

Joy turned around and shot him eye-daggers.

He chuckled and went back to humming. For some reason he felt amazingly spirited.

## CHAPTER NINE

AFTER ALL THE FOOLING around earlier, Joy was surprised by how quickly the boys finished their shopping once they finally got down to business.

Their half siblings finally had age appropriate gifts. Jamie might be the store's Personal Shopper, but Joy couldn't help but feel a bit like a shopper extraordinaire as she surveyed the boys' pile of gifts, including the jewelry box with their mother's gift in it.

Joy felt choked up all over again looking at it.

From their expressions, the three boys were obviously just as pleased with themselves.

"Let's go upstairs to the lounge and wrap everything, and then you're done."

"Joy, that's not necessary. We can wrap them at home," Ed interjected.

"Not necessary, but at Harrington and Vine's if we do something, we do it right. We'll see to it these are ready to be opened tomorrow morning."

The boys didn't need more prompting than that. They started noisily distributing the bags filled with gifts between them as Joy and Ed started toward the escalator.

Ed looked concerned. "Are you sure about this?

We've taken up almost your whole day, and I'm pretty sure we can manage the wrapping at our place."

"I'm sure. I have to tell you this has been the highlight of my holiday. The boys' enthusiasm has helped me regain some of my own holiday spirit. Plus, I'm thinking about buying my own gaming system after hearing them sing the various games' praises."

He chuckled. "Oh, they got to you all right." He glanced back over his shoulder.

"Yeah, they sure did." She looked at the three bagladen boys racing up the escalator and couldn't believe it—she actually felt a stab of regret that the day was winding down. She liked the trio.

At that particular moment, T.J. punched Tim, and Jake, obviously feeling the part of big brother, thwacked T.J. who looked a bit teetery for a moment.

"Be careful," Joy called, visions of boys tumbling down the escalator dancing through her head.

"Rule Number Thirteen," Ed barked without looking.

"How do you do that?"

"When people become parents, they're given eyes in the backs of their heads."

She laughed. "And what was Rule Number Thirteen?"

"Boys?" Ed called.

"No physical contact with your brothers. Ever. Especially in public," they parroted in unison.

"Have I mentioned that I really like these rules?" Joy asked Ed.

"I don't know if they're the best form of discipline. I mean, my ex was never much of a fan of them. But hey, they seem to work. I'd rather parent with a sense of humor than with a stern hand and this seems to do the job."

They walked by Betty's station. "Did you boys have fun?" she called.

They all shouted out yes.

"The lounge is back here." She led them down the hall and past her office. She threw open the lounge door.

Betty had gone to town, bringing up wrapping paper galore, premade bows, ribbons, gift bags and tape into the employee break room.

"Wow," the boys cried, setting their presents on the long break table.

"Have at it," Joy said.

She and Ed stood in the doorway watching the frenzy.

"We're going to need a cleaning crew in here when we're done," Joy said, laughing as Tim stuck a bow on his head.

"Who's your favorite son, Dad?" Jake called out, batting his eyes.

"You, son…on any given day."

"Is today one of the days?"

"You know I never tell that part," Ed scolded, laughing.

"Yeah, he doesn't tell because we all know I'm the favorite," Jake assured his brothers.

Their response was to wing wadded-up wrapping paper scraps at him.

"Good answer, Dr. Hall. You know, they really are great kids," Joy told Ed, voicing her earlier thoughts.

"I thought you had an allergy to boys?"

"Maybe I did, but I seem to have recovered. Maybe your kids are like allergy shots...they've built up my immunity."

"Better yet, they're like a fungus, they grow on you."

"Or—" The phone in the break room rang, interrupting the silliness. Joy picked it up.

"Joy, you've got a call on line three," Betty said.

"I'll run across the hall and take it in my office." She smiled apologetically at Ed. "Give me a sec and we'll pick up with our analogies for your boys when I return. I'll be right back."

Ed nodded that he'd heard, the boys were too busy to miss her.

Her office seemed almost too quiet as she walked in. She punched line three and said, "Hello?"

When she finished the call, she noticed Ed was standing in the doorway. "Everything okay?"

She smiled her reassurances as she nodded. "More than okay. That was Mrs. Jeffreys. The family came home and was overwhelmed. Anne came over to see if Mrs. Jeffreys knew who left the gifts, but she denied all knowledge. But Anne knew. Mrs. Jeffreys said she broke down and cried."

He stepped into the office, moving closer. "You did a good thing."

Joy's heart sped up, racing wildly as he closed the space between them.

"We did a good thing," she corrected. "You and the boys were such a help. I couldn't have done it without you all."

"Speaking of all of us..." Ed started, then stalled.

"Yes?"

"I know you said you're new to the area, and I asked earlier if you had plans for tonight. You didn't answer, so this leads me to believe you might not, in which case, I wondered if you'd be interested in joining the boys and me for dinner?"

She knew she'd enjoy spending more time with the Halls, but didn't know if she liked the idea of horning in on the holiday. "Ed, I don't know. I mean, it's Christmas Eve."

"I know, I know. The idea of eating with my three is daunting, but I have rules that cover mealtimes," he reminded her.

"Rule Number Fifteen, no food fights, right?"

He smiled and nodded. "Right. We'd really like to have you join us." He paused a moment, smiled and added, "*I'd* really like to have you join us."

Joy liked Ed's smile.

To be honest, there was a lot she liked about Dr. Edward Hall.

She liked how he handled his boys.

Liked the concern he had for his patients.

Liked his sense of humor.

Liked his rules.

And she was pretty sure that she'd like having dinner with the Halls.

"You've been so kind to spend the day with us," he continued, "and I'd like a chance to repay you."

"Oh, repayment." She felt let down. She didn't want to be his charity case dinner invite. "I don't think so. I mean, it's a family sort of holiday, after all. Not quite the proper venue for repaying a debt."

"Joy," he said, his voice all soft and amused. "There's maybe an element of repaying you, but there's something more. We'd enjoy your company and would love to have you join us. And…" He paused and looked decidedly uncomfortable. "Listen, I'm really out of practice. I mean, I've got three boys, one of whom occasionally dates girls—you'd think if nothing else his experiences would serve as a refresher course, but…"

Ed ran his hand through his hair. "Listen, I'd just like a chance to spend an evening with you. More than just an evening, I suspect, but I hate to push you too fast, so let's just start with tonight. I'd like to have dinner with you. And it's Christmas Eve. We've got a huge catered meal coming, and I swear I won't play any Christmas music."

She could read his other reasons in his eyes. It wasn't parent-speak, but man-speak. He was saying that this wasn't about repayment. She thought about the kiss under the mistletoe and realized that was what it was about. He was as attracted to her as she was to him.

"Well," she said slowly, grinning, "maybe a little Christmas music wouldn't be so bad, I mean as long as it wasn't rap."

He smiled in return. "That means you'll come?"

She nodded. "Yes."

He blew out a long breath, as if he'd been holding it as he waited for her answer. "Great. That's just great. Let's go see how the boys are doing. I'll confess, I'm concerned about your employee lounge."

She started toward the door, then realized that Ed wasn't following her.

She heard him clear his throat and she turned.

He was standing underneath the mistletoe.

"We have a rule about mistletoe, remember?" he asked in a mock-scolding sort of tone.

"Does it have a number?" she countered.

He didn't even pause to think, just nodded. "Number Twenty-eight."

"Twenty-eight, eh?" she said, stepping into his open arms. "I guess I know better than to mess with the Hall's Family Life Lessons."

She stood on tiptoe and pressed her lips to his. And at that moment, for the first time since leaving San Diego, Joy O'Connell felt as if she'd come home.

As the kiss ended, Ed pulled her closer. "I'd like to say something poetic and eloquent here, but the best I can come up with is, wow."

"Wow will suffice."

"What time did you say you were closing the store?"

"Six."

He glanced at his watch. "It's almost that time. What if we hang around and wait for you? You can follow us to my place."

She knew she should probably protest, should tell Ed that he didn't have to wait around. But instead, she simply smiled and said, "That would be nice. There shouldn't be that much that can't wait until I get here the day after Christmas."

"Then it's a date." He took her hand. "Let's go see how the wrapping has progressed."

They walked across the hall to the employee break room.

"Oh," was all Ed said as they peered in the room.

Joy couldn't have been any more articulate. It

looked as if someone had exploded Santa's bag of toys in the room.

Three faces turned to them both as they stood surveying a whirlwind of paper and ribbons.

"Tell you what, you go finish up your work, and I'll just help the boys see if we can locate the furniture under all this paper."

"Really, Ed, you don't have to."

"I think we'll be adding another rule to our list. What do you think, guys? If you make the mess, you get to clean it up."

The boys' response couldn't exactly be called enthusiastic. Actually, as the three surveyed the havoc they'd wreaked, they groaned.

"That was a yes, of course we'll clean up, in case you were having trouble translating," Ed assured Joy. "Just leave this to us and go get your work done. The sooner you finish, the sooner we get to go."

"I'll be back soon."

Joy hurried through the items on her desk that couldn't wait until the day after Christmas, and made a very important call to the electronics department and arranged to have the game she'd had them hold wrapped and sent up to her office.

It was an extravagant gift for kids she'd just met today, but she'd been so touched that they'd given up their gaming system for their mother, that she couldn't resist.

Maybe she could talk Ed into letting them open it tonight. They could teach her the finer points of the system after dinner.

Gift delivered, urgent work completed, she gathered

up her things. This morning she'd been in such an Eben-ezette mood, bah-humbugging the whole holiday season. But now? Thanks to the Halls, she felt almost giddy with anticipation.

She hurried down the hall and opened the door to the break room, not sure what she'd find. She sucked in a breath as she surveyed the scene. The room was sparkling.

"Wow, when you guys set your mind on something, you do it right," she said.

The boys beamed at the praise.

Jake spoke up. "Dad said you're coming to dinner."

"If that's all right with you?" She didn't have long to wait for a response.

"Sure," T.J. said. He eyed the wrapped box in her hand. "Uh, Ms. Joy, what's that?"

"Oh, just a little something for three kind of special guys I know."

"Did you get Dad anything?"

She reached into her briefcase where she'd put the frames. "I didn't get this one wrapped but…"

Ed pulled his out of its box and turned it around to show it to the boys. "My new favorite picture."

The boys groaned as they studied the family with a particularly grumpy-looking Santa.

"I thought it really captured your true essences," Joy assured them. "I think your dad should keep it on his desk in his office."

"My poor patients," he said, shaking his head. "Okay, guys, gather up your stuff and take Ms. Joy home for dinner."

"You're lucky Dad's not cooking," Jake said. "We'd be eating hot dogs and macaroni and cheese for sure."

The boys all chatted about Ed's less than stellar favorite dishes as they moved out of the store, which seemed eerily quiet now. Joy realized she sort of missed the Christmas carols.

The security guard stood at the door, ready to lock up when the time came.

"Good night and Merry Christmas," Joy told him.

"You, too, Ms. O'Connell."

"She's coming to eat at our house tonight," T.J. told the man.

"Well, I hope you all have a wonderful dinner."

"Dad's not cooking so we will," Jake assured the guard.

They all stepped outside, the sky seemed even darker than when they'd left to deliver presents earlier. The air was brisk and heavy.

"We've settled tonight's plans, but there's still a question that needs to be asked. You see, I've got to make a trip to Raleigh. It's a long drive there and back. And I wondered what you were doing tomorrow?"

"Spending my day taking a ride with a certain rheumatologist and his three sons?"

"Make that a statement, not a question, and you've got it right."

Joy laughed as she repeated it as a statement this time. "Spending my day taking a ride with a certain rheumatologist and his three sons."

"Good answer. Now, how about New Year's?" he pressed as they started out into the now almost deserted parking lot.

"I don't know. What am I doing New Year's?"

He leaned in close, his breath a whisper on her ear lobe. "Maybe a real grown-up date, no boys allowed?"

"Make that a statement, not a question, and you're on."

He draped his arm over her shoulder and pulled her tight.

"Ew," the three boys chorused.

As they walked through the practically deserted parking lot, it started snowing in earnest. There was more than Christmas music playing, as far as Joy was concerned. A sense of possibilities and potential seemed to echo all around her.

"So, what are you doing the Fourth of July, Dr. Hall?"

For an answer, Ed pulled her into his arms and kissed her. There was more than potential and possibility in the kiss…there was a sense of recognition. A sense that this…this man was what she'd been waiting for.

"Gross," was the boys' response this time as they made gagging noises.

At that moment, wrapped in Ed's arms, listening to a trio of joking boys, Joy realized she was very…very joyful, that is.

# SPECIAL EDITION™

Silhouette Special Edition brings you a
heartwarming new story from the *New York Times*
bestselling author of *McKettrick's Choice*

# LINDA LAEL MILLER

## Sierra's Homecoming

*Sierra's Homecoming*
follows the parallel lives
of two McKettrick women,
living their lives in the
same house but
generations apart,
each with a special son
and an unlikely new
romance.

December 2006

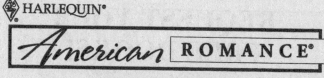

### HARLEQUIN®

## *American* ROMANCE®

### IS PROUD TO PRESENT

# COWBOY VET
## by Pamela Britton

Jessie Monroe is the last person on earth
Rand Sheppard wants to rely on, but he needs
a veterinary technician—yesterday—and she's the
only one for hire. It turns out the woman who
destroyed his cousin's life isn't who Rand thought
she was. And now she's all he can think about!

"Pamela Britton writes the kind of
wonderfully romantic, sexy, witty romance
that readers dream of discovering
when they go into a bookstore."

—*New York Times* bestselling author
Jayne Ann Krentz

**Cowboy Vet** *is available from*
*Harlequin American Romance in December 2006.*

# REQUEST YOUR FREE BOOKS!

## 2 FREE NOVELS
## FROM THE ROMANCE/SUSPENSE
## COLLECTION PLUS 2 FREE GIFTS!

**YES!** Please send me 2 FREE novels from the Romance/Suspense Collection and my 2 FREE gifts. After receiving them, if I don't wish to receive any more books, I can return the shipping statement marked "cancel." If I don't cancel, I will receive 4 brand-new novels every month and be billed just $5.24 per book in the U.S., or $5.74 per book in Canada, plus 25¢ shipping and handling per book plus applicable taxes, if any*. That's a savings of at least 10% off the cover price! I understand that accepting the 2 free books and gifts places me under no obligation to buy anything. I can always return a shipment and cancel at any time. Even if I never buy another book from the Reader Service, the two free books and gifts are mine to keep forever.

185 MDN EF3H   385 MDN EF3J

Name _____ (PLEASE PRINT) _____

Address _____ Apt. # _____

City _____ State/Prov. _____ Zip/Postal Code _____

Signature (if under 18, a parent or guardian must sign)

### Mail to The Reader Service:

**IN U.S.A.**
P.O. Box 1867
Buffalo, NY
14240-1867

**IN CANADA**
P.O. Box 609
Fort Erie, Ontario
L2A 5X3

Not valid to current subscribers to the Romance Collection,
the Suspense Collection or the Romance/Suspense Collection.

**Want to try two free books from another line?**
**Call 1-800-873-8635 or visit www.morefreebooks.com.**

* Terms and prices subject to change without notice. NY residents add applicable sales tax. Canadian residents will be charged applicable provincial taxes and GST. This offer is limited to one order per household. All orders subject to approval. Credit or debit balances in a customer's account(s) may be offset by any other outstanding balance owed by or to the customer. Please allow 4 to 6 weeks for delivery.

BOB206